DARK INTERLUDE

"Sissi . . ."

"Yes?" With a surge of excitement, she felt his warm mouth press against her neck. Slowly his arms encircled her, and he turned her to face him.

His kiss was hungry, full of longing as he pressed her body to his with a passionate need she longed to fulfill.

Sissi was drunk with pleasure. Her heart was hammering wildly against his chest as his passion inflamed her aching soul. She moaned in languid bliss.

Percy could feel her eager body molding softly against his. Her sigh pierced his muddled thoughts, and he was instantly furious with himself.

He shouldn't be kissing her. He shouldn't be alone with her. *She was marrying someone else. . . .*

BOOK YOUR PLACE ON OUR WEBSITE AND MAKE THE ARABESQUE ROMANCE CONNECTION!

We've created a customized website just for our very special Arabesque readers, where you can get the inside scoop on everything that's going on with Arabesque romance novels.

When you come online, you'll have the exciting opportunity to:

- View covers of upcoming books
- Read sample chapters
- Learn about our future publishing schedule (listed by publication month *and author*)
- Find out when your favorite authors will be visiting a city near you
- Search for and order backlist books from our online catalog
- Check out author bios and background information
- Send e-mail to your favorite authors
- Meet the Kensington staff online
- Join us in weekly chats with authors, readers and other guests
- Get writing guidelines
- AND MUCH MORE!

**Visit our website at
http://www.arabesquebooks.com**

DARK INTERLUDE

Dianne Mayhew

Pinnacle Books
Kensington Publishing Corp.
http://www.arabesquebooks.com

PINNACLE BOOKS are published by

Kensington Publishing Corp.
850 Third Avenue
New York, NY 10022

Copyright © 1998 by Dianne Mayhew.

Pinnacle, the P logo and Arabesque, the Arabesque logo are Reg. U.S. Pat. & TM Off.

First Printing: December, 1998
10 9 8 7 6 5 4 3 2 1

Printed in the United States of America

Chapter One

The soft rays of the setting sun filtered through the long bright corridors of the Liberal and Fine Arts Building of the university campus. The hour was growing late and, for a Wednesday evening, the building was unusually calm and deserted. The only sound was the echo of a woman's heels clicking steadily over the freshly waxed parquet floors. She was a slender woman, regal in height and stature. Making no attempt to be discreet in her approach, her eyes remained fixed straight ahead and full of purpose as she strutted down the empty hall toward her fiancé's office.

As she neared the professor's office, she paused, suddenly unsure of her decision to confront him only two days before their engagement party. He said he had to grade papers, Sissi remonstrated. And she was sure that's what he was doing. Shaking off her momentary uncertainty, she lifted her chin and began walking again, her pride revived. There was nothing wrong with her actions. If the woman who called her earlier that day was lying, then the professor would have nothing to worry about. But if she was telling the truth . . .

The door was closed when she reached it. Framed in the middle of the door was a small window. She raised her hand to knock on the glass when, incidentally peering into the window, she paused in shock. It was with disbelieving eyes, although she had been forewarned, that she saw the man she had given her trust and devotion to, the man she thought could do no wrong, in the arms of another woman.

A black leather chair that was partially hidden behind the desk was the basis for the lovers' passionate binding. The couple was facing away from the door, but the blond hair was clearly visible as it lay sprawled on the desk and around the face of the professor. The professor's head could clearly be seen as well, although the blond hair hid his face from view. A pair of long pink legs peeked over the huge black desk. And between those legs was a glimpse of the professor's heavily starched white shirt flapping back and forth over his dark brown buttocks that rose and fell without pause. Momentarily frozen with disbelief, she gripped her bag against her bosom until the sound of the cloth crumpling between her fingers galvanized her into action. The sight of her husband-to-be making blatant love to another woman disgusted her. It was like a bucket of cold water to her system. Determined to give the couple the same shock they had given her, with dramatic emphasis she swung the door open, causing it to bang loudly against the wall.

The professor froze, his buttocks still in the air as he tentatively lifted his head and saw his fiancée staring at him in wide-eyed outrage. The young woman peeped from beneath him and gaped in surprise at the sight of Sissi Adams.

"Sissi!" the professor cried. Sissi stared at him in disgust, flung her bag over her shoulder, put her hands on her hips and asked sardonically, "So this is how you grade papers. What grade does she get?"

The professor was dumbfounded, moving away from his lover only after the embarrassed young woman's giggle from Sissi's comment filtered through the room.

"It's not what you think," was the age-old denial. Sissi raised her carefully arched eyebrows and scoffed, "No, Professor Phil Richardson, it's exactly what I think."

Philip slowly dressed, keeping his eyes on Sissi as if he were afraid moving too quickly would frighten her away. She watched in increasing stoicism as he reached down and pulled up his pants and quickly zipped them. Steady was her gaze as he tossed the young white girl her short-sleeved pink sweater and black miniskirt.

"Sissi, I don't know . . . I never meant for this to happen," Philip stammered, tossing impatient glances at the young woman who was dressing in frustratingly slow movements.

"Well, it did," Sissi retorted. She hadn't moved since entering the office and had no intention of coming any farther. Philip's relationship with the young woman was too much of a betrayal, and she had gotten her share of betrayals to know when to call it quits.

"Uh, Professor . . . should I go?" the young woman asked timidly as she scooted into her black stack shoes. The professor frowned as if to say of course she should go.

"Yes, Nancy. I need to talk to my fiancée . . ."

"Not anymore," Sissi abruptly retorted. Philip's expression was renewed with panic as he looked up at Sissi in shock.

"Sissi!" was all he could sputter. Nancy picked up her book bag that had been tossed next to the desk and walked fearfully toward the door. Sissi saw her expression of concern and almost felt sorry for her.

"You don't have to worry about me. He's the one that made the mistake—right, Phil?" Sissi added, stepping aside to allow Nancy to leave. But as Nancy entered the hall, Sissi recalled the phone call she had received a few hours earlier. The young woman on the phone had warned her that Phil Richardson was having an affair. She wondered if Nancy could have been the voice on the phone.

"Nancy!" she called with impulsive curiosity. She peered out the door at the young woman who was just about to dash down the hall. Nancy jumped in nervous agitation then cautiously turned around, her wide blue eyes fearful as she stared into Sissi's dark brown stern eyes.

"Yes?" she whispered, her light voice barely audible.

"Did you call me this morning?" Sissi asked, her tone almost sympathetic at the notion that the young Nancy had foolishly fallen in love with Philip Richardson. Sissi knew about that kind of love, that desperate love that would take a woman to any heights to obtain it. She was just fortunate that she didn't feel that type of love for Philip. No, it was another man who had stolen her heart—only she could never be with him.

"I . . . I . . . don't know what you're talking about," Nancy responded in a timid voice. Sissi considered her for a moment longer, then nodding, turned away from Nancy, keeping a whisper of a smirk from coming to her mouth at the sound of Nancy running down the hall.

"Someone called you? Who?" Philip demanded, his guilt forgotten in his anger that Nancy could have deliberately betrayed him.

Sissi considered Philip with keen eyes. He wasn't a handsome man by any means. But he had come to her aid many times, especially after her heartbreaking separation from Percy Duvall. Still she was enraged by Phil's betrayal. She had trusted him, believed in him. It hurt that he could be so cruel as to make love to another woman only two days before they officially announced their engagement to all of their friends. Just the night before he had professed his undying love for her, his complete devotion to her. *"I'll always love you, Sissi,"* he had said. A threat of tears sprang to her eyes at the memory of his words. Feeling resentment at the hurt he had caused her, she blinked away her tears. In that moment she knew there was nothing he could say or do to change her mind. The marriage was off. There would be no engagement party.

It was as if Philip sensed her instant decision to call off the wedding. He became desperate and, with agitated movements, he walked back and forth, glancing from Sissi's impassive stance at the door to the black leather chair where he had committed the love crime.

"Sissi, I love you," he began in a fierce whisper, barely able to look at her as he spoke.

"I don't want to hear it, Phil," Sissi snapped, refusing to give him even an inkling of a chance that she could ever forgive his betrayal.

" Just . . . just hear me out!" he grunted. "I said I love you," he complained, glancing at her from beneath his sad dark eyes. Sissi was not moved by his pathetic puppy-dog glance.

"It doesn't matter, Phil. It's over." At her words he stopped walking and stared at the floor in utter despair.

"You can't end it like this, Sissi. We have guests coming, a lot of your friends. What will they think?" he tried to reason with her.

"They'll think I'm doing the right thing," she responded easily.

"But you're not."

"Oh, really?" She laughed harshly, although her eyes remained unamused. If she had been wearing the diamond engagement band he had bought her, she would have thrown it in his face. But she had been so proud of the beautiful ring. She wanted to have it sized to fit her perfectly and had dropped it off at the jeweler's the day before.

"You're not making the right decision. I can help you, Sissi. The renovation isn't totally complete, you know that. And where are you going to find the money to fix up the cottage? You know you love that cottage. I can do that for you, Sissi. I want to take care of you. I love you," he added in a flurry of words to keep her from interrupting.

Without any hesitation, Sissi said stoically, "I don't need your help. I can do it alone. And you don't love me—if you did, this moment wouldn't be happening. The engagement's off, Phil. The wedding isn't going to happen. It's over." Her words were emphatic with her determination not to be swayed. Phil always had a way of convincing her that everything was all right. He was the one who was at her side when she and Percy Duvall separated just two years earlier. Phil had convinced her that it was for the best, and slowly he had won her over with his seemingly total devotion. He was always willing to help and had—even before she accepted his proposal of marriage—put up the funds she needed to renovate her grandmother's old mansion. He had done a lot for her, and she was grateful. But nothing he had done was worth selling her heart and soul, especially in the face of this cruel, blatant betrayal.

"Give me a chance. You just need to calm down."

"Oh, come on, Phil. Do I look upset?" Sissi scoffed, folding her arms across her chest.

"No, but that doesn't mean you're thinking rationally," he answered hastily, walking toward her.

"Rational? You just finished screwing your student in my face—"

He stopped short at the explosion of words that came from her. "You weren't supposed to be here!"

"My apologies," she retorted. They both fell silent, then

Phil turned away from her and sat on the edge of the desk, his hands limp in his lap. His shoulders were slumped, his expression sour. He had lost her—he knew it, but he could not give up without a fight.

Sissi didn't move from the door. She watched him, curious about what he was going to say next.

"Okay. Let me just say this," Phil began cautiously. "I . . . we both have a lot of people coming out Friday night and I mean, I know your relationship with your friends doesn't affect your career, but my colleagues will be there."

"And?" Sissi smirked, narrowing her eyes in disgust as she captured the meaning behind his selfish reasoning.

"And I can't . . . I need you, Sissi." His tone fell to a whine. "I could lose my job over this."

"Good," Sissi said testily. The nerve of him. After he had betrayed her? Was he was worried about his position at the university? What about her pain, her suffering, her heartache?

"It's not good. I know you're angry, but you're not that kind of woman, Sissi. Just give me a few days, after the engagement party, and then we can talk about this."

"No!"

"Listen, . . . just pretend then. Okay? I can't tell my colleagues what has happened. You know how it is here. North Carolina Central Tech is so conservative. If anyone finds out, if even one person suspects anything, I'm ruined. Is that what you want?"

"Yes, that's what I want," Sissi whispered.

"Don't be heartless," Phil groaned in agony.

"Why not? You were," Sissi muttered, lowering her eyes in tired frustration.

"I'm not asking you to forgive me at this moment. I know I hurt you. I'm just asking you to wait a moment, think about what breaking off our engagement would mean."

"That's enough, Phil. Enough!" Sissi snapped, holding

her bag so tightly that her hands started to hurt. "I . . . I'm going home. I can't do this." Her voice was choked with pain. Before Phil could speak, she swiftly left the office and hurried back to her car. She was getting emotional, and the last thing she wanted to do was cry. He didn't deserve her tears, she thought bitterly.

She drove toward home in a stupor, stopping at red lights and stop signs mechanically, her thoughts on Phil's betrayal. She had known him for almost ten years during her years as a student then as a freelance employee at the university's TV station. Phil had always been a friend to her, a confidant. She knew he was attracted to her when she was a student, but her heart was with Percy Duvall at the time. Still whenever she had problems, she took them to Phil. His ten-year age difference and status as a professor at the university made him more of a big brother than a potential lover, and he always knew the best way to handle a problem. He was smart and kind, not only to her but to others as well. But when she and Percy broke up, Phil was at her side and, through his loving considerate actions, she learned to turn her appreciation into trust for him.

A bitter smirk spread across her lips. She had thought, in Phil, she had found the perfect man. He was intelligent and strong. He was considerate and generous. When she thought she was going to lose her grandmother's old mansion a year earlier because of back taxes, Phil offered to co-sign for a loan to stop the foreclosure on the property. But he took his generosity even further and began renovating the mansion until it was like new. She sighed heavily. With Phil she felt at peace. It wasn't the earth-shattering love she had found in Percy's arms, but at least she could trust Phil's assertion that he believed in her. That was a quality that Percy never had. He never believed in her. Thinking of Percy only caused Sissi to feel even more pain and confusion. He was supposed to come Friday night, but with the engagement off she had no chance of seeing him.

She was so caught up in her disappointment, she didn't notice the red light ahead of her and nearly drove through it. The vehicle to her left beeped its horn, shocking her alert. She slammed on the brakes, causing her head to jerk forward. When the car stopped, she sat up, breathless and shaken.

"Oh, Lord, I have to get them off my mind," she whispered, glancing at her surroundings in embarrassment. She was several miles from home. Rolling down the window, she maintained a stern attention on the road until she reached the house. She had just put the key in the front door when Phil's car skidded into the driveway. The dust hadn't settled before he jumped from his car and raced up the front lawn to her, breathing heavily. The last thing he wanted for Sissi to set her mind to was ending their engagement. He had to talk some sense into her.

"Sissi," he breathed heavily. She gave him a long, disgusted look before opening the door and walking calmly inside.

"Baby, I can't let you end it like this," he groaned, walking beside her through the house as she set her bag on the foyer table. She stood at the foot of the stairway and slipped out of her high heels. Picking them up, she started up the stairs.

"Sissi, I know you're mad. But I don't love that woman. I love you." At his words, Sissi became incensed and swung around to face him.

"You conceited fool," was all she could muster, then in a fit of frustration she threw one of her shoes at him. He ducked, covering his head as the shoe whizzed by.

"What? What?" he yelled in confusion. "I said I love you."

"Phil, I'll tell you what, love me enough to pack your

clothes and get out of my house," she bit out before continuing up the stairs. She was on the top stair when Phil decided he would risk approaching her.

"Baby—"

"I'm not your baby!" she snapped as she passed a few doors before reaching her bedroom.

"Sissi, don't do this," he groaned softly. Sissi stopped and stared at him, her eyes wide in disbelief. He seriously believed he was right, she could see it in his eyes. He thought there was hope for them. He was as foolish as he was arrogant.

"There is nothing you can say to change my mind, Phil. I am not going to marry you. I am not going to forgive you. I gave you my gratitude, my devotion, my trust. I set aside my doubts because you promised me you would never hurt me. When Percy left me, I swore I would never let another man hurt me. And you swore you wouldn't. But you did anyway. You had sex with a student, Philip. In your office with the door unlocked. That's blatant disregard for the so-called love you have for me. It's over. It's just plain over." Her words held such a note of finality that Phil gulped.

"Sissi," he began painfully. "I know . . . I accept that I was wrong, okay. But you can't possibly compare today with Percy's betrayal of you. He left you after you lost the baby and accused you of lying about it. I have never doubted you and would never have let you carry such a burden alone. Can't you see that?"

Sissi frowned and leaned against the door. It was only on very rare occasions that she or Phil spoke of her miscarriage. It pained her to hear about it again. It weakened her and made her feel vulnerable.

"But it isn't the same thing," Sissi murmured softly, looking at the floor in shame. Percy had made her feel guilty for having the miscarriage. He never believed her.

And she wondered for a moment if he still thought that she had aborted their child. Seeing her distraction and vulnerability at the mention of the baby, Phil pushed on.

"Just keep our plans for now, Sissi. Don't let everyone think we couldn't make it. You know how your friends are. And I promise you, if you still want to end the engagement after the party, I'll leave you alone. I promise!" he added in a heated murmur at her dubious expression. Sissi sighed and Phil brightened, believing he had won. But her next words quickly dispelled that idea.

"Fine, Phil. I'll go on with the party. I'll let everyone think that we are still engaged. But it isn't because I care what they will think about me. It's because, as bad as what you did today was, you have done a lot for me and I'm grateful. I don't want to see your career ruined, although a little earlier I would have gladly done that to you." She sighed, weighing her options as she spoke. "I'm going to let Michelle and Nicole come over Friday morning as planned and pretend that all is well between us. But Phil, don't misunderstand. It's over. I am not going to marry you. I can't forgive you. Come Monday morning, after everyone has left, I expect for you to do the same. When you feel the time is right, you can tell all of your friends that we broke up. Tell them what you want, I don't care. Just don't think that I'm going to marry you after what I saw today. Because truth be told, you're no better than Percy!"

Before Phil could respond, she closed the bedroom door in his face. He stared at the wood as if it had committed an offensive crime. He stood there a moment longer, then sighing with regret, he walked back down the stairs, unbuttoning his shirt as he went to the first floor bathroom. He needed a shower. He needed to clear his head. The bad news was that Sissi had caught him in the throes of passion with a young student. The good news was she was going to give him a few days to smooth it over. Even if she thought their engagement party was going to be a fake, for him it was a chance to win back her respect and gratitude.

"You'll change your mind, Sissi," he whispered to himself as he stepped into the bathroom and ran a hot shower.

The night of the party had come far too suddenly for Sissi. She could barely contain her mixed-up emotions each time she saw Phil. She had been successful in avoiding him totally on Thursday, but now he was capturing every moment he could to be close to her, and she was regretting her decision to pretend the engagement was still on. From the moment Michelle and Nicole arrived, he began holding her in fond embraces, caressing her shoulders and kissing her cheeks. She was disgusted and gave him long, evil glares. She was no fool and, if he thought that he would change her mind through the magic of the evening, he was a poor judge of her character.

Several of her guests had already arrived, and the basement was lit with soft lights, mellow music played and the easy sound of laughter and cheer was heard. But Sissi had grown impatient with mingling with the guests and at having Phil always at her side. She was tired of smiling, and every now and then the picture of Phil with his Nancy entangled in a lovers' embrace swept into her mind.

It was with relief that Phil found himself caught up in conversation with a few of his old colleagues from his tenure at Maryland University. Discreetly she left the party scene and went upstairs to her room. She lay on her bed in frustration. She needed to talk to someone. But Nicole was so animated about the entire idea of her getting married she didn't dare dampen her romantic impressions. And Michelle, one of her best friends from college, she wouldn't share a secret of any kind with her because she couldn't keep her big mouth closed.

As she lay there, she heard car after car arrive and grew curious. She wondered if Percy would actually come. She had invited him in hopes of seeing him one last time. But now, with her engagement to Phil off, she played with the idea that they could somehow get together again. She frowned, as she had been doing nearly most of the day. Percy didn't want her anymore, he had made that clear. All through the day she toyed with the memory of him and found herself dressing and preparing herself just for his arrival. She sighed. He was even worse than Phil. Why should she even want him to want her? Not able to answer the question, she got up, freshened up a bit, and stepped out into the hall. She heard voices in the foyer and stood still, not wishing to put on her smile just yet, not willing to go back down to the party until she had witnessed Percy's arrival.

At the top of the stairway in the soft silhouettes of the long hall, she watched with growing anticipation as guest after guest arrived. Her long dark eyelashes unwittingly hid her eager gaze as she observed the front door. With each new arrival, she drew closer to the stairway and scoped the faces of the guests for the tall, sun-bronzed frame of Percy Duvall. As the hour grew late, her confidence rose and she was sure that Percy would come. And she would be the first to greet him. She would be the first to look into his keen dark-brown eyes, the first to capture his full, passionate mouth in a sweet hello.

She blinked in consternation at the direction her thoughts were taking her and shook off her romantic fantasies of their reunion. After all, their parting had been bitter and two years had gone by. It was whimsical and foolish of her to portray him as a man who would easily come back into her life. But as she stood earnestly awaiting his arrival, she could not stop her wayward heart from toying with the idea that he still loved her, that the passion they had once shared could heal the wounds of his betrayal.

She sighed, noting with a pang of guilt that she was supposed to be portraying a woman happily engaged. She frowned. Subdued by the loyalty she promised Phil, she sighed heavily at her foolish decision to help him in the midst of his betrayal to her. But her gratitude to him kept her loyal. After all, when she fell, he was always there for her. She owed him the weekend at least. She dawned her cloak of honor, prepared to smother any feelings she had for her ex-love even as she continued to stand in the shadows to watch for Percy's arrival.

Chapter Two

The white lines streaked by in a blur beneath the beaming headlights of the old dark blue Nova. The road was barely visible in the darkness. It was a lonely road, dark and deserted without another car in sight. In its isolation it seemed to stretch on without end. And as if jealous of intruders, the trees appeared to reach out into the night to barricade all other exits. The windows were rolled down, but there was barely a breeze flowing into the car so still was the humid North Carolinian summer air.

The car was moving with a will of its own, speeding down the dark freeway, carrying its three male passengers toward Sissi Adams' home. Percy Duvall was no fan of hip-hop music, but it was his best friend's car. Besides, it graciously served to divert the attention of Craig and Eddie from noticing his dark mood. He was also glad for the loudness as it served to diminish his brooding over Sissi, who, no doubt, had not given him a second thought after writing his name on her lovely pink and almond invitations to come out and party with her and Philip Richardson in honor of their engagement.

Percy groaned inwardly, wishing he could relax and stop thinking of Sissi for just a moment. He tried to focus his attention on the old car, noting then that they had gone past only one gas station since leaving the train depot. He darted a worried glance at the gas gauge. Seeing that the gauge read over half full only slightly consoled him. Fighting his impatience with the time that it was taking to arrive at Sissi's home—he refused to think of it as Phil's house, too—he sank deeper into his seat and folded his arms across his muscular chest.

His continuous struggle to find comfort by stretching out his long legs was a partial blessing as it distracted him from the purpose of the ride. Still he wished that Eddie, who was used to sitting in the backseat, had not taken the backseat on this particular trip.

Eddie couldn't be blamed for his habitual behavior. In all the years of their friendship, Eddie never sat in the front. It was an unspoken rule between the three men that either Percy or Craig would drive and Eddie was designated to the backseat. Of course this evening Percy would have gladly taken the backseat himself as he didn't really care to be involved in any conversation. He was sure that Craig and Eddie didn't fail to notice his despondency. He usually expressed animated interest in their trivial discussions of the latest music or talk of women they had met, but his enthusiasm was overshadowed by nervous energy that he chose to call restlessness. After all, he thought stubbornly, he hadn't slept in almost twenty-four hours. He refused to admit that his agitation had anything to do with the fact that soon he would come face to face with his beautiful Sissi Adams.

He closed his eyes, appalled that he still thought of Sissi as his woman. The thought of seeing her knotted his gut with dread. Yet he had to admit that just the thought of her could still incite an excitement deep in his loins. It was natural, he thought grudgingly. He was a man and Sissi was a beautiful, sensuous woman. Any man would want to love her. He resented the rush of tingling sensations that flowed through his veins at the thought of seeing her and wished he could replace the word *love* with loathe, despise, hate. But he knew he could never hate Sissi even though she had scorned his confession of undying love for that of another man, none other than his number-one rival, Philip Richardson.

Phil was the last man Percy would have expected Sissi to marry. The professor had a reputation on campus for being a womanizer, and Percy recalled how Phil would watch Sissi with his beady little eyes. Sissi had even laughed about Phil's attempts to get her on a date. She would never consider going out with him—she wasn't his type, she had claimed. How she could turn to a man who had proven he was a womanizer, Percy could not fathom.

Percy sighed heavily then glared at the dark road ahead of them. His eyes shadowed with frustrating images of Sissi with Phil. It shouldn't bother him that she would choose to love Phil. She was a grown woman. He wouldn't dwell on his loss now. She was happy where she was. And now they were getting married.

Married!

He wanted to grind the word between his teeth and spit it out of the window. He was miserable with the deeply etched emotions that filled his gut at the thought of Sissi's impending marriage. He closed his eyes for a moment, exhausted with the foolish concern he harbored for a woman who had scorned him. *Damn her for still being able to get under my skin!* he swore under his breath, thankful that the loud music kept Craig and Eddie from noticing his gloom.

As if reading his thoughts, Craig said a moment later, "Man, you're too quiet." The words were shouted over the bass of the radio and caught Percy by surprise. Until that moment Craig's and Eddie's voices were no more than a hum in the background of his thoughts. He frowned, giving Craig a puzzled glance.

Craig laughed at the bewildered expression on Percy's face and asked sarcastically, "Lost?"

"Huh? Oh," Percy responded before sitting back in his seat with a nonchalant shrug. "I was just wondering why you won't get rid of this beaten-down car."

Craig grinned, not believing for a moment that Percy was giving any thought to his vehicle. But he glanced around the interior of his Nova with pride and said, "Someday I will, but so long as Nicole allows me to use her Sidekick, my Nova's all right with me." When Percy didn't respond, Craig gave him another curious glance and asked, "So what else is on your mind besides my sweet car?"

"My accounts," Percy answered easily. "I'm just thinking that this trip is a bad idea. I should be in New York poring over the details of my new accounts," Percy explained in a sullen mutter.

There was no way he was going to admit to Craig or Eddie just how intense his thoughts were of Sissi. He would never hear the end of it. It was only a year ago, just before he discovered that Sissi had moved in with Phil, that Percy had determined he still loved Sissi and wanted her back, no matter what had happened between them. He had behaved like a madman, calling all of Sissi's girlfriends in an attempt to find her and plead with her to forgive his selfish pride, to give him another chance to prove his love for her. But in the wake of his search, he discovered that she had returned to her grandmother's home in North

Carolina—and Phil was now living with her. Keeping his impulse in check, he had to resist the urge to go to Sissi and shake some sense into her, to confess that he still loved her and would do anything to get her back.

He nearly scoffed at the intensity of his emotions for Sissi. He was just thankful that he had never shared his passion with her or told Craig and Eddie of his intent. He was more thankful though that he had not followed his impulse to seek her out, knowing now that her heart belonged to someone else.

"New York big shot, ain't you, Percy." Eddie laughed, his high-pitched voice caught somewhere between adolescence and manhood.

Over the music, Percy barely heard him but responded in a disgruntled sneer: "I work hard and play hard, Eddie. I'm not trying to be anybody's big shot here," he finished firmly, not in the mood for Eddie's childish mockery.

Eddie was a big kid in Percy's sight. He was always making light of serious situations. Percy couldn't recall the last time he had heard of Eddie being on a date or at a party, or in any atmosphere outside of his job at the hospital. No, Eddie could no more relate to the serious emotions that Percy was dealing with than Percy could relate to Eddie's choice of becoming a physician. Percy knew one thing: If ever he needed a physician, he wouldn't go to Eddie!

"Yeah, yeah. So you've said. Whatever," Eddie responded, his tone still mocking although Percy's words held no jest when he spoke. Seeming oblivious to Percy's dark mood, Eddie shifted his glasses on his nose and smirked up at Craig, expecting to find an alliance in his ridicule of Percy's rebuff. He always considered Percy and Craig the charismatic ones, the men women always went after, the kind of men that other men enjoyed discussing football and beer with. Eddie felt awkward from his too thin frame to his ill-fitting clothes to the eyeglasses he always wore. Although, he had to admit with appreciation, Sissi had helped him pick out two sweet pairs of frames which he still wore. At least in that department he did not appear clumsy.

His only consolation and comfort at not being the charismatic one was that he was on his way to becoming a successful doctor, having just finished his last year as an intern at Southern Maryland Hospital. He was proud of his accomplishment and found that, for all his lack of charm, women were showing much more interest in him now.

He fought back a proud grin, not wanting to come off as a chump in front of his long-standing brothers, as he so often called them. It was a wonderful feeling to finally have gotten up the courage to ask one of the nurses at the hospital out to dinner. The fact that she had said yes was still amazing. For Eddie, the weekend couldn't be over fast enough. Tuesday night was supposed to be their dinner date, and he was anticipating it with high expectations.

It was funny, he thought with dry humor as he settled back in his seat, asking the nurse out to dinner had completely wiped out his years of infatuation with Michelle. He felt confident that for once he was going to be in a room with her and not feel like a complete buffoon. At least. he hoped.

"Hey, Eddie," Craig called with a laugh as he peered at him through his rearview mirror. "What's that big grin for?"

Eddie blinked in surprise, catching Craig's eyes in the mirror. He hadn't realized he was grinning. He shrugged, his grin broadening and said with his boyish charm, "Didn't even know I was grinning."

Craig nodded in appreciation, pleased that for once Eddie seemed relaxed and cheerful.

Percy, on the other hand, was killing him with boredom. Craig couldn't wait for the man to see Sissi and get it over with. Percy wasn't fooling Craig for one moment, either. Craig had perceived from the moment that Percy had gotten in his car how anxious Percy was about confronting Sissi. It was amazing and somewhat amusing to see Percy so preoccupied with anyone or anything outside of his New York clients. When Percy and Sissi first broke up, Percy had vowed that he was finished with Sissi for good. And Craig was rather envious at how well Percy seemed to handle their breakup. Percy had gone on to move up at his brokerage firm, rolling in the accounts, working like a dog without a sign of missing Sissi, until he discovered that Sissi had gotten involved with the professor. Now that was a strange twist, Craig thought with a quick glance at Percy.

A slight frown creased Craig's forehead as he thought of his own problems. With his fiancée, Nicole, on his right arm, whining about her ruined reputation, and Michelle on his left, begging him to leave Nicole, he was headed for a long weekend himself. He sighed heavily, wishing Michelle would just disappear, at least for the weekend. The last thing he needed was a battle between those women.

The drive was nearly over and the men had long since fallen silent, each preoccupied with his confounded emotions at the impending reunion with their friends from college. They would be at Sissi's place any moment, and Percy took a deep breath, leaned back in his seat, and closed his eyes.

The bottom line tonight, Percy decided resolutely, was that Sissi had made her choice. She was getting married. She had invited him to her party as a goodwill gesture, and he would handle it like a man. It didn't matter that Sissi was without a doubt making the biggest mistake of her life. He shook his head in misery, wishing he could be happy for her, happy that she was happy, even if it was with the professor. But he couldn't feel even an ounce of joy for the couple. With a scowl, he knew the best he could offer was civility and a short congratulations.

Chapter Three

"Ah, man, look at that. Look at that house! Can you believe Sissi's grandmother left that to her? I wish I had a rich relative," Eddie blurted as Craig cautiously drove onto the property, then traveled the long driveway that led to Sissi's newly renovated mansion. Craig put his foot on the brake and with Percy and Eddie, they all stared at the mansion.

Settled deep within the embrace of the trees, the manor seemed to leer down at them. Except for a few shaded windows on the top floor, the house was bright with the sound of activity and merriment. It was four stories high and seemed to stretch half a block long in width. The porch stretched nearly the length of the front of the house and had several deep stairs leading up to the impressive oak doors. There were gray and white marble pillars on every corner of the house and thinner pillars on both sides of the door. The men were all equally awed by the grandeur of the house, having visited homes that size only when touring historical museum homes.

"Her grandmother wasn't rich. But it's creepy," Percy muttered. He did not—would not—admit that it was a beautiful mansion. Not so long as Phil shared in the glory of its renovation.

Craig whistled in admiration and finally parked the car behind several other vehicles. Judging by the dozen or so cars in the lot, Craig guessed that most of Sissi's guests had already arrived. Slamming the doors shut, Craig and Eddie started up the stairs. Percy paused, envious and annoyed at the dazzling home Phil had been able to offer Sissi. *And what did any two people need with that much space anyway?* He glared at the house as if it were the sole cause for his grief.

"Hey, you coming?" Craig asked, glancing back at Percy with a raised eyebrow.

Percy rolled his eyes, smirked his lips, then squaring his shoulders, hurried up the stairs to join Eddie and Craig at the door. The weekend was just getting started, but he couldn't wait for Sunday. He could see the days ahead of him as being long and torturous. Agreeing to stay over had been a foolish mistake, he knew that now. He was burdened too much by the past. He didn't trust Phil's so-called love for Sissi. Phil's true colors would shine through eventually, Percy believed, if it hadn't already happened. Knowing Sissi, she would smoothly sweep it under the rug. He promised himself that after this weekend, he would never put himself at Sissi's mercy again.

"Hey, we forgot the gifts," Eddie muttered just as Craig rang the doorbell. Craig shrugged, shoved his hands in his jeans pockets, and said, "I'll come back out later and get them."

The doorbell was unusually loud, Sissi thought as excitement speared through her veins. But Percy was here! From the hall window, she had seen the car pull into the driveway and instantly recognized Craig's Nova. A smile curved her lips as she momentarily recalled all of the good times she and her friends had shared driving around from club to club in that old car.

At the sound of the car doors closing, Sissi started down the stairway only to stop in midstride at the sight of Phil. A tug of guilt assaulted her senses at spotting him. She had promised to pretend the engagement was real. To greet Percy with too much enthusiasm would surely give her away.

Phil stood with his arms folded across his chest, his eyes disapproving of her hurry to answer the door. He was a big man with his stalwart build—his six-foot-tall stocky frame stood practically guarding the doorway. He stared up at her, his eyes sadly imploring her to remember her promise as the bell chimed again.

Their eyes locked, and Sissi frowned at his sullen gaze. Yes, she had made him a promise but had he forgotten his indiscretion? She was the hostess, she reasoned in growing annoyance. It was natural for her to welcome her guests with open arms. She squared her slender shoulders, lifted her chin proudly, and lowered her eyes in an attempt to smother her disgust with Phil's pathetic attempt to win her sympathy. She was playing his game, he should be content with that.

With the will of a conqueror, Sissi asked in a low, husky voice that belied her excitement at the prospect of Percy walking through the door, "Well? Aren't you going to answer it?"

Phil neither moved nor responded to the question. He kept his composure, although he wanted to yank open the door and beat Percy to a pulp. And he had no doubt that Percy was on the other side of the door. He had made a major mistake, he knew that. But with Percy present, it would limit his chance to win Sissi again. He regretted his earlier macho decision to allow her to invite the man to their party.

Percy Duvall had stolen Sissi's heart a long time ago. It had taken a lot of effort and patience from Phil to get her to even consider a real date with him after leaving Percy. But he had finally won her over and resented the very idea that Percy could so easily recapture her heart. Jealous resentment surged through him like molten liquid, causing him to use all of his will not to explode at Sissi. He admitted that he was wrong, that his cheating undermined their impending marriage. But he was a man, and Sissi had to understand that it was sometimes hard to resist temptations that women like Nancy threw at him every day. Besides, he didn't love Nancy, and what he had done did not compare to Percy's betrayal after Sissi's miscarriage, he reasoned.

Wasn't it Percy who had left Sissi stranded and alone after losing her baby? Wasn't it Percy who had proven his selfishness for his own needs over Sissi's needs? Phil was sickened at the thought that he could lose the woman he loved. That she still cared for Percy was so obvious a blind man could see it. That Percy was undeserving of Sissi's love only infuriated Phil more. She could have at least had the decency to keep her promise and contain her anxious desire to see Percy. Did she believe he hadn't noticed her two-hour toilet? Her repeated changes of dress? Her anxious glances at the clock from the moment she had risen until this moment? And instead of playing hostess to their guests and his colleagues, she was waiting like a lovesick schoolgirl for Percy to walk into her life.

Stifling his rising anger, he pulled his crushed gaze from Sissi. With tense furrowed eyebrows, he swung open the door. Even before Phil said hello, he turned a last sad glance up the stairway at Sissi and knew instantly from her strained gaze, her slender hands balled into anxious fists at her side, that she was still harboring love for Percy Duvall. It hurt him to the core of his being, his own infidelity forgotten.

"Hey, bro," came Craig's instant greeting. Craig was just beginning to grow annoyed at the long wait and was relieved when Phil finally opened the door, even if the host's expression was sour and uninviting.

Before Phil could speak, Michelle's loud high heels clicked onto the hardwood floors and she asked in a loud, slightly slurred voice, "Phil! Where in the world is Sissi?"

Craig glanced at her for only a moment, instantly averting his gaze when her whining voice faded into silence at the sight of him. Percy caught Michelle's suddenly bright eyes and shook his head slightly, disappointed to find that Craig was most likely still secretly dating Michelle. And the man had said it was definitely over.

"I'm right here, luv," Sissi responded easily, too involved with scoping Percy's half-hidden figure to notice the quick exchange between Michelle and Craig.

Michelle glanced behind her at the stairway and, at seeing Sissi, she let out a shrill, pretentious squeal of delight that she no doubt thought was sweet and feminine.

"I was missing you downstairs, but I can see what the delay is now," she added lightly, now fully admiring Craig.

Craig rolled his eyes, refusing to acknowledge Michelle's mute greeting. He was not going to trip over Michelle again, of that he was determined. He had warned her before he came down that he was going to be with his woman, Nicole, and didn't want her hounding him. When was she going to get the picture?

Ignoring Michelle's inquiring gaze, Craig offered Phil a quick handshake and congratulations on his engagement to Sissi. Eddie followed suit before gingerly squeezing past

Phil's stocky form that was blocking him from having smooth access into the house.

Phil's return greeting was marred by his keen glance at Sissi, who was still eyeing Percy. Her large almond-shaped brown eyes could not conceal her desire, and Phil could not control an annoyed frown. Was she crazy? She was going to blow the whole evening. People would guess that all was not right between them if she kept up her idolizing gazes on Percy.

"Tell me, Percy, you didn't bring a companion for the weekend?" Phil asked loudly. All eyes fell on Percy, and he frowned, thinking it wasn't any of Phil's business if he was alone or not.

"No," was Percy's blunt answer.

"That's a shame. But don't worry, I'm sure you'll find a willing companion among the young ladies downstairs," Phil said crudely. Sissi was shocked at his comment and wanted to berate him, but she could only stare in embarrassment at Percy.

"I'm sure I could. But I don't roll like that," Percy responded easily. He was ready to leave. He could tell what kind of an evening he was up for. Phil grinned smugly, and Percy managed not to frown, even as he silently admonished Sissi. He wanted her to stop staring at him before he was compelled to pull her to him and give her a passionate kiss right in front of Phil.

He just wished she wasn't so adorable.

She had cut her hair into a short shaggy tease of sassy hair that she had slicked back from her face. On Sissi's slender face, the hairstyle was perfect; it was sexy and very appealing, and Percy instantly liked her new look. She seemed a little thinner than when last he had seen her, but her figure was still exceptionally curvaceous and beguiling, especially in the brown, spaghetti-strap short dress that she wore. It hung like a negligee and, with her swanlike movement, it flowed elegantly against her skin. All in all, she was blooming and appeared to be in good company with Phil's help. It seemed that there would be no déjà vu, and he would not have a chance to win her love again. He was disappointed.

"Hey, Michelle, honey. Give me some love, baby," Percy said in a loud boisterous voice as he pushed past the men and broke the hypnotic hold Sissi seemed to have over him.

Michelle grinned, happy to accept Percy's jovial greeting. Her goblet of champagne in one hand, she wrapped her arm around Percy and gave him a hug, whispering, "Percy, you are just as fine today as you were yesterday."

"Did I see you yesterday?" he inquired cheerfully, tossing Craig and Eddie a wide grin.

"In my dreams, as always." Michelle laughed, giving him a hearty squeeze. Percy's grin widened, although he wanted to tell Michelle to cut the pretentious act. She was madly in love with Craig, and everyone knew it. Hadn't she made it painfully obvious over the years?

"Me, too?" Eddie asked in a puppy voice, coming around Craig to give Michelle a hug as well. Michelle gave him another of her big smiles, if not as bright, before giving him a sweet peck on his cheek.

"Of course, you, too, my sweet Eddie. How is that doctor business coming? I was in Annapolis a couple of weeks ago," she went on, not giving him a chance to respond. "Meant to call you."

"Yeah, yeah, Michelle. Before you go on about nothing, I want to get my hugs and kisses, too," Sissi said with a beaming smile at her friends.

Percy used that moment to avoid Sissi's request and turned to Phil. The two men locked gazes, and Percy said in a deep, almost stern voice, "Congratulations, Phil. I wish you the best." He leaned toward Phil to give him a pat on his back, then extended his hand.

Phil could barely contain his disdain for Percy. He managed to nod his head and accepted Percy's handshake, then immediately released his hand as if Percy had the plague. Percy didn't fail to notice either that Phil, obviously hating the contact with him, seemed to choke on even the smallest acknowledgment. His short "Thanks," tore from him as if an apple were caught in his throat. Percy didn't know whether to be amused, annoyed, or feel sympathy for the man's obvious suffering.

"What about me, am I not getting married, too?" Sissi asked in her husky low voice, her eyes challenging Percy to ignore her any further. He could at least have the decency to acknowledge her, she thought indignantly, disappointed at his lack of enthusiasm at seeing her. She had been so eager to see him again, to possibly renew their friendship, if not their love. She wasn't expecting him to fall madly in love with her, especially while he believed that she was going to marry Phil, but to be friends again, that was all she wanted, she tried to convince herself.

Percy's cool glance left her a little puzzled. *Why is he so bitter?* she wondered. He had changed, had hardened, she thought, but she managed to maintain her smile even though it threatened to waver beneath his cold gaze. But when he reached out his hand and had the audacity to offer her a formal handshake, Sissi's eyes narrowed and her qualms set aside, she considered him with open indignation. Smugly she ignored his hand and leaned toward him, forcing him into an uncomfortable embrace.

"Congratulations," he muffled stiffly in her ear. He had to resist the urge to kiss her cheek, knowing how easy it was to get lost in Sissi's provocative web. For Sissi, his reaction couldn't have said more clearly how disappointed he was at her engagement to Phil. Intuitively Sissi sensed that, although Percy might never admit it, he regretted losing her. The idea consoled her aching heart after being so cruelly distressed by first Percy and then her cheating ex-fiancé.

As they released one another, Sissi managed to lock her gaze into Percy's eyes and felt a flurry of butterflies attack her senses at his unveiled yearning for her. It didn't matter that it was quickly snuffed out, she had seen it. An almost timid grin spread across her mouth as she flushed. That slight spark that had flared was dangerously close to inciting a flame between them. Uncertainty caused her to run her fingers through her hair. As she did so, her gaze happened to fall on Phil and she paused, noting with growing impatience Phil's silent berating of her performance. So she wasn't the best actress. He was lucky he was still in her home having a party at all, she thought.

Phil shut the door after greeting Sissi's friends. Once it was locked, he leaned against it to shrewdly consider the group of men and women exchanging hugs and warm kisses. He hadn't missed the exchange between Percy and Sissi. It irritated him to see them together. And to know he had put himself in the position where there wasn't much he could do to stop Sissi from rekindling her love with Percy was a distressing realization. It was going to be a long night, and he was determined that if he did nothing else, he wasn't going to give Percy a chance to be alone with Sissi.

Sissi carefully drifted her focus from Phil back to Percy and, not missing a beat, chose to ignore Phil's sullen expression. She would deal with him later, if need be. But for now it was her moment, and she had to admit a small part of her was enjoying making Phil suffer at what he had done. It was only fair that she have a moment with Percy. It was just a little less than a year since she had seen him. During the times when they happened to be at the same gathering, Percy wouldn't allow her near him. He would find an excuse to leave or simply not talk to her. In fact, the tension between them was so bad, she had chosen not to attend the party Nicole had thrown for Craig's twenty-ninth birthday several months earlier. She knew Percy, as one of Craig's best friends, would not dare to miss the event. Of course, Percy was so stubborn, like a child. Sissi had guessed some time ago that he knew how wrong he was by now, but he still refused to discuss the miscarriage. He would never hear her out. So, fed up with his blatant intent to avoid her, she chose to avoid him instead. But he was on her territory now, and she was determined that if nothing else, whether he liked it or not he would admit that he was wrong about the miscarriage.

It was a dreadful discovery to hear that, just a month after she agreed to allow Phil to move in with her, Percy had begun searching for her. She had moved out of the apartment without a word to her friends, but she was so excited about renovating her grandmother's house, she couldn't wait to get to North Carolina. It was bad luck that Phil had just moved in with her as well.

It was very frustrating. Percy hadn't spoken to her in less than a year, and then suddenly he decided he had to talk to her, he had to find her—but she had already come to the sad conclusion that they would never be together again. She had given up hope, never dreaming that Percy would change his obstinate mind or at the very least want to hear her recounting of the miscarriage.

She peered up at Percy behind her thick dark eyelashes and allowed her gleaming white teeth to dazzle him. He had searched for her once before, he had wanted to talk. Why not believe that he could still have a desire to clear the air between them. There was nothing wrong with talking. Surely no one would think just because she and Percy spoke that her engagement was off, even if it were the truth.

"Thank you," she said to Percy before stepping aside to accept Eddie's brief hug.

"I'm happy for you, Sissi," Eddie chimed in a boyish voice Sissi had grown to love. Eddie was like a little brother for Sissi, and she doted over him, returning his warm hug as he bent over her.

"I'm sure you'll be next, Eddie," Sissi whipped out before turning finally to Craig. Craig was one of Sissi's dearest friends. They had met through mutual friends on campus and had hit it off more as brother and sister than boyfriend-girlfriend. It suited them both just fine. Sissi just wished that Craig was more discreet with his passions as he was breaking the heart of her other dear friend, Nicole, Craig's devoted girlfriend. Of course, Nicole loved Craig without question, and at least Craig was still around even if he had never completely given up his other woman.

Craig smiled at Sissi with pride as if she were his little sister. The last time he heard from Sissi, she was saying her regrets for not attending his birthday party. She was ill, she had claimed, but Craig knew better. Like Percy, Sissi couldn't bear to be in the room with her ex for fear that he would discover that she still loved him. The problem was, Craig could see clearly that Percy also still loved Sissi. If they weren't so stubborn, Craig suspected they would have the greatest love a couple could imagine.

"Craig." Sissi grinned, opening her arms wide for his hug. Their genuine friendship gave them both liberty to hold each other in a warm embrace that would cause no eyebrows to raise, no hearts to race in wild jealousy.

"So, Sissi is getting tied down. Watch her, Phil, she ain't no Mary Poppins, that's for sure." Craig laughed.

Sissi playfully shoved Craig aside, gasping indignantly. "He wouldn't love me if I were—"

"Okay, you guys, enough of the greetings stuff," Michelle interrupted. "There's a party going on, and you must see the beautiful decorations I created . . ."

"And Nicole," Sissi added pointedly, keeping her gaze on Craig as she spoke. She wanted Craig to treat Nicole kindly tonight. Nicole was going to need his support, and Craig couldn't allow Michelle to make the evening worse. Sissi was determined to make sure Craig didn't get caught up in Michelle's wanton wiles.

"And Nicole, of course. So come on, you're missing the fun. Come on, let's go," Michelle finished, her hyper tones masking her irritation at Sissi's mention of Nicole. She also was annoyed at the warmth Sissi and her guests shared. In particular she resented Craig's adoration of Sissi, as if Sissi were some kind of an angel or something.

"Michelle's right. Let's go," Phil agreed, walking up to Sissi and taking her hand in his. Sissi smiled at Phil, and he instantly released a relieved breath, happy to see that she had not forgotten her promise to him. For a few minutes, watching her admire Percy, he had grown concerned. But her easy acceptance of his hand relieved his fear, and he happily walked by her side down the stairs.

"You know, Craig, Nicole is already here." So happy to see her best friends all together again, Sissi began chatting to Craig, glancing over her shoulder at others with a cheerful grin before entering the basement hall as she spoke. Craig let out a loud guffaw.

"Now you know I know," he responded heartily.

Marvin Gaye's song "Sexual Healing" was filling the air, and Percy sighed, following the group to the party. It was going to be one of those types of parties, where the music would leave him feeling blue and alone. He didn't need to hear those tunes, not tonight, he groaned as the seductive tune grew clearer at their approach. Loud hip-hop music would have been preferable, he thought moodily.

Percy's eyes followed Sissi's graceful movement through the basement doorway, and he tried to quell the surge of regret that filled him. From the moment she had left his embrace, her attention had drifted completely from him. He felt rebuffed, and it irritated him that he felt used. She obviously wanted to get a reaction from him, to see if she had it like that. Well, she did! But he wasn't going to slip up twice. He was going to put his emotions in check. Still he wished, as he looked around the crowded basement, that he had asked someone, anyone at all to come with him as his date. The problem was, since he had lost Sissi he had dated many women, but he always failed to make a commitment, no matter how close to perfection they came.

He noticed, too, how Phil was keeping his flamboyant fiancée close to his side. With a keen observation, Percy decided that Phil must have an idea that he was all wrong for Sissi. Why else was the professor guarding Sissi like a Secret Service agent guarding the president? The man hadn't left Sissi's side since they entered the basement. Yes, it was obvious that Phil Richardson was not completely confident in himself, and Percy pitied him for it. Sissi needed a strong man, not someone hovering over her like a guard dog.

Chapter Four

The sweet, sexy melody of Marvin Gaye's voice rang throughout the lavishly decorated basement. It was brightly lit, with spotlights beaming from each corner of the room. The room was boldly decorated in black, cream, and shocks of pink. A mountain of food was presented on a long buffet table. There was a bar set up near the back door and several tables, covered with cream-colored tablecloths, were situated around the large room. It was an impressive crowd of Sissi's and Phil's friends. Everyone was engrossed in animated conversations. A few men were gathered by the bar singing off-key with Marvin Gaye's "Sexual Healing," raising their drinks in a high toast. Then the song changed, and Otis Redding's "Tramp" blared out of the speakers. The women shouted, got on the dance floor, taking their partners with them. It was a mixed crowd, equally divided between Sissi's and Phil's friends, but Phil's preference dominated the music. It was his choice of music that set the mood of the evening.

But no one seemed to mind. They were too busy mingling, dancing and drinking, and whispering, "Girl, did
you hear?" and responding, "Yeah, I heard," and laughing, "Oooh, wait until he finds out what she did last
weekend."

They hung around the room like a pack of hungry
wolves, waiting maliciously for a scene to break out among
the hostess and her guests. Of course, the kind of friends
that Sissi had held nothing sacred. It wasn't Phil they were
talking about, either, but his fiancée, Sissi, and her ex-
lover, Percy Duvall.

"I heard she was pregnant," one woman exclaimed with
excitement in her voice that couldn't be restrained.

"No, not Sissi. She's hardly the type to accidentally get
pregnant," another whispered, her greedy eyes flapping
about the room in hopes of spying on the much envied
Sissi Adams.

"Shoot, forget Sissi. What about Nicole? Now you know
what she did?" a voice rang out from the huddle of women.
Like snapping turtles they turned in unison to stare at the
speaker, their eyes expectant in the wake of juicy gossip.
When the speaker, a tall older woman, hesitated, like a
chorus they rang out in unison, "What?"

"Slept with Keith, that's what. Girlfriend slept with her
cousin's man," the older woman heaved as if relieving a
great burden from her chest.

"I had heard that, too," another of the women chirped
in agreement, and pretty soon they were all accepting the
rumor as fact, eagerly believing that Nicole Burns could
have easily slept with her own cousin's husband.

"And they were supposed to have been close, too,"
another said. "Like sisters."

"And you know Donna's going to let Nicole have it when
she gets here," a voice edged with unbridled delight rang
out.

"Yeah, 'cause Donna don't play like that."

"Who said she was invited?" another asked.

"Please, with a bash like this, you know Sissi had to invite everyone to show off. Besides, the guest list must have been done a long time ago," responded the tall older woman.

"Nicole's too classy to have done something like that. Saying she slept with her favorite cousin's husband is hard to believe," a voice of reason dared to speak. As if betrayed, the other women glared on the short round girl who defended Nicole's honor. Grear cringed beneath their contempt, regretting her words and wishing she had kept her opinion to herself. The last thing she needed was for her friends to think she was siding with Nicole.

"What?" the older woman snapped, her eyes narrowed, daring Grear to repeat her comment.

Grear blinked nervously, her eyes lowering in shame as she mumbled, "I mean, she could have . . . done it."

"I know she did. She was busted, girl!" the woman insisted. They all fell silent, their eyes landing on the object of their discussion with envy and dislike.

"Forget Nicole for a moment. Look at Percy over there. He is still as gorgeous as he was in college," a giddy woman said with a wink at her comrades.

"Oh, he is fine. I saw him at Nicole's and Craig's party a few months ago. And I know he's not rich like Philip, but Sissi was a fool to let him go," another of the women agreed.

"And he was in love with her," the older woman added, shaking her head and pursing her lips as she recalled in envy the way Percy had called her, demanding to be told where Sissi had moved.

In the corner, near the patio doors that allowed a sweeping view of the lavishly decorated landscape, the huddle of women fell silent as they stared into the crowded room. They watched the couples on the floor, and each imagined that she had the attention of Percy Duvall, the gossip and curiosity about Nicole all but forgotten for the moment.

Nicole was usually laughing and boasting along with the other women about her strong black man, her handsome lover, her fiancé, her Craig. Normally at a party she would dance and cheer, her petite body working the dance floor. She enjoyed life and knew how to have fun as well as how to relax just like everyone else. But with all of the confusion and disgusting lies that had been spread throughout the room regarding her relationship with Keith, her cousin Donna's husband, Nicole thought she would burst with frustration. The rumor couldn't have occurred at a worse time, either. She was in a financial bind. Her truck was in danger of being repossessed, her mortgage was going to be foreclosed on soon, not to mention credit cards way over the limit. Craig knew nothing of her problems. She had been so careful not to let him know how desperate she was becoming. He had made it clear that he didn't want any burdens, and she had seen to it by hiding her bills and manipulating their joint finances. How could she come to him now, when he was in the process of moving in with her, and tell him that she was thinking about filing bankruptcy?

More irritating than the gossip and her money issues was the way Keith allowed the rumor to continue without defending her. It was almost two weeks since the rumor began, and Keith had not once denied it. And then he had the nerve not to show up at Sissi's party to help clear up the lie. Of course, Nicole knew Keith wanted a divorce from Donna. Keith also knew that it would incense Donna if she believed he had slept with Nicole. But that was the wrong way to do it. Donna was more determined now to remain Keith's wife, just to make him writhe, no less. What

Nicole resented most was that not once did Keith consider how Craig would react at hearing the tasteless lies.

Just because Keith's uncle had died didn't give him the right to play king of hearts with everyone else. If Keith had any sense at all, he would have realized that letting Donna believe that there had been a romantic encounter between them would only make Donna more determined to hurt him back.

Nicole sighed, sipping her champagne without tasting it. She could practically hear the nasty whispers about her as the crowd milled around her. Coming to Sissi's and Phil's engagement party was supposed to be fun for her, because Sissi was her best friend. Now she wondered if it was a foolish mistake instead. The worst part about the slanderous gossip was that most of the women encouraging its continuation were her so-called friends—the same women who had come to her home only a few months earlier for Craig's birthday party.

She felt betrayed and fought the tears that stung her eyes. She wouldn't let them get the best of her. With stubborn pride she subdued her fragile impulse to cry. Batting her eyelashes as if she was flirting with one of the men, she managed to overcome her tears just as Grear Meyers and three other women sauntered by her.

Grear was a short woman, no more than five feet tall. Her long thick brown hair that she wore in heavy bouncing curls nearly hid her face from view and made her appear even smaller and more timid. But it wouldn't have mattered. Grear had a way of never looking directly at anyone when she spoke. With such a large crowd of people, Grear was certain to hide in her shell of insecurities.

"Nicole, hi. You remember Maryl, Bridget, and Keisha," Grear said, hesitantly tossing an uncertain glance at the other women as if she was looking for their approval to speak to Nicole.

Nicole nodded with clear indifference, although she became temporarily amused from her pessimism by the women's blaring attire. The three women and Grear were all old college friends of Sissi's. It was obvious to Nicole that their attire had been carefully, if not in complete tacky taste, chosen for the occasion. They were spandex-down, she thought in cynical amusement.

Maryl, who wasn't much taller than Grear, but dumpier, wore white spandex tights with two-inch black leather high heels and a sheer black lace blouse that showed off her thick stomach and small breasts. Her hair was cut short, similar to Sissi's haircut but did nothing to complement Maryl's strong, manly features. Bridget, the girl on Maryl's left, wore a glaring orange spandex miniskirt with an offensively dull orange blouse that enhanced the orange-gold highlights in her hair. Her bright blue eyeshadow and scarlet lipstick made her appear clownish, and for a moment Nicole actually smiled.

Most offensive, Nicole decided with narrowed eyes as Keisha had the nerve to smirk at her from behind the other women, was the dark purple monstrosity that Keisha was wearing. Keisha, whose weight definitely called for more demure attire, was much too grossly built to have even attempted to squeeze into the tight purple spandex cat-suit she was wearing. Her flab could not be concealed by the confines the spandex offered, nor did the black blazer that she had chosen help in subduing the awkward wardrobe.

"Ladies," Nicole greeted with an obvious snub on the word. Her amusement faded at the sly glances the women gave one another, and again she cringed inwardly as her shame resurfaced. Michelle had successfully ruined her reputation. The lying hussy! Of Michelle's role in instigating the rumor, Nicole was sure. She was the only person who even knew Keith well enough to begin such a malicious lie.

". . . got such nerve to show her face," she heard Maryl whisper as they tottered away. Nicole shifted her gaze as casually as she could, hating what she was hearing in the muffled conversations, determined not to run and hide as her heart was crying out to do. She hoped Donna would come out to the party. Donna's presence would prove to everyone that the gossip was untrue and unfair.

Nicole frowned. This would hurt their relationship, of that she was sure. They had grown to have such a trusting and close bond, even though it was years before they even knew the other existed. Nicole was seventeen when her father came home with his fourteen-year-old niece and simply said, "Here, watch your cousin. I have to get back to work."

Nicole closed her eyes for a moment, recalling her shock at having a cousin she had never heard of. And they looked so much alike that for some time Nicole thought her father was lying and had fathered a child out of wedlock. In truth she discovered that her father had a brother who had left home years before Nicole was born. Her uncle, Donna's father, had married, had a child and was living his life as an insurance salesman when he died from a heart attack. Unfortunately he was driving at the time, and his wife was riding with him. They were both killed when the car swerved off the highway into an oncoming truck.

It was a sad situation, and Nicole had tried to comfort her young cousin, thinking Donna was completely alone in the world. It wasn't until Donna's sixteenth birthday that Nicole discovered how big her extended family really was. Donna had grandparents who adored her. They had been trying to contact her and get her back from Nicole's father. But it was Donna who wanted to get away from the Joneses. She wanted to be with her uncle, her father's family, having heard wonderful stories about his growing up. So Donna had painted a horrible picture of her grandparents and two uncles. When Nicole finally met them she was shocked, embarrassed even, at the lie Donna had so well planted.

Donna's grandparents were the sweetest, jolliest old couple Nicole had ever met. Her two uncles, Michael Jones and Waymer Jones, weren't much older than Nicole's father and too kind for words. They lived in a quiet area in the heart of Fredericksburg, Virginia. And Nicole was instantly envious if not completely baffled by Donna's relationship with her mother's family.

Nicole sipped her wine and frowned, recalling how it had been she, not Donna, who visited the Joneses. She had grown to love Donna and the Joneses as her own family. It was through the Joneses, too, that Donna met her husband, Keith. He was a neighbor of Michael Jones and when Michael had taken ill, Nicole and Donna would visit often. Together the cousins came to know the boy next door. But it was Donna, not Nicole, that Keith was interested in. And that was fine with Nicole. Her cousin was finally happy. Why should anyone think that after nearly fifteen years, she would suddenly sleep with Keith?

With a swift glance around the room, Nicole wondered in mild irritation what was delaying Craig, Eddie, and Percy. As if on cue she spotted Craig near the fireplace. The sight of him caused Nicole to tense, especially when she caught sight of Michelle hovering over him. She averted her gaze from them, trying not to show how humiliated she was that Michelle was the first to greet Craig. She took a deep breath and tried to focus on the happy occasion of Sissi's upcoming wedding.

Searching the crowd, she looked for just one friendly familiar face to help her forget the ordeal of seeing Michelle's controlling hold over Craig. It came soon when she saw Janice, another of Nicole's good friends, laughing heartily with one of Sissi's male guests. Seeing Janice helped Nicole to relax almost instantly. Janice was always lively and jovial, befriending everyone with the same enthusiasm. It was Janice's sense of humor and fun that eased Nicole's despondency. Not once did Janice ask if the rumor was true. Even Sissi had asked if the rumors were true, Nicole noted.

Nicole wouldn't know what to do with herself if Janice hadn't called her a few nights earlier and said in her bubbly voice, "Girl, you know I don't believe none of that nonsense Michelle's started. Don't you let her get to you. She's been trying for years. Okay, honey?"

Nicole had agreed and with a little nudging between Janice, Sissi, and Craig, she had kept her original plans to help decorate for the party and to stay the weekend in celebration. At least a small part of her was happy she had come. If nothing else, she was showing her head, proud and sure of herself. In the end, none of them mattered anyway. It was her life and her future that she was concerned about, and she wouldn't let Michelle interfere with her plans for even a second longer, Nicole decided resolutely.

"Why in the world did Sissi invite Michelle? I can't stand that sneaky hussy," Janice ranted, coming up to stand at Nicole's side, having witnessed Nicole's silent cry for support.

Nicole blinked, amazed at how impromptu Janice's comment was. They both glanced up and watched Michelle.

"Look at her, thinking she's all snazzy in that loud red dress. She needs to do some sit-ups."

"Well, she is pretty," Nicole confessed softly, not wanting to appear jealous of Michelle.

"If you say so," Janice heaved, although she refused to acknowledge that Michelle's long legs were dazzling in her black stockings or that her full, flowing hair was attractive over her slender face. So Michelle had large, clear green eyes. So often people told her that she could be Vanessa Williams's sister. It was her nasty, sneaky, gutless attitude that Janice was seeing, and there was nothing pretty about that.

"But a few sit-ups wouldn't hurt," Nicole added, noting the small pouch that was threatening to fill Michelle's girth.

"Now that's more like it," Janice said, laughing. "Sit-ups, push-ups, and running in place wouldn't hurt, either."

Nicole smiled although artfully averting her gaze from Janice's own rather full girth. Michelle and Janice were in fact about the same height. Overall Janice was well built, but in the latter years her stomach had grown fuller and her hips wider. Still she was attractive, and the weight she had gained only enhanced her beauty, Nicole decided.

"And if you could have heard her lying to that guy," Janice gushed on in a barely hushed voice, completely unaware of Nicole's observation.

"What's she lying about now?" Nicole asked, holding her champagne in a hand that threatened to tremble with rage.

"You know the kind. That she used to date some guy from NBC. Was engaged to some producer. She's such a trip. And look at her, she's all over Geoff."

"Geoff?" Nicole asked with casual curiosity, darting her glance around the room until it fell on the man standing in deep conversation with several women. Nicole recognized him as the same man whom only a few minutes before, Janice had been engaged in conversation with.

"Yeah, girl. You know, the new weather guy at the station. He's Sissi's friend. I think he's also a part-time professor at the university with Phil or something like that. Anyway I wouldn't worry about Michelle, she's such a sleaze. To have the nerve to start a rumor about anyone, let alone you and Keith . . . I can't stand her. Why Sissi deals with her is beyond me," Janice added heatedly.

"Speaking of Sissi, what's going on with her anyway?" Nicole whispered, looking around the room for Sissi's familiar sleek form. Janice frowned and shrugged.

"I don't know. But I'm glad you noticed it, too. She's been acting . . . distracted," Janice answered with a worried glance in search of Sissi.

"Maybe it's because Percy's here," Nicole pondered.

"Maybe nothing. I know it is. What I'm concerned about is her engagement. I don't want her to give up Phil to return to an old problem, you know?" Janice hissed, her gaze now on Percy standing in a small group by the fireplace. Nicole twitched her mouth, looking dubious.

"Do you really think it would be a mistake?" she added, considering Phil. "I think Phil is the mistake. He seems so wrong for her. He's so . . . so dull. And Percy's so in control of everything," Nicole said, trying to search for the right words as she weighed the two men.

"Yeah, but at least Phil never accused her of murder," Janice snapped heatedly.

"Murder?" Nicole looked confused.

"The miscarriage, remember? Percy thought she had aborted the baby. I thought that was so low," Janice muttered. "If he weren't so charming, I would have dropped all ties with him a long time ago."

"But that's what I mean. He's so perfect for Sissi," Nicole tried to explain.

"He's only as perfect as we imagine him to be. The reality is Percy is not the man for Sissi. Otherwise they would be together. I mean, look at you and Craig. With everything that has happened between you two, you're still together. Now that's love. That's belonging," Janice added emphatically.

Nicole didn't respond, not wanting to encourage Janice any further. She completely disagreed with Janice's notion of love. And worse yet, to use her and Craig's situation only made the issue worse. Besides, as Janice got more involved in discussing her emotions, the louder her voice became. It was Janice's one big flaw. She couldn't control her tone of voice when she became excited or anxious. So Nicole simply agreed with her as she allowed her gaze to follow Michelle.

Michelle Lifkin was hot with frustration. Craig was keeping his word. He was having nothing to do with her. Annoyed by the cold shoulder he was giving her, she rolled her eyes as she scanned the room. Feeling Nicole's pitiful gaze on her, Michelle looked across the room with a malicious smirk twisting her full mouth.

Her piercing green eyes fell on Nicole mockingly, as if to say, *Go ahead, deny it. I know the truth.* After all, Michelle thought smugly, it wasn't her problem that Nicole couldn't keep her legs closed. Always in some man's face while faking like she was a sweet little thing in love with Craig. But now everybody knew just what kind of sweet girl Nicole truly was, especially with the in-laws. If she could just get Craig to see the light, Michelle was sure he would be hers.

It seemed from the day they met they were rivals, and everyone was always on Nicole's side. Michelle blamed Sissi as much as Nicole for her problems. After all, it was Sissi who introduced Craig to Nicole and ruined what Michelle considered a beautiful relationship. Michelle fumed even now in the face of her triumph. That Nicole always managed to be so needy, with her petite frame, so desperate with her round big brown eyes, so frail with her sweet, light voice, yet so wonderful for befriending an orphaned cousin, infuriated Michelle.

Michelle frowned in disgust The only thing desperate about Nicole was her inability to clear the smear of tramp from her name. Michelle had caught Nicole in the dead of the night coming out of Keith's hotel room after Donna had kicked him out of their home. How was Nicole going to explain the fact that she lived in Virginia and Donna lived in Mitchellville, Maryland? Yet she saw Nicole and Keith at the Marriott in Washington, D.C.

She couldn't explain it, Michelle decided, because she was guilty. Nicole could deny that they had slept together to her death, but Michelle would never believe it. It was Nicole's story that she was consoling her cousin-in-law, that she was trying to help him get over the pain of his bad marriage with Donna. That's why she had embraced him, she explained. Sure, Craig may have believed that, but Michelle was proud that Donna hadn't fallen for it.

A wicked grin spread across Michelle's mouth as she thought of Donna. Nicole was so sure that Donna believed her, but Donna had already informed Michelle that when she arrived at the party all hell was going to break loose and her cheating cousin was going to be sorry. Michelle couldn't wait.

Her face clouded with a temporary bout of resentment. It was Nicole who had stolen Craig from Michelle, not the other way around. But no one could see past Nicole's innocent frame and bright smile. She seemed too demure, too nice to be the conniving witch that Michelle knew she was. Well, how sweet was she now?

Michelle's thrill of at last having the upper hand on Nicole wasn't complete though. She glanced for a moment from Nicole to Eddie, Percy, and then Craig. They had found a quiet space by the large unlit fireplace. And a twinge of despair shadowed Michelle's eyes as she recalled Craig's burning words the day before.

"Don't come near me, don't speak to me. Don't even look at

me, Michelle. You disgust me." She winced at the memory of his words, knowing even as it pained her to hear him speak so harshly to her that he would be short-lived in his anger. He would find his way to her before the weekend, if not the night, was over, she was sure. She sighed, feeling uplifted at the idea of Craig's weakness for her love. He might want to marry Nicole because of her well-spun web of sweet innocence, but it was Michelle that stirred his blood. Hadn't he said so just a few weeks ago? He loved her, even if he thought it was over between them. She knew better. Her smug victorious expression returned, and she again gave Nicole a penetrating gaze of triumph.

Chapter Five

Nicole cringed inwardly beneath Michelle's piercing stare. It was irritating that after all these years, Michelle was still able to crumple Nicole's composure with one belittling gaze. Michelle was the woman who was trying to steal Craig from her, without any discretion, Nicole swore under her breath. So it was Michelle who should be quivering with discomfort!

Refusing to allow her bitter thoughts to control her, she forced her hands to remain steady and brought her champagne to her lips. It was dry and tasteless as the sourness she was feeling numbed her senses. That Michelle! She had singularly managed to ruin Nicole's life. First she seduced Craig, as if Nicole was unaware of their affair. Then she had the audacity to spread the rumor about Keith. And everyone was believing it! It wasn't as if Michelle had pictures or anything to back up her nasty claim. It wasn't as if Michelle even had any credibility. It didn't matter, Nicole decided. Donna would arrive shortly and all would be cleared.

Nicole's gaze left Michelle and embarked on a hopeful search of the crowd for Donna, but there was no sign of her. Again she wished she hadn't come. She was just plain tired. It was a mistake to subject herself to everyone's snide glances and spiteful comments that they must have known she could hear.

Craig had urged Nicole to come to the celebration, asserting she had nothing to fear. He believed in her and that should be good enough for her, he had insisted.

"Haven't they been claiming I'm Michelle's lover for years? You don't see me hiding from her," he had said dryly. At his comment Nicole wanted to fling her hairbrush at him, but then she realized how right he was. At least he hadn't let the rumor or the truth of it keep him locked inside. Yes, he was right, of course, but after all she was only human—and she was tired of being hurt.

Nicole groaned inwardly before raising her gaze from the gray carpeted floor. It was a coincidence that her eyes landed on Craig. He was standing in his usual group with Eddie to his right and Percy to his left. With dark narrowed eyes, she considered her fiancé with an almost hypnotic gaze, torn between disgust at his betrayal with Michelle and affection at his belief in her.

Craig was the tallest of the three men, though only by a slight difference. His smooth brown complexion always appeared as if someone had run a film of gloss over his skin. He had a sleek, well-trimmed mustache and kept his hair in a military short cut. His eyes were dark and seductively shielded with a wealth of thick eyelashes any woman would die to have. He was clean-cut in fashion and precise in his mannerisms, from his combed eyebrows to his polished alligator shoes.

Oh, he was smooth, and Nicole guessed that was why

she had stayed with him all these years. And he treated her well, giving her everything she asked for. Plus he had the image she craved, the style she admired, but his heart was selfish when it came to loving her and Michelle.

And that was where he had failed her.

When he informed her that he would meet up with her after picking up Eddie and Percy at the train station, Nicole's first reaction had been blinding anger. He was leaving her alone, at the party, with those vultures? Alone. With everyone spying on her, watching her every move. She knew what they would think—that she and Craig had broken up over her blatant affair with her cousin's man. Just another point for Michelle to add to her triumph bag.

Nicole sighed in regret. For a moment she wished that she were Janice or Sissi. Janice, who was smart enough to date outside of her college buddies, never seemed to have a problem with men or money or her career. She was so carefree. And Sissi, she had men falling at her feet. She could handle any man, it seemed. It was so obvious that Phil was madly in love with her. He had barely left her side all evening, and whenever Nicole noticed Phil watching Sissi, his expression was full with concern and obvious devotion to his fiancée. Even Percy was enamored with Sissi. Poor Percy, Nicole thought. Sissi had all but ignored the man since he arrived. And Percy was obviously sulking over his loss, his gaze either staring into the fireplace or searching for Sissi.

Nicole sighed. She never found Craig watching her the way Phil and Percy watched Sissi. But it didn't matter, she decided. Whatever Craig did now, she would always doubt him. Their relationship wasn't the same. It had long since lost its innocence, and there was no recapturing the old love. Her feelings had changed, and it was time for her to make decisions for her future. She wondered if Craig would be a part of it.

Craig felt Nicole's downcast gaze on him and considered her in appreciation. She had no idea how beautiful she was. His Nicole. She was courageous, too, he thought in admiration. He darted a glance at Michelle. He never believed for one moment that Nicole slept with Keith. But Michelle had no credibility with him. He didn't believe a word that came out of her mouth. Ever since his last year in college when he met Nicole and broke up with Michelle, Michelle hounded Nicole like an unrelenting beast, waiting to snare her up the moment she tripped. It just so happened that it took over seven years for Michelle to find something negative about Nicole that people would believe. So what if Nicole and Keith were close? She had known Keith years before they started college. Besides, Keith was Donna's husband and would have never asked for a divorce had Donna not flaunted her blatant affairs in the man's face. So Donna was no more reliable a source than Michelle, at least not for Craig.

More important for Craig was Percy's opinion of the whole sordid story. Percy was nonchalant and completely confident that it was a lie. In fact, Percy had thoroughly scolded Craig, saying, *"Don't make the mistake I made, man. Trust your woman."*

And Craig definitely did trust Nicole. She was far too mild tempered and consistent by nature to cheat on him, he rationalized. Of course, he noted in mild exasperation that Nicole hadn't moved far from her discreet position near the patio door since he arrived. She was like a butterfly: petite, gentle, and awaiting escape. It was her vulnerability that kept Craig by her side. She was so precious with her big brown eyes that were watchful and sad as she scanned the room. It hurt him to see her that way.

But at least she had taken time to look her best, he thought in appreciation. She had worn her hair loose and flowing, his favorite style. On her petite frame it looked heavy, like a burden, but still it was beautiful and silky. She wore little makeup, mostly eyeshadow and mascara. Her lipstick was a soft mauve that matched her long pink dress. She had slender legs, not as shapely as Michelle's, but alluring in their petite way. In fact, there was no similarity between Nicole and Michelle. They were as different as night and day.

Craig's gaze fell from Nicole to Michelle. He wondered in silent contempt if their blaring difference was the handicap that kept him torn between both women. If he had listened to Percy's good sense, he would have dropped Michelle a long time ago before everything had gotten out of hand. His gaze fell back on Nicole and he took a step toward her. He was going to get her out of here, at least for a breath of fresh air. She looked like she could use a respite from everyone.

"So, Craig, I didn't get a chance to do much talking upstairs, but I'm pleased you all made it. Thanks for coming," Phil said with a wide grin as he came up to Craig.

Eddie and Percy looked up from their examination of one of the African artifacts that was positioned over the fireplace at hearing Phil's words. Phil ignored the other two men, particularly Percy's mocking gaze, and kept his attention on Craig, although beneath Percy's penetrating gaze, he wondered for a panicky moment if Sissi had told them about his tryst with Nancy and their sham engagement

Craig was about to go to Nicole's side when Phil approached him. After a quick glance from Nicole to Phil and back to Nicole, Craig shrugged. Janice was at Nicole's side now, his girl would be all right. Offering Phil a broad grin Craig said, "That's cool, bro."

"I was concerned about the long ride you took from D.C. You didn't get lost, did you?" Phil continued.

"You know how Sissi's directions are," Craig laughed.

At Phil's concerned expression, Craig quickly added, "Just joking. I found your place just fine. Man, I was doing eighty . . . ninety miles an hour coming from the train station." He glanced at Percy and Eddie for confirmation. "Had a cop been smooth enough to catch me, he would have had a field day with his ticket quota."

They chuckled, though Phil shook his head, saying, "He would have had a field day hauling you to jail. You're not in the big city now."

"More to your liking, ain't it Phil?" Percy drawled, adding a mock southern twang to his speech. He pierced Phil with a taunting gaze. Phil literally winced, his dislike for Percy so potent that his contempt instantly showed across his face. Percy's every word was growing proof that at some stage, Sissi must have given Percy insight on their engagement.

"I like the quiet, if that's what you mean," Phil responded, his mild tone in conflict with his tumultuous urge to kick Percy from the party.

He thought he knew what Percy was leading up to. So he had made a mistake. One lousy, foolish mistake. It didn't mean he didn't truly love Sissi. At least what he had done wasn't a cruel rejection of the woman he loved when she needed him most, as Percy had done. And Nancy meant nothing to him. She was a siren, a pliant, passionate . . . He grunted, shaking his thoughts from the memory of sweet Nancy in his arms. No, he was determined that he would not lose Sissi—especially not to Percy Duvall.

"That's exactly what he meant," Craig smoothly interceded, tossing Percy a reprimanding glance. Percy raised an arrogant eyebrow at Craig, his attention temporarily distracted from Phil as a glimpse of Sissi's slender form caught his attention from across the room.

"Oh, right, right. Well, again, thanks for coming, Sissi's

real happy to see you," Phil added with another smile. Craig nodded, trying not to stare at Phil's large teeth.

The man was a bull.

Phil's head was considerably large and round. He was a smooth, deep chocolate-brown shade although of a dull tone. His hair was unruly and lifeless, though he kept it shaved close to his head. He had a faint mustache which did nothing to hide his full, bitter mouth. He was a hulking, brooding animal, and Sissi didn't seem to notice. It was amazing that a beautiful woman like Sissi would trap herself with Phil.

If they weren't beauty and the beast, Craig didn't know what to call them. Subduing his mean thoughts, he managed to maintain a sober expression as he said, "I'm sure not as happy as she is to be marrying you."

"Sure she is," Percy said sardonically, unable to restrain himself. He had promised himself he would be civil, nice even. But it was difficult to watch Phil, or talk to him without recalling just what kind of a womanizer the older man always had been and respect the professor's role as Sissi's fiancé. Phil Richardson did not deserve Sissi. Sissi could no more seriously be happy about marrying that ostentatious pompous man than a cow enjoyed being slaughtered, he decided with a keen glance across the room at Sissi. She seemed completely oblivious to his glance as she laughed heartily with a few of her friends.

"Ignore him, Phil, you know Percy is just being sarcastic. Anyway," Craig added quickly, "you know I wouldn't miss your engagement party."

"But Phil would miss your birthday," Percy said dryly, his attention on Sissi's elegant flowing form as she moved through the room, holding brief conversations with different groups of people.

"Well, you know, hey, I got to nap a bit during the train ride. So I'm refreshed and ready to party!" Eddie chimed in, also trying to divert trouble from stirring between Percy and Phil. He couldn't believe how nasty Percy was behaving. Not Mr. Smooth himself. It wasn't as if Percy could not find another woman to spend the evening with. From the moment he walked into the room, the women began flaunting themselves at him. Smiling from ear to ear, provoking him with their deliberately planned words. They wanted him and were even more enticed by his complete disinterest in them. Poor Percy, Eddie thought. If he couldn't let go of his love for Sissi, he was doomed to be alone and miserable.

"Michelle's right over there. Go dance with her. Everyone else has," Percy snapped, his dislike for Phil sharpening his tongue. It had been a while since he had been in the presence of Phil Richardson, but now that he was at the party, he recalled all of the rumors and dislikes he had for Phil Richardson, the campus womanizer. How he maintained his career was beyond Percy. What made the engagement worse for Percy was that Sissi was just as aware as he of Phil's reputation. They had commented on it several times during their dating years on campus. How she could choose to marry such a disloyal womanizer was beyond Percy. Sissi disappointed him. So caught up in his own turmoil, Percy didn't notice Eddie's reaction at his words.

Eddie was hurt. Everyone had to be in his business, he thought, furious. He had news for Percy. He wasn't thinking about Michelle. In fact, the few flurries of excitement he had experienced prior to leaving Maryland were completely gone. He just wanted to get to a phone and call the nurse at the hospital. He only hoped the nurse hadn't changed her mind about dating him. With a worried frown, he glanced at his watch and wondered if she was on her break yet.

"Hey, Phil, can I use your phone? I need to check in at the hospital," Eddie asked.

"Of course you can," Phil stated.

"Just keep it short. The man's got a lot of bills to worry about now," Percy said dryly, glancing in sardonic awe about the decorated basement.

Phil tossed Percy an impatient scowl but evenly responded, "There's a private phone upstairs, two doors down on your right."

"Cool. Be right back," Eddie muttered then hastily left them, moving quickly through the crowd until he reached the doorway and disappeared up the stairway, happy to escape the unpleasant tension.

"I thought he was an intern or something?" Phil asked Craig a moment later.

"Yeah, but he's been getting paid. Man, it can take years before you earn your respect as a doctor. So you know he's got to play that role. You know how it is." Craig chuckled.

"Sure Phil, you know how it is, playing that role. That's what got you your reputation back in the old days, right? That's how you got Sissi, playing that role."

Phil started slowly, turning his beady hard eyes on Percy with dead resolve. "What I do for Sissi and how I do it is none of your business, Percy—"

"I wasn't trying to find out," Percy interrupted, his tone just as hard and determined, all signs of humor faded.

"You sure about that?" Phil asked, his tone full with warning.

Percy paused and stared straight into Phil's eyes, saying with stoic calm, "Question is, Phil, are you sure about it—"

"Hey, hey. Cut it short, man. We don't have to go there," Craig interrupted hotly, exasperated with both men for allowing their tempers to flare. Percy looked at Craig. He knew that he had been provoking Phil from the moment he had approached them. He felt a tug of guilt at his behavior. He was allowing his emotions to drive him into an unnecessary confrontation with Sissi's fiancé. To Craig's surprise, Percy backed down first.

"The only place I have to go is to the bathroom," Percy muttered, avoiding Phil's gaze out of an attempt to remain subdued.

Phil was surprised at the sudden change in Percy's tone but relieved that his rival was leaving, even if for just a moment. The only reason he allowed Sissi to invite him was because he was one of Craig's best friends, and Craig was all right with Phil. Plus, when they were creating the guest list, he had Sissi's complete devotion. His only concern was Percy, and he had wanted to be sure that Sissi had gotten over him. Now, in light of his affair with Nancy, he was regretting his arrogant confidence that he could handle Percy. The man was proving to be a true threat.

"I didn't miss your birthday party on purpose," Phil explained to Craig the moment Percy walked away.

From across the room, Sissi looked up so sharply that Phil caught his breath. Her dark eyes penetrated through him and he had the oddest feeling that she didn't see him standing there. Phil gave her an uncertain smile. She returned it, although with a stiff effort. Still he exhaled a sigh of relief, counting his blessings every moment that she continued to pretend that their engagement was real. A triumphant grin spread across his arrogant face as he stared at her. He was determined that she was still his wife-to-be. No matter how many stinging remarks Percy hurled at him, he still had Sissi. He still had time.

Chapter Six

Percy was burning with frustration. Just seeing Sissi in the same environment with Phil was annoying. He wanted to go to her, pull her out of Phil's ostentatious life-style and bring her to her senses. He closed the bathroom door and stared at his face in the mirror. He was being irrational. Sissi looked perfectly happy, completely at ease. He rolled his eyes then turned on the cold water. Cupping the water in his hands, he splashed his face several times until the heat of frustration simmered to a mild irritation, and he was able to face himself again.

Sissi Adams was a grown woman. If she was happy with a man like Phil, then there was nothing Percy could do. At least that was what he wanted to believe. But he couldn't shake the notion that all was not right between Phil and Sissi. Perhaps it was wishful thinking, but Phil appeared very uptight, even bewildered. Percy was aware that he was adding to the older man's flustered behavior, but Phil Richardson was not a man easily flustered—unless he had done something to make himself nervous. Sissi was a totally different story. She didn't want to talk to him, that was apparent. Had she so easily seen through him that she was trying to tell him that there would be no chance of their ever getting together by keeping her distance all evening? He feared that if given the chance, she would curse him for being a fool two years ago and throw in his face that she had found the perfect man in the professor.

Percy sighed, staring down at the running water in a mute daze. He would never forget how he had reacted at discovering Sissi had miscarried. He was sick with grief and thought in an irrational rage that she had betrayed him. He wanted the child so badly that he grieved for weeks before coming to his senses and finally accepting that there was no way Sissi would deliberately abort his child.

It had been the worst moment of his life. He had gone out to purchase an engagement ring and surprise Sissi. He was going to marry her, to make his family complete. But that same day she came home dry-eyed and cold, or so she had appeared to be. It was just her way of maintaining her composure. Percy believed he was more devastated than Sissi. After all, she was the one who had confessed to not wanting children. How could she expect him to believe that the miscarriage wasn't deliberate? He scowled, hating himself for how rash he had been. How blind he had been not to see that Sissi would never have betrayed him. He should have held her when she came to him in distress about their loss. Instead he scorned her. He had so much regret. If only he had believed her, trusted her more completely.

He groaned, sickened by his own foolish pride. He had lost Sissi in the worst possible way. He had abandoned her coldly, left her to suffer the loss of their child alone. The last thing he could do was to fault her for turning to Phil.

Percy smirked at his image, unable to believe that Phil

could have changed so easily. Phil had never quite stopped wanting Sissi. Even when Percy and Sissi lived together in New York, Phil would call every so often, checking on Sissi, patiently biding his time until Percy slipped up. And Percy grudgingly admitted that he definitely slipped. He gave Phil the ammunition to go for Sissi full force.

A knock on the door snapped Percy out of his brooding. He dried his hands then quickly opened the door.

"Janice!" Percy grinned the moment he saw Janice impatiently standing outside the door. Janice had been staring at the hardwood floors and looked up with a silent scowl when the door opened, prepared to tell the slow patron of the bathroom just what she thought about him. When she saw that it was Percy she, too, grinned from ear to ear.

"Percy, baby." She laughed, about to wrap her arms around him in a warm greeting, then she hesitated. Glancing at him with a dubious smirk, she glanced at his hands and asked, "Did you wash your hands?"

Percy laughed, glancing at the towel still in his hands. " Are you saying I'm triflin'?" he asked, pretending to be offended.

"It's been years since I've seen you." She laughed, giving him a hug.

"I know. Why didn't you come to Craig's party?" he asked, giving her a quick kiss on her cheek.

Janice shrugged and answered. "Now you know work comes first. But man, wow. I guess I haven't seen you since you and Sissi were . . . together." Her voice faded off in uncertainty, and she blinked up at him in mild discomfort. "Sorry. I didn't mean to bring it up."

Percy shrugged, stepping aside to allow Janice to enter the bathroom. "You don't have to apologize, Janice. Sissi and I were together for a long time."

"Two and half years as I recall," Sissi's husky voice added

from behind Percy. Percy felt suspended in limbo as he turned around and looked at Sissi.

"Yeah, two and half years, and it's over now," he continued in a mocking drawl in an attempt to conceal the excited rush he felt at her presence.

Sissi's heart sank at his words, certain that he was giving her a clear signal that he unequivocally was not interested in her. She could easily guess what he must think of her after all they had been through. If only he could for once put someone else's feelings first. But he would never understand her. Just as he probably wouldn't believe her if she told him that the entire engagement party was a sham instigated first by Phil's affair and then his plea that she wait until Monday to end their relationship. And with the engagement hovering between them, there wasn't anything she could say.

"It certainly is," Sissi finally whispered. A moment of nostalgic silence fell over them then Janice, sensing their dilemma, gave them a gentle hint. "Excuse me you two, but I have got to go," she chirped then closed the bathroom door and shut them out. Standing alone in the hall, Sissi and Percy continued their appraisal of each other until Janice's hearty shout caused them to smile at one another.

"Can I get some privacy? Go talk somewhere else," Janice called out, breaking the tension.

Percy grinned before taking a hesitant step back to the party. They were just outside the basement door at the top of the stairway when Sissi muttered, "You don't have to avoid me all night, Percy. We can hold a conversation."

Percy paused, his hand on the doorknob when he considered Sissi with an almost amused glance. "I am not avoiding you, Sissi Adams. I just don't want any misunderstandings between us. Not again."

"Well it's a little too late for that," Sissi retorted, annoyed at his condescending air.

"Maybe. I just want to make sure you know that I came here as a friend. If you need me . . ."

"I needed you once before, remember," Sissi again retorted.

"I was there for you," he said as calmly as he could, knowing instantly what she meant.

It was Sissi's turn to frown. She had lost a precious gift—her child—and Percy was not there for her. Had he gone senile?

"No, you weren't. You turned your back on me, left me alone, Percy. I needed some understanding, some affection. . . ." Her voice trailed off in bitter resentment.

Unable to find the right words, Percy could only mutter, "Well, it seems Phil solved that problem."

Sissi lowered her gaze at his comment, believing he judged her poorly for turning to Phil for affection. Percy would never understand. At the time Phil soothed her, he understood her pain, he proved he loved her with an open, trusting heart. At that time he hadn't yet shown his devious cheating side. It pained her to realize that Phil had not charged as much as she thought he had. Had she not owed him so much for all he had done during her painful miscarriage, in renovating her grandmother's home, and helping to rebuild the old cottage where she was born, she would have instantly broken up with Phil. But he deserved this last show of appreciation from her. But in giving him her loyalty, she confined herself from openly talking with Percy. The sad truth was, what she had once felt for Phil had died completely after seeing him in Nancy's arms. And seeing Percy had finally put a name to the void in her heart. *Love.*

She hesitated then said in a soft, defensive voice, "I know what you are thinking. But Phil loves me, he's very

. . . sweet," Sissi whispered, trying to explain her decision to marry Phil. But even as she spoke of Phil, she saw flashes of Nancy's blond hair on his desk and Phil's white shirt whipping in the wind as they made love. It sickened her, and Percy didn't miss her blanch.

"Sure he is," Percy responded dryly. From what he had witnessed in the few hours he'd been there, Phil was a paranoid, hovering jerk who had no faith in Sissi. If he did, he wouldn't be so guarded, Percy decided.

Sissi closed her eyes for a moment, hating his tone, wishing he could understand the pain she had felt after he left her. But as usual, Percy could think only of himself. And he had such nerve judging Phil when he himself had a lot to answer for. At least Phil was there for her when she needed him most. Where was Percy?

"I'd better get back to the party," Sissi said, suddenly bitter as she opened her eyes and stared into Percy's searching gaze with regret.

"Wait, I want to talk to you," he pleaded softly, going against all of his instincts to stay clear of her. He felt compelled to explain himself, to answer for his mistake, to apologize.

"I think we should," Sissi responded easily, her gaze steady. He would hear her out this time, but on her terms. She would tell him how wrong he was to think she could hurt their baby. He had made the ultimate mistake, and she wanted him to know it.

"Actually now's not the time," Janice stated, strutting up to them, looking refreshed and ready to party again.

Sissi and Percy both looked at Janice in surprise, so intent on each other, they had not heard Janice's approach.

She smiled brightly, shrugged her shoulders, and said in a reasonable voice, "Phil will come looking for you at any moment. You're going to have to find another time to talk. Come on, you two, and leave it up to ole Janice. And shall we remember," Janice added in a secretive murmur, "all is fair in love and war. Now back inside."

Sissi was hesitant, tempted to tell her secret, to confess the lie about Phil and her, but then she thought better of it. Like contrite children, she and Percy followed Janice into the party.

Janice was right, they realized. Phil was so determined not to let Sissi out of his sight it was questionable that he hadn't searched for her during the few minutes she had stepped away. Percy appeared to want to speak again, but Sissi didn't look his way, she didn't even glance backward as she and Janice milled through the crowd and escaped any questions that Phil might have had about their whereabouts.

"There's my baby, working the crowd as usual," Phil said proudly.

Craig looked up, long since bored with conversation with Phil. He wished Eddie or Percy would return and get him out of the awkward conversation he was being forced to hold with the professor. Phil's demeanor and role as a professor at the university where Craig had graduated still unnerved Craig. Phil was a role model, of sorts. He wasn't the type of guy that Craig wanted to spend an evening with, unless it was to get a job. Trying to keep his disinterest from showing all over his face, Craig nodded and returned a broad smile to Phil as he followed Phil's gaze and spotted Sissi in the crowd. Sade's sultry song "The Sweetest Taboo" was playing. Sissi was holding a glass of wine and as natural as a siren queen she was gently swaying her hips to the music, trying to lose herself in the song as she stood laughing and talking with Janice and a few other friends.

"And a beautiful girl she is," he said easily, watching Sissi with appreciation.

Sissi's smooth chocolate-brown complexion stood out well among the guests. Her keen gaze and almost royal air was out of both Nicole's and Michelle's league. She was classy, sassy, and way too sexy to be ignored. Craig needed a girl that was attractive in a low-key kind of way. Nicole was that key for him. But unlike Nicole, who could sometimes be more sobering than fun, Sissi had a constant flair of excitement about her.

Craig and Sissi were very close friends. They were such good friends that it took some convincing to get their friends to believe they weren't dating while they were still living on campus. That was their bond, their genuine friendship. Craig recalled how Sissi had confessed her admiration for Percy months before Percy seemed to notice her. But when Percy and Sissi finally got together, everyone thought it would last forever. They were such a perfect match, well tempered for each other. Sissi's leaving Percy to marry Phil was mind boggling, and Craig still found it strange to think of or watch Sissi with Phil. But, Craig had to admit, Phil had charisma and he had Sissi Adams.

"I'm just amazed that I got her." Phil's voice was like an echo in the back of Craig's mind, as if he could guess Craig's amazement that Sissi and Phil were together. Unconsciously agreeing with Phil, Craig nodded as his attention returned to Phil.

Percy walked up to them just as the words escaped Phil. Phil regretted his choice of words at seeing Percy's rude smirk curve his mouth. But Percy smoothly looked into the fireplace as if his thoughts were elsewhere.

Phil instantly stiffened at Percy's presence and was annoyed at Percy's sardonic expression. So caught up in watching Sissi engage her girlfriends in conversation, Phil hadn't noticed Percy's return. He chose to ignore Percy, resolving that he wasn't going to make a scene this night, of all nights. He had too much to lose.

Disappointed with his unsatisfying encounter with Sissi in the hall, Percy resolved to avoid any further confrontations with Phil. He had to talk to Sissi. Tossed to the wind was his determination to steer clear of her. It was foolish to ignore Sissi as if she weren't in the room. It didn't matter that she was engaged, she wasn't in prison. She was a free woman able to make up her mind as to whom she held conversations with. There was no penalty for talking with an ex-boyfriend. With a mischievous grin, Percy looked up from the fireplace and considered Sissi from across the room, oblivious to the murderous glare that gleamed in Phil's eyes once the professor spotted the direction Percy's attention had gone.

Craig caught wind of Percy's new attitude and frowned, instantly concerned. But as Percy adjusted his tie, Craig could only mutter, "What are you up to?"

"Nothing, man, just going to have a short conversation with Sissi," he stated, feeling more relaxed now that he was openly choosing to talk with Sissi.

"Be cool, Percy," Craig warned.

"What?" Percy scoffed, glancing at Craig in mock innocence. "I'm just going to speak with Sissi for a few minutes. It's been a while, you know?" If he couldn't talk privately, then they could talk in the open. It was a party, he was a guest, not an invader. Talking with Sissi was as natural as all outdoors. It shouldn't be a big deal.

Before Craig could detain Percy with an anxious "Wait," Percy strutted across the room.

Craig sighed, trying to pretend that he didn't notice Phil's agitation. He couldn't refrain from a sympathetic glance at Phil and felt almost apologetic for Percy's crude behavior. Still, Craig decided firmly, Phil didn't have anything to really worry about if Sissi loved him. Sissi was pretty consistent and knew what she wanted. Sure, Percy was handsome and charming. Percy's career was going well, his success was broadening, but Percy had broken Sissi's heart. Being the sensible girl that Sissi was, it was not likely she would trip over that same brick again. All the charm in the world couldn't erase Percy's lack of understanding when she needed him after the miscarriage. As Craig recalled, it was a pregnancy that Sissi had been looking forward to, much to everyone's surprise.

Thinking of Percy's and Phil's success caused Craig to slightly frown. Craig hadn't been so ambitious either in his career or with women when it came to gaining wealth. He had gone to college to be an engineer, and was doing all right now as a computer technician. Steady work was how he justified it. He didn't complain much that fixing computers was what he really did because he wasn't a complainer by nature. But once Eddie landed his internship at Southern Maryland Hospital, and Percy's reputation as a shrewd stockbroker grew on Wall Street, he realized his friends were destined for the kind of success he would never have. Proud as he was of them, he couldn't help but envy them a little.

Still his Nicole was proud of him, Craig thought. She was proud that he hadn't let his envy interfere with his friendship with Eddie and Percy. She was proud that he hadn't let himself down by just giving up. In fact, next fall he planned to go back to school to get a degree in architectural construction, a spin-off of his engineering degree but a higher-paying field. He was sure that would help to advance his career.

Of course he knew had he been more involved in his studies and not in his romantic entanglements, he might have been as successful as his friends. The problem was when he wasn't studying he had his hands full between breaking up with Michelle and keeping her at bay while trying to win Nicole. To this day, he thought with a roguish pride that would have caused Nicole to slap him and Michelle to gasp with indignation, he didn't know which woman he was more attracted to. He only knew that Michelle was not the kind of woman he would marry, although she was the best lover he had ever been with.

"Percy's an arrogant little punk!" Phil scowled, flushed with fury. His sullen comment distracted Craig from his conceited thoughts. Craig put a reassuring hand on Phil's shoulder, sympathetic to Phil's rage.

"Don't let him get to you, Phil. It's late and well you know," Craig said in an effort to ease Phil.

"Damn right I know," Phil hissed, his beady eyes pinned on Percy. "And he needs to know that Sissi doesn't want him anymore."

"He knows that. Everyone knows that." Craig tried to sound confident, nonchalant. "Like Percy said, they're just talking. It's been a long time since they've seen each other," Craig added.

"I don't believe that," Phil snorted, crossing his stocky arms over his chest.

"If I were you, I would want them to put the past in the past and move on, you know."

Phil scowled instantly at the remark. "Their past is already in the past. They don't need to rehash anything." Riled up, he stormed away from Craig and headed directly for Percy and Sissi. He wasn't going to be made a fool of by Percy, he didn't care how late it was!

Phil's approach was so brusque that he nearly stepped on Sissi's foot and caused her to stumble slightly. Phil caught her arm, whispering, "Excuse me, baby."

Sissi glanced uncomfortably at Percy then offered Phil a tight smile, hating how he purposely moved his hand from her arm and around her waist in a show of intimate possession. She almost pulled away but then thought better of it, knowing that his colleagues would notice and wonder and gossip and ruin his career. She sighed, recoiling at his very touch, disgusted with the images of him and Nancy that continuously invaded her peace of mind whenever he was near her. And worse, she somehow did not feel that he was truly regretting his mistake. She regretted her promise and was feeling drained from the constant congratulations she was receiving for a marriage that would never take place. When Phil placed a warm kiss on her cheek, she could not help but turn away even if the move was subtle. Phil felt her draw back and with snapping, beady eyes, he tossed Percy a sour glance before smiling warmly at Sissi.

"Can I talk to you for a moment?" he murmured, clearly planning to stay with Sissi regardless of her answer.

"Of course," Sissi said quickly, glancing uncomfortably at Percy, wishing she could tell him everything at that moment. She was losing Percy. He had barely reached her side when Phil joined them. Percy hadn't even had the chance to say one word before Phil joined them. Sissi was growing impatient and was determined, the moment she got the chance, she and Phil would have a serious talk about the liberties he could take with her. After all, the engagement in fact was off.

Percy watched the couple in stoic silence. Sissi appeared completely relaxed, calm, even loving. He felt foolish standing beside them. She was lost to him, he could see it in her eyes, he could hear it in her soft voice, feel it in the intimate way they were bound together. What point did it serve to tell Sissi he was wrong about the baby? He changed his mind in that long agonizing moment as he watched Sissi settle by Phil's side. Giving Sissi a look that clearly stated his opinion that further conversation between them was useless, he strolled calmly away.

The moment Percy was gone, Phil said in a barely audible hiss, "I want him out of this house." Anyone watching would think he was talking about the weather so expressionless was his face.

Sissi didn't blink, she maintained her composure even though her blood boiled in searing anger at his command. "Oh, do you?" she asked with sarcasm dripping from each word.

Phil frowned down at her, knowing in an instant he had made the wrong statement. But he continued. "He acts as if he thinks you're free. Taking liberty to say whatever he pleases, as if he's running the place."

"Ah, feeling hurt. A little confused," Sissi murmured, giving him a sidelong glance. "Well, join the broken hearts club, Phil. You know? The one you started."

"Come on, Sissi. Don't go there, not while my friends are around. You promised," Phil whispered, instantly contrite. She was so bitter, so cold. Where was his vivacious sweet Sissi? Had he lost her for good, or was she just trying to punish him to see him sweat? He would sweat if that would keep him from losing her, he thought vehemently.

"Yes, I made a dumb promise to help you," Sissi bit out. To anyone watching them, the pair appeared calm and at ease as if they were discussing the grocery list for the next day. But Sissi was steaming inside. And Phil had the sinking feeling that he should shut up and stay clear of her throughout the rest of the evening. But he could not resist the comment.

"I was just concerned that maybe, in your frustration with me, you hadn't noticed what was going on with Percy," Phil blurted, giving her an imploring look.

"And what's going on with Percy, Phil?" Sissi asked, her tone indulgent.

"He's a sarcastic ignorant punk. I'm not blind, Sissi, and

neither are you. He wants you back, and I'm not going to let that happen," Phil added without thinking.

Sissi's eyes widened and with a hint of a smile that could be taken as a sneer, she retorted barely above a whisper, "And how are you going to stop him? By offering Nancy to him in a truce? Maybe you think he's like you, but he's not. As long as he *believes* that I'm engaged and belong to you, he won't touch me. Besides, I haven't yet decided what I want to do." Sissi's tone was harsh, her words final, but her heart was beating wildly. Did Percy really want her back? Had he made a comment to Phil to make Phil nervous, or was Phil just on edge because of the fake engagement party?

He felt a moment of panic at her cool disdain and whispered, "Please, Sissi, I'm just saying . . . don't be so obvious. If you haven't told him, then he must have guessed. If he can guess, everyone else can."

Sissi wanted to add, *"And what if I want him back as well?"* At any rate, she didn't get the impression that Percy wanted her back at all. Phil was looking at them through lovesick eyes, and everything they did would appear suspicious to him. Realizing it would be futile to argue the point, she fell silent.

Eddie was heading toward Craig when he heard fragments of their conversation. He was embarrassed to hear their very subtle argument and continued on as if nothing was ever said.

"I'm glad I don't have that problem with Nicole," Craig said as Eddie came up to him. Eddie winced, his expression clearly stating that he thought Craig did have a problem with Nicole. Craig scowled at Eddie's reaction and snapped, "What? You don't believe that crap Michelle started, do you?"

"No. Not about Nicole, but Donna . . . well, they are

cousins. If Donna believes it . . ." Eddie began hesitantly. Craig raised his hand as if to say, "Stop."

"Cousins or not, I don't care what Donna believes. You know how she is. Paranoid. And you know why she believes it, too," Craig added with a wary glance across the room at Nicole.

Eddie nodded, one arm resting on the mantel above the fireplace while he stared at the carpet. "Yeah," he dragged out grudgingly. He regretted offering his opinion to Craig. He was more comfortable pretending ignorance of the entire situation. The nurse had taken the night off, and he was stupid enough not to bring her home phone number with him. So now he was snared between the romantic entanglements of his best friends. He sure wished he were somewhere else.

"Then don't fall into that trap. Michelle's poison. And I'm not one for calling women names, but Michelle is a witch," Craig insisted. Of all the people he knew, he didn't want Eddie to believe Michelle, too. Nicole needed all the support she could get. If she knew that Eddie believed Michelle's lies, it would hurt her deeply.

"Yeah," Eddie dragged out again. "But what about Donna?" he asked tentatively.

Craig scowled. He despised Donna. She was as bad as Michelle. Calling Nicole all the time, crying about that loser husband of hers. But what really infuriated him was Donna's accusation that he was sleeping with Michelle. How would Donna know anything about him? He wanted to wring her little neck every time he saw her. Donna was conniving and two-faced, and the little hussy had even come on to him before. He was just glad he knew her slick type. She wanted to help Michelle and hurt Nicole. But he wasn't going to play her game. If Nicole weren't his woman, he thought, it would serve Donna right if the rumor were true. Of course, he didn't believe it at all.

"Donna's not important," he bit out, taking a swallow from his drink. Eddie shrugged and appeared uncomfortable. He was about to find someone else to talk to, feeling Craig's mood change. He hated being around Craig when he was so gloomy. Craig's problem was he had too many women in his life. Michelle alone was like having four women. Again he wished he had stayed in Maryland.

"I'll tell you what," Craig added, finishing his drink in a last hearty gulp. "For two women to look so much alike, Donna's nothing like my sweet Nicole. Nothing. I wouldn't put any faith in anything she says. I'm tired of her, always in my face, in my business and upsetting my woman. You know?" he asked, giving Eddie a questioning look. Eddie didn't know how to respond, so he just nodded before allowing a sympathetic gaze to stray to Nicole.

Nicole felt the glances from Craig and Eddie and frowned. What now? She was tired of being peered at and made uncomfortable, even if it was her fiancé who was watching her. Two things kept her at the party, Craig's pleading that she come out and stay the weekend since they hadn't seen each other all week and her hope of seeing Donna and explaining what really happened. The latter hadn't occurred, and she was growing tired of the stares and whispers. And wasn't it funny that Sade's song "Jezebel" had played twice in the last hour. No doubt, Michelle had encouraged someone to repeat that tune. She hated Michelle. Feeling hot with frustration, she turned to Janice who had engaged herself in deep conversation with some male colleague of Phil's.

"Janice," Nicole whispered, lightly placing her hand on Janice's arm. Janice glanced over her shoulder and became instantly alerted to Nicole's strained expression. Nicole appeared extremely uncomfortable, almost on the border of hysterics, and her face was unusually animated.

"What's wrong?" Janice murmured, her voice dripping with concern.

"I just need some fresh air. I'm going out into the yard. I thought I should let someone know, although I'm sure everyone will be watching me when I leave," she added testily.

Janice nodded, understanding Nicole's need to escape. She patted Nicole's arm and searched quickly around the room for Michelle. She didn't see her in the crowd.

"Go. The coast is clear. But don't walk far, it's creepy out there. Why Sissi chose to move here after her grandma died is beyond me," Janice added, hoping to distract Nicole's burden with her trivial observation. Nicole gave her a little smile then scurried from the party, feeling certain that everyone was indeed watching her.

Chapter Seven

The night air greeted Nicole like a warm shawl. Once outside the house, she paused, relieved to be away from the unfriendly crowd. Still her cheeks were flushed with aggravation. It had taken all of her resolve not to seek Michelle out and slap her silly in front of everyone. "How dare that hussy pursue Craig as if I'm not even in the room!" she mumbled to herself.

What she needed was a breath of fresh air and a moment of quiet. The night was still and peaceful, giving a sensation of solitude that suited her mood perfectly. In its serenity, the crickets sang their songs of glory and seemed to follow Nicole as she walked an aimless path away from the house. Down the slope of the property, less than a half mile away, Sissi owned a guest home. Nicole stared at the small cottage in longing. She could use a few hours of rest away from everyone and their leering.

The number of guests was overwhelming and Nicole, even knowing Sissi's popularity, hadn't expected such a gathering. Nicole was just glad that almost all of the guests were leaving tonight. She only wished that she had not committed to staying. She wanted to get away from everyone, in particular, Craig. He had trodden on her pride far too many times. Tonight was the last straw the way he was allowing Michelle to hang on to his every word and follow him around. And no one had anything to say about Michelle. No, they could focus only on Nicole and the outrageous rumor that she had slept with Keith.

Nicole walked carelessly across the lawn, unable to appreciate the beautiful foliage as her thoughts strayed to Keith and his disloyalty. He had begged her help in divorcing Donna. Now that his uncle was dead, and he was getting the bulk of the man's insurance, he wanted to be free of Donna before she found out about his new fortune. Oh, she was an idiot to trust him. It was no accident that Michelle happened on them at the hotel. Nicole was confident that Keith had set the whole thing up. He wanted Michelle to find them. When he said he needed Nicole's help to divorce Donna, he had not said at what price.

For years he and Donna were having problems, but it was his uncle's death that finally flamed him into action. He was ready for a divorce, to live his life free of Donna's wayward ways and to possess all of his inherited funds solely by himself. Problem was, his little trick backfired. Now, not only had he ruined Nicole's reputation but he had infuriated Donna to the point where she wouldn't give him a divorce if her life depended on it. Donna had sworn to make him pay for embarrassing her.

So he needed Nicole again. He promised her a nice sum of money when he received the insurance money but with all of the confusion and lies about her now, she couldn't be sure that anything she said to Donna would work. And time was running out. Sooner or later, Donna would find out about the insurance money, and she would definitely make sure she got at least half. Donna was shrewd that way.

"Kinda late to be out here alone, isn't it?" Geoff Roberts asked, striding casually up to Nicole.

Nicole was startled and turned sharply at the sound of his voice. A slight scowl crossed her delicate features as she considered him in unveiled irritation. She wanted to be alone.

"I can take care of myself," she responded with a haughty roll of her eyes.

Her reaction didn't daunt Geoff. He had found her attractive from the moment he saw her and was determined to get to know her. Sissi had told him a lot about Nicole, from her petite slender figure to her brazen, stubborn personality. Sissi hadn't lied one bit. When he finally saw Nicole, he immediately sought out Sissi and insisted that he be a part of her weekend plans.

"There's no way I can get to know her in just one night. Come on, Sissi. Let me stay the weekend. I promise to stay out of Phil's way," he had practically begged. When Sissi's smile peeked forth, Geoff knew he had won.

Geoff grinned now, staring at Nicole's petite frame with a smug grin that clearly expressed his doubt that she could actually protect herself. But his gaze was full with more than just concern over her welfare. Nicole would have blushed beneath his warm appraisal if she weren't turning one of her own on him.

He bore a remarkable resemblance to Craig. The biggest difference between Geoff and Craig was in their grooming. Geoff had a casual neat quality, sported an after-five shadow over his strong jawbones, and was thin although of a firm build. He might not be as suave as Craig, but he was charming all the same, she decided, allowing her irritation to diffuse.

There was one major distinction between Craig and

Geoff. Geoff's eyes. They were assertive, keen, and direct eyes—there was no wavering in his gaze. Nicole found that pleasing if not somewhat disquieting, as if he could see into her soul. Of course, it could all be a false impression. He could very well be as untrustworthy as Craig. "I'm sure you can take care of yourself, Nicole. So tell me, have you been here before?" he asked as he crossed his arms over his chest and leaned casually against a tree. He seemed so relaxed, so in control.

Nicole allowed herself to smile at his pleasant attitude before she responded with an easy, "Sure. A few times, mostly during the renovation process. And what about you, have you been here before?"

"No. But Sissi described the place quite thoroughly to me." They both fell silent and then Nicole started strolling again. Geoff quickly fell into step beside her.

"Everything okay? You seem a little sad," he said hesitantly when they had walked for several moments without sharing a word.

Nicole glanced at him sideways before replying dryly, "I just needed to be alone."

He nodded at her response, not sure if she was hinting for him to get lost or if she was just giving an honest response.

"So I see," he said quietly. "I'll tell you, Sissi sure knows how to draw a crowd," he said, trying to strike up a different conversation.

Nicole shrugged and continued to walk until she came upon the man-made pond. She stared at her barely visible reflection on the water for a moment before responding. "Sissi always draws a crowd."

"But they're not all staying over the weekend are they?" he asked, as if he wasn't already aware of the weekend guest list.

"Oh, no way. Sissi's not that generous." Nicole laughed.

"But you're staying, correct?" he asked bluntly.

"Yes," she drawled, looking up at him. "Craig and I plan to stay until Sunday afternoon," she added deliberately, looking directly into his eyes for any reaction. There was none. "And you? Are you staying all weekend?"

"Sure am," he responded quickly then in a daring move, he leaned over her to whisper in her ear, "I'm glad we'll be here together."

Nicole laughed and moved away from him before retorting, "I don't think so. I told you, my boyfriend and I will be here, together."

He smiled and considered her through captivating eyes before carefully choosing his next words. He began slowly, holding her gaze as he spoke. "Maybe it's just me, but I don't get a vibe between you two. Craig's the one who came in with Sissi and Michelle, isn't he? He doesn't strike me as the kind of man who would keep your attention for long—all stuffed up with himself the way he is." He stopped, wondering sheepishly if he had gone too far when she snapped her head back and scoffed at him.

"It sounds as if you have been misinformed," Nicole said evenly.

"He just doesn't appear to be the kind of man who could hold on to a woman like you," he repeated, holding her gaze steadily.

Nicole was by no means flattered, the first thought in her mind, that he had heard the rumor and was looking for an opening to discover the truth As if it were any of his business.

"Actually Craig's perfect for me. He's reserved, confident—"

"Confident? Are you assuming I'm not confident?" he interrupted, incredulous that she could see him that way.

"No." She chuckled at his appalled expression. "As a

matter of fact," she added in an indulgent tone, "I believe you're probably a little too confident."

He smiled at her suggestion, took a few impudent steps up to her until his body overshadowed hers, and asked in a husky voice, "In what way?"

Nicole looked into his brazen dark eyes, trying to control a responsive smile as she answered, "I can think of a few ways, but it wouldn't be appropriate to assume such things."

"Please do assume. That's what makes us all interesting," he murmured. As he spoke, he leaned over her, closing the minimum space between them until his face was only a breath away from hers. Instinctively she wanted to take a step back, but she had started this game. She couldn't handle him.

"I believe," she said softly. "I believe that you are confident that I'm attracted to you. I believe," she added then hesitated.

"You believe?" he prompted, curiosity animating his face.

"I believe you think before the weekend is over, you could be so overconfident as to kiss me." She gave him a challenging glance before quickly lowering her gaze again.

Geoff grinned wolfishly and cast a glance over his shoulder at the house before responding. "I wonder if you would believe that I will kiss you before this night is over?"

Nicole paused and glanced up at him. Her lips were slightly parted in response to his comment. She was amazed by him, intrigued by his gall. Before she could react, swift as an eagle, he bent forward and captured her mouth in a tender kiss. Nicole didn't resist, although she was shocked at her own behavior for enticing him. She didn't pull away either when his arms wrapped around her. Shamelessly she returned his kiss, defiance and rebellion against Craig and everyone filling her soul as she allowed Geoff's passionate kiss to invade her senses.

"Umm, you're beautiful," he whispered against her mouth. His words broke the spell, and Nicole instantly pulled away from him, a little flustered from the long moments that he had held her in his arms.

"What's wrong?" he asked, puzzled by the unexpected rejection.

"What do you think?" she retorted, smoothing her dress and taking a few steps away from him. Her eyes were haunted as she wondered how he saw her. Did he believe the rumors now, like everyone else? He certainly had cause. She sighed.

"Hey, it was a harmless kiss. That's all," he added, sensing that she was ready to flee—like a captured dove was this woman.

"What made you think you could kiss me?" Nicole demanded, furious with herself for allowing Geoff's charm to seduce her. At Geoff's bewildered glance, Nicole rolled her eyes. He need not say he knew about the gossip for her to know what he was thinking!

"I thought you wanted me to kiss you," he answered slowly, not understanding her meaning.

"I didn't," she said nastily.

He frowned, obviously taken aback by her antagonism. He was a man used to getting his way, especially with women. They fawned over him, and vied for his attention. And here was this slip of a girl—one moment she was leading him on, something he was used to from women he barely knew. The next moment she was an angry bitter young woman itching to slap him, if he had any understanding of body language.

"I could be wrong, but I know when a woman wants to be kissed. And you wanted it," he said dryly, refusing to believe that he had read her signals wrong.

"I can see you're as blind as you are confident," Nicole said snidely.

"Why wouldn't I think you wanted to be kissed. You were practically puckering up for my kiss," he observed.

"I'm engaged to be married in just a few short months—August, that is," she lied. "I have no interest in another man, especially a stranger who is sleeping with Michelle Lifkin!"

"Michelle? I just met her tonight, like you," he said. "And she isn't my type. I prefer my women petite and beautiful, like you.

"Compliments will get you nowhere, Geoff. Perhaps you should practice your lies a little longer before hitting on involved women," she retorted, giving him a contemptuous stare.

Geoff was confused by her reaction. He wasn't sure where the tables had turned, when she had become angry, but she had managed to take their flirtatious kiss and blow it completely out of proportion. He considered her, his eyes narrowed as his frustration faded and he became amused.

She was like a child, a little girl playing womanly games. She didn't know anything about him. And she could deny it all day long, but she had wanted him to kiss her. She had returned his kiss in fact. He grinned then, thinking perhaps she was intimidated by him.

In an attempt to soothe her fears and ease her mind, he said, "I like you. I came out here after you because I find you attractive. And you know something, I like you even more now that I've met you." He grinned at her wide-eyed stare, believing she was amazed by him. "You're like a wild kitten, just waiting to be tamed. I think I'm the man to tame you," he added boldly.

"You think so?" she retorted then sauntered past him to head back to the party. He hastily moved aside to allow her to pass. Nicole was mildly puzzled. She had to admit, a small part of her had expected him to attempt to stop her, to perhaps kiss again. Ignoring her absurd desire to have him chase her, she walked briskly toward the house.

"Nicole, wait," Geoff called. She kept walking, hearing the muted merriment coming from the house more clearly as she got closer.

"Nicole," he gasped, grabbing her arm just before she could step out of the shadowy path.

"What?" she snapped breathlessly. It was difficult walking through the grass with two-inch heels and a long, tight dress. She nearly lost her balance when he grabbed her and had to grab hold of his arm to keep from tumbling over.

"I'm sorry," he apologized.

"Look, Geoff. Let me solve your problem right now. Anything you heard about me sleeping with Keith is a lie. We didn't kiss, we didn't hold hands, we didn't screw. Okay?" she blurted, releasing him as she regained her balance.

"I don't know—"

"Oh, don't pretend with me," Nicole snarled, knowing he was about to deny hearing the rumors. "I know why you're here. I know what they're saying. But it's all a lie. I should have never allowed you to kiss me," she added bitterly.

"I don't know what you're talking about," Geoff snapped, not wanting to be cut off again. His eyebrows furrowed together. He stared into her angry brown eyes as if she were crazy before her words suddenly sank into him. His expression slowly changed from impatience to comprehension. She had thought he was trying to seduce her because of the nasty rumor about her and Keith. He became exasperated with her. What did she think he was, desperate?

"Well?" she demanded at his continued silence. Suddenly she wasn't so sure that her outburst was fair. He appeared genuinely confused. Maybe he hadn't heard the rumor, but no one was that daring, not without having some opinion about her. Blinking, her long lashes covering her regret, she couldn't back down now—it would send the wrong message.

"You have a nice walk, Nicole," he said gruffly, making the decision for her as he turned sharply away and headed back to the house with stiff determined steps.

Nicole dropped her head in humiliation, standing sadly in the middle of the lawn, her heels digging into the grass. Once again she regretted her decision to come to the party. Craig had distorted her opinion of men. He had taken her pride and dignity, allowed the woman who endorsed the gossip to be at his side, and now he had caused her to push Geoff Roberts, an innocent bystander, aside.

Chapter Eight

Craig finished his rum and Coke in long swift gulps. He was tired and ready to go to bed. It was after eleven, and most of Sissi's guests were just beginning to dance. In the midst of the crowd, he had long since lost sight of Nicole. She probably stole out of the house, knowing her. He glanced at the faces in the crowd, searching once more for her. Instead he found Michelle.

She was laughing and looking beautiful and carefree. For an instant, he wished Nicole was more like Michelle. Michelle always appeared to not have a care in the world, where Nicole was on the brink of depression sometimes. Of course, there were times when Nicole would let go and ease up. But it was becoming more and more rare to see Nicole completely happy. The problem was, he knew what kind of a woman she was when they first started dating. At first, her vulnerability made her more attractive. She needed a strong man to hold on to, and he enjoyed playing that role. But it was becoming tired and old, and he wanted someone with more desire to enjoy each day. So the same vulnerability that made him come to her was what had pushed him back into Michelle's vivacious arms.

They were two completely different souls and, after all of these years, he still was torn between both of them. Of course, just after Percy and Sissi broke up, Craig had proclaimed that he wanted Nicole and Nicole only. He just wished he had been able to sustain himself when Michelle seduced him only a month later. And they were right back into their old ways.

He sighed, feeling more tired than guilty. Michelle was a handful, uncontrollable, demanding. Nicole was safer. She made few demands and her manners were nonthreatening. Still Michelle was exciting in bed. She was always willing to try something new and experiment with making love. Making love to Michelle always proved to be an adventure. He missed that excitement when he was with Nicole. But Michelle was too excitable. She was threatening, possessive, and devious. He couldn't trust her as far as he could see her. And for that, he would never be able to completely give himself to her. But Nicole was a different story. Loving Nicole was safe and carried no pressures. As long as he was by her side, Nicole would love him forever.

A smug smirk curved his dark full lips as he allowed his gaze to linger on Michelle. She looked up, feeling his eyes on her and smiled provocatively at him. Craig didn't respond and, without turning his head, shifted his eyes away from her until they fell on Phil and Sissi.

Sissi and Phil were standing intimately close. It was a shame that Phil was so obviously uncomfortable with her. Even with his fiancée at his side, giving him her complete attention, he appeared miserable. The problem was, Phil had no faith in Sissi. It didn't take much to read into his fear of Percy, although most of his concern was brought on by Percy's attitude all evening. As Craig watched the pair, Phil's dark beady eyes rose from Sissi and fell first on Craig then on Percy, who was standing across the room.

Percy was engrossed in conversation with a few gentlemen who worked at the university. Phil wondered if Percy was discussing him. Of course, the thought was irrational. But Phil couldn't put aside the thought that Percy was out to ruin his reputation. The very idea that Percy could be discussing him made him cough in discomfort. Two women glanced at Phil when he coughed and smiled in greeting. Phil, unable to resist the flirtatious smiles, returned their gazes. He wasn't handsome, he knew that. But women were attracted to him, something he had discovered in his early teaching days. Perhaps it was his brawn, or his direct manner. He wasn't sure, but he enjoyed the attention and even in his fear of losing Sissi he couldn't help but notice when women flirted with him.

Phil recalled he had first thought Sissi was attracted to him when she was a student at Maryland University. But he soon discovered that she had eyes only for Percy Duvall, her fellow student at the university. It was disappointing but a challenge to gain her interest. She kindly but firmly put him in check whenever he tried to ask her out on a date. But he did manage to become her friend. And it was with unbridled pleasure that, after Percy made the ultimate mistake and accused Sissi of lying about her miscarriage, Phil was able to at last draw Sissi to him. Hadn't he warned her that Percy wasn't man enough to take on the responsibility of becoming a father? Hadn't he warned her that Percy was self-centered and was unable to be gallant for any woman?

Percy had proven to be everything Phil claimed. And once he had Sissi in his arms, he had no intention of losing her, especially not to Percy.

Craig witnessed Phil's suffocating demeanor with sympathy for Sissi. He understood how it was to be with someone who was always depressed and easily provoked into a jealous frenzy. He knew that problem all too well.

"Can't take your eyes off her, huh?" Michelle whispered slyly as she snuck up behind Craig. Craig rolled his eyes at her, knowing full well she knew he wasn't interested in Sissi. But he didn't bother to explain himself. He was simply not in the mood to play any of Michelle's petty games.

He glanced over his shoulder at her, clearly not pleased that she was there. He stiffened when she put her chin on his shoulder and stared up at him as if they were deeply in love. All night she had found a way to stand near him, to make it appear as if they were somehow together. As attractive and intriguing as she was at times, the very sound of her voice irked him now. She had the nerve to make herself comfortable in the nook of his back after what she had done to Nicole. He yanked his body away from her and faced her with fierce dark eyes. The brusque movement caused her chin to bump against his shoulder.

"Get lost, Michelle," he spat out though careful to keep his voice low. Michelle hesitated for a moment, running the back of her hand against her chin, a little shocked at his vehement reaction. She self-consciously scoured the room to see if anyone had heard him. Comfortable that no one was watching them, she asked in feigned innocence, "What's wrong with you?"

"You know what's wrong with me, Michelle," he replied in hostility. "That lie you spread about Nicole and Keith."

"Oh, it's true enough, but I didn't start it," she denied adamantly. His displeasure was evident in his tense shoulders and the strained veins popping out of his taut neck.

"Bull, you know you started it. Donna spoke with you, and then she told me. And the first thing you did is lie on my baby. Let me tell you something—"

"No, let me tell you something about your baby," Michelle interrupted scathingly, incensed at his blind devotion for Nicole. Her eyes were wide with frustration. He dared to use an affectionate term for Nicole, after all they had been through.

"I *witnessed* Nicole and Keith kissing. I was not lying about that. She pulled away as if she didn't want it to happen, but I'm no fool. If you're too blind to see just what kind of tramp she is—"

"Don't kid yourself. Nicole is nothing like you," Craig said nastily. Michelle's mouth gaped open in shock, then impulsively she swung forward and slapped Craig squarely across his cheek. The impact brought immediate attention to them.

Percy watched the quarreling couple in silent censure of their behavior. Nicole might not be visible but as tiny as the woman was, she could be anywhere in the room and not be seen. In exasperation, he considered Michelle's vehement face and Craig's stunned look. They had no sense of discretion at all.

"I'll be back," Percy whispered to the two people he'd been talking to then hurried to Craig's side, much to their disappointment.

"Wow. That was loud. What did you do?" Percy asked the moment he reached Craig. Craig's cheek was red from Michelle's angry slap. He narrowed his eyes and glanced around the room. Most of the guests had gone back to their conversations and dancing, although there was still an underlying tension in the air. Thankfully there was still no sight of Nicole.

With Percy standing to his left and Eddie staring sheepishly at the floor, Craig growled between clenched teeth, "If you weren't a woman, I would pop you in your face."

"What? Are you threatening me?" Michelle demanded, her green eyes flaring, daring him to act out his threat.

Craig rolled his eyes, gave Percy an enraged glance, and

demanded, "Get her out of my face, Percy, before I show
a side of me I didn't even know existed."

Michelle was indignant and sputtered, "Oh, forget it.
You know why I slapped you," before pushing her way
between Craig and Percy leaving the basement in a rush
of anger and embarrassment.

Sissi watched the indiscreet exchange between Craig and
Michelle with mild irritation. Nicole and Michelle were
her friends, but she was finding it increasingly difficult to
tolerate Michelle—especially in the wake of discovering
her own fiancé was sleeping around. It hurt her, even if
she wasn't in love with Phil the way Nicole was in love with
Craig. The principle was the same. It was wrong. And Craig
. . . She sighed. He should be ashamed of himself to allow
Nicole to be embarrassed by his relationship with Michelle.

Sissi was sure that by now Nicole was fully aware of Craig's
relationship with Michelle. He had claimed that his and
Michelle's relationship had ended a long time ago. But
everything that happened this evening showed differently.

Sissi slowly sipped her champagne, adjusted the strap of
her dress then glanced at Percy, who, in his usual bravado,
intervened for the couple. She wished he had changed.
She wished he wasn't so handsome. She wished he wasn't
everything she wanted in a man. But he was—from his
successful career at the brokerage firm down to his suave
mannerisms, even in the way he avoided her because he
thought she loved Phil. She sighed, lowering her gaze in
agony.

Having Percy so close was painful. She wanted to break
down and tell him everything. To tell him that she still
loved him. That they could work out the pain of the past
and start fresh. That she still wanted to have his child and
marry him, not Phil. If she could just pour her heart out
to him and forget the promise she made Phil. The engagement was off—she had the right to at least tell Percy. But

she knew she would never betray Phil that way. He had done too much for her and, despite his cheating, when she was depressed and alone and starving for understanding, Phil was the one who helped her through. He deserved this last kindness from her in spite of his affair with Nancy. She would just have to get Percy out of her system, off of her mind, she decided firmly.

But feeling Phil's arm around her waist, listening to him discuss the renovation of their home, left her feeling somehow dirty. She felt gratitude to him for all he had done, yes, but the image of him and Nancy was implanted in her mind so deeply that she could not bear the feel of him against her. He had gone from being a man she could depend on and trust with her innermost secrets, to being a stranger whom she knew nothing about.

In hindsight, Sissi realized that Phil carried all of the signs. She was so hurt from her heartbreaking relationship with Percy that she could not see beyond Phil's kindness. He was like a snake, waiting and biding his time until he finally struck her. And she fell, like a fool, for his pretentious innocent ways. Oh, he had kept the promises he had avowed when he courted her after Percy's desertion. But he was worse than Percy. Because in Sissi's heart, she knew that Percy would never sleep with another woman while confessing to love her. No. Percy was too much of a man to play with her heart. If only he had been man enough to trust her love when it mattered most.

Feeling the threat of tears moisten her eyes, she squared her shoulders and lifted her chin proudly. She would not cry. Not for her lost love with Percy. Not for her foolish belief in Phil.

Phil was watching her closely, and Sissi blinked rapidly, trying to hide the pain she was feeling. He didn't deserve to believe he was the cause for her show of tears. And he was so suffocating. Such a jerk. She had made the promise, but she had not counted on his paranoid hovering over her. She had no privacy, no room to breathe. Though she had thought as the evening wore on he would relax, he proved to react differently. When the party was over, what was he going to do then? Try to convince her to stay with him, she thought sadly. She could only hope that he would realize she could never forgive him. Never.

"Can you believe Maryl?" Phil commented in disgust as Maryl stumbled against one of the tables and spilled her drink on another woman sitting near her.

"She wasn't always like that," Sissi managed to say as she gingerly stepped out of his embrace. She was highly annoyed with Phil's deliberate attempt to caress her. She was sure he believed that since she made the promise she would allow his intimacy. She was losing patience with him and, if he wasn't careful, she would snap and tell everyone that the engagement was off and had been even before the party!

Sissi's irate expression unnerved Phil. He wasn't sure if her frown was directed at him or Maryl. He knew only that since Percy had arrived, his hopes to change Sissi's mind had been dashed. It was just unfortunate that he had been arrogant enough to encourage Sissi to invite him. Now she was fidgeting and ready to escape, he could sense. On impulse, before he could be discouraged, he bent over her and planted a full kiss on her mouth.

It was all Sissi could do not to sputter and gag in disgust. After he had his mouth all over Nancy, how dare he! Eyes blazing with anger, Sissi gaped at him in disapproval. Phil grinned sheepishly down at Sissi.

"Why did you do that?" Sissi demanded, trying to maintain her composure.

"I felt compelled," Phil whispered back. His eyes were sad yet hopeful. Sissi had to turn away, so annoyed was she that he thought his pathetic attempt to look doleful would soften her. Believing her silence was acceptance of his affection, Phil possessively placed his arm around Sissi's waist. He was instantly brought to reality when Sissi shot him an enraged look.

"Move your arm from my waist," she spat. This time her voice rose slightly, and Phil looked around plaintively, hoping no one heard her biting command.

"Sissi, calm down," he whispered urgently and hastily removed his arm.

"I will not calm down. All evening you've been crowding me, pretending that everything is all right. It isn't. Just stop . . . touching me," she sputtered, so enraged she could barely speak. Phil was crestfallen. He loved Sissi, beyond Nancy, beyond his career, beyond his pride. He loved her and would do anything to win her back. If he just had more time.

"I'm sorry, baby. I know it—"

"Don't call me baby," Sissi swore, interrupting him in utter exasperation.

"Sissi, I'm sorry. If you would just lighten up. I'm trying to keep up appearances, that's all," he blurted in frustration. So now he couldn't call her baby. What next? Did she want him to leave tonight with the other guests?

Sissi was tired of Phil standing at her side, pretending that he was the perfect man when he was lower than a dog. He was crazy if he thought she could keep up such a sham all evening, especially with his hands all over her at every chance he got. She wanted the evening over with and to be alone—or at least away from Phil.

"I'm tired. I think I'll call it a night," Sissi murmured, her steam fading.

"You can't," Phil said hastily, glancing around the crowded room.

Sissi gave him an impatient glance. "Why not?"

"What would everyone think if you left now? The cake

hasn't been cut. We haven't toasted each other. At least let me toast our engagement—"

"Fake engagement," Sissi corrected.

"Fake then. But we should give each other a toast before you leave. Please," Phil pleaded.

"Fine, you can give a toast. But I can't play this game that far. I will have to be speechless tonight, honey," she added sarcastically.

Phil nodded, ignoring her sarcastic tone. He didn't want to risk changing Sissi's mind or upsetting her more. In the state of mind she was in, she could easily throw caution to the wind and tell everyone.

A delicate frown creased her forehead as she walked side by side with Phil to the honorary table where cake and a champagne fountain had been set up. A toast was the last thing she wanted to do right now. But she held back a sigh and forced a small smile to her lips to add realism to the performance she was about to give.

Phil asked one of his guests to turn down the volume on the stereo. When Anita Baker's sultry "Body and Soul" was barely audible, and the voices of the guests began to fade into silent curiosity, Phil cleared his throat and announced, "Everyone. Can I have your attention?"

All eyes turned to Phil and Sissi. Percy narrowed his eyes, his hand gripping his brandy with a tension that he wasn't aware of as he waited for the dreaded announcement.

Grinning proudly, Phil put a large hand on Sissi's narrow waist, holding her close to him, and said, "I hope you all are having a good time." They all cheered. Sissi maintained her tight smile, trying not to feel foolish as she stood there, her hand in Phil's.

Phil continued. "I'm glad you came. I just wanted to say that the woman I've loved for some time now has consented to marriage." There was another loud whoop and hollering cheers. Phil chuckled but waved the crowd silent and, with his next words, his eyes fell directly on Percy. "I want to toast my future wife, Sissi Adams." He turned to her, his eyes clearly stating his love for her. "I'm a proud man tonight. And I know I'm going to make you as happy as you have made me. I love you, baby. To our future!" Then he kissed her, and everyone cheered again, shouting, "To Sissi and Phil!"

A moment later the music started again and Al Green's "I'm Still in Love With You" filled the air. Percy turned his back to the crowd, his face granite as he stared into the fireplace, not wanting to watch Sissi and Phil slow dance.

"Thank you, Sissi. You're a jewel," Phil whispered in Sissi's ear as he held her in an intimate embrace. The floor was crowded with couples dancing around them. The lights were low and the mood romantic. But Sissi was cringing inside, bitterly accepting his embrace, knowing that despite her disappointment in him, she would see the evening through. However, feeling overwhelmed with her overpowering need to be free of him, she stopped dancing and said abruptly, "I need a breath of fresh air."

Phil looked worried and asked hastily, "What about the cake? You're not going to cut it?"

"You cut it. I don't want any," Sissi answered briskly.

"Do you want me to go with you?"

"Can't you see I need to be alone?" she asked impatiently.

"Yes. I just thought . . ." Phil paused, uncertain what he thought.

"Phil, that was a pretty big announcement. I just need a moment alone—all right? I've been through a lot, as you know. And you've been smothering me all evening," she added in exasperation.

Phil hesitated then took a step back and, releasing her

hands, nodded toward the balcony. "I understand, and you're right. Go. I'll be here when you get back," he said so kindly that Sissi frowned. That was the old Phil. The man she thought she could marry and learn to love because of his kindness and generosity. But he was a fake, a phony and she wouldn't let the sweet words he offered blind her. Licking her lips, she hastened away.

Phil stared after her sultry form in aggravation, watching her until she disappeared outside the door. Standing alone he looked back. Percy and Craig had been talking, but Phil soon found that Percy had disappeared also. Panic filled him as he searched the crowd. The last thing he wanted was for Percy to follow Sissi outside. A moment later he spotted Percy engrossed in conversation with Janice. He relaxed, sipped his drink, and found a new group of guests to mingle with, all the while his eyes alert for Sissi's return.

"Nicole, girl. What are you doing out here?" Sissi asked, spotting Nicole leaning despondently against one of the trees.

Nicole slowly looked up, her eyes dull with exhaustion. She had remained outside, hoping that Geoff would return. She had seriously turned him off and was highly annoyed with herself and Craig. After all, if it weren't for Craig's repeated betrayal, she wouldn't be in the predicament she was in. Feeling overwhelmed with her problems, she unexpectedly broke into tears.

Sissi was stunned but immediately shook it off. Nicole needed her. A moment later she was holding Nicole, gently rocking back and forth as she whispered,. "Don't you let her lies get to you, Nicole. That's what Michelle wants." Nicole continued to sob, and Sissi added in a firm voice, "Who believes her anyway? We all know what kind of a person Michelle is."

Nicole sniffed and gently pulled herself free of Sissi's hold. "I know. But I'm so frustrated, I could scratch her eyes out, Sissi," she sniffed and dabbed at the tears on her cheek.

"I understand," Sissi replied.

"Do you think . . . have you ever considered her relationship with Craig? I know that he said it was over for good. But something happened, and they started their affair again. I'm not crazy, Sissi. I know they're still involved." Nicole whispered, wanting to cringe and hide.

Sissi sighed. She understood Nicole's grief better now than ever. When she lost Percy, it had nothing to do with another woman. But for the first time in her life, she fully understood how a woman could stay with a man when she knew he was cheating on her. Of course her relationship with Phil was different, and she was not going to be foolish enough to give him a second chance to hurt her—but if she had loved Phil, really loved him, Sissi honestly believed she might have been like Nicole and found excuses to stay with her man. It was a pitiful state she and her best friend were in.

"Why don't you do something about it?" Sissi asked softly, wanting to share her secret about the false engagement. But as she considered Nicole's solemn expression, she knew that telling Nicole about Phil's indiscretion would only sadden Nicole more. So instead, she added, "You're a beautiful person, Nicole. You're pretty, intelligent, and a strong black woman. You don't have to deal with Craig's selfishness. You need to step up to him and let him know that you're not going to deal with it anymore."

Nicole nodded in agreement. She wasn't even sure if she was in love with Craig, she couldn't honestly say why she stayed with him. She was just used to being with him. After all, she had several years invested with him.

"I could break Michelle's neck," she said bitterly with a sideways glance at Sissi. She knew she wasn't answering

Sissi's questions, but she couldn't. She didn't have an answer.

"That would at least solve the problem at hand, but," Sissi added contritely, "you would play right into her hands and lose Craig for good." They fell silent, and Nicole stared at the ground in remorse.

"I'd better get back inside before my hound dog searches me out," Sissi said dryly, pushing away from the tree.

"I'm coming with you," Nicole said, falling into step beside Sissi. Before they reached the house, Nicole paused and Sissi glanced at her expectantly.

"What is it? You're not letting her get to you again, are you?" Sissi asked gently. Nicole smiled, a mischievous light in her eyes.

"No," she drawled. She glanced around them then stepped closer to Sissi. Sissi was curious now. She, too, glanced around and with a grin, asked in a perceptive whisper, "What? Come on . . . what's the big secret?"

"Your friend, Geoff Roberts—"

"Yes," Sissi answered quickly.

"I was just wondering—I mean, I don't want to step on your toes—"

"My toes are fine." Sissi laughed.

"Okay, then, here I go. Tell me about him. What's he like? Shoot, you know what I'm asking." Nicole laughed again, uncomfortable now.

Sissi considered Nicole with a broad grin. "I knew it. I knew it. All this time, little Ms. Faithful," Sissi said proudly. At last someone had drawn Nicole's attention, and it wasn't that fake Craig. Sissi was pleased.

"I haven't done anything, Sis. I just wanted to know more about your friend," Nicole said defensively, recalling the rumor about Keith. Sissi didn't notice Nicole's chary attitude.

"Let's see," Sissi began, tapping her chin thoughtfully and staring at the night sky. "He's single. In his early thirties. He's got a kid, five or six years old, I think. He has a great job at the network. Oh, did I tell you he's the weatherman or meteorologist, whatever?"

"Janice told me," Nicole replied.

"Well?" Sissi probed.

Nicole had started walking again to the house. It was her turn to pause and look curiously at Sissi. "What do you mean, well?" Nicole asked, feigning ignorance.

"You know what I mean, Nicole," Sissi snapped, though she was laughing. "Are you going to go for it or play the little innocent with this guy? 'Cause I'm telling you, he's not only everything I said he is, but he's looking for someone to love. I can see it in his eyes."

"Yeah, I'll bet," Nicole said sarcastically.

"No, I mean, I know him. He's not just looking for a one-night love affair, Nicole. He's looking for someone special. You're just his type. Give him a chance," she added, desperately wanting so much for Nicole to be happy. Geoff was a good man, Sissi was sure of it. And he would be perfect for Nicole. If Craig couldn't be the man that Nicole needed, he should let her go.

Nicole narrowed her eyes then stood back on her heels as if a light had shone on her. "You didn't," she whispered in shock.

"Didn't what?" Sissi asked innocently, though a smile escaped her full lips heavenward.

"You sent him out here, didn't you?" Nicole accused.

"No," Sissi answered.

"Oh, sure you didn't. Always the matchmaker, for heaven's sake. And here I was beginning to think that Janice had sent him out. Just what did you expect to accomplish? I'm already in love."

"With a jerk, a cheater, and a liar," Sissi stated flatly,

her smile fading at the thought of Craig. She loved Craig dearly but for her friend Nicole, he was absolutely worthless.

"That isn't true. You don't know if he's a cheater or a liar," Nicole said defensively.

"You admitted it yourself a few minutes ago. Well," Sissi sighed impatiently. "At least you admit to the fact that he's a jerk."

Nicole glared at Sissi, trying to appear stern, then a smile broke the tension and she laughed. "Yes, Your Honor, I admit to that fact."

They walked to the back door and stood there a moment in silence, neither relishing the idea of returning to the party.

"He is attractive," Nicole whispered, her thoughts wandering back to Geoff.

"Of course he is. Would I give you less to consider?" Sissi responded with a haughty shrug.

"You troublemaker," Nicole muttered playfully before they entered the house.

"Angel," Sissi countered, leading the way in.

"And you know that dress is hot. You should be ashamed of yourself, can practically see your butt," Nicole drawled softly as they joined the party. Sissi glanced up at her, a wide grin brightening her eyes.

"That's all right, my man likes it," Sissi retorted then sauntered past Nicole and headed for the bar, her hips swaying outrageously left to right. Nicole laughed, the scandal temporarily forgotten.

Chapter Nine

Geoff was baffled by Nicole. She had come on to him one moment then spurned him the next. He should have expected her to be flaky. He was exhausted and ready to sleep even though it was barely past midnight. Sissi was going to think he was crazy if he left though, especially after he had begged to stay.

He had no idea why he hadn't left after Nicole spurned him. Phil had pointedly snubbed him, and the others just simply ignored him. He stood near the bar, drinking vodka and grapefruit juice. They were a strange crowd, Sissi's friends. In particular, Craig. At first he thought Nicole was married to him, but Sissi had quickly cleared up that matter. Nicole hadn't made the big mistake yet, was how Sissi had put it.

Geoff allowed a semblance of a smile to form across his face. He knew what Sissi's friends thought about their relationship, especially Michelle. They all looked at him as if he were some creep from the backwoods. But it was his motto never to date on the job, and he and Sissi worked together, although rarely since she freelanced one week out of the month at the station. Still, even if Sissi were interested in him, and he was sure she wasn't, it would be a problem.

He had an affair with a woman on his job years earlier, and he had learned a valuable lesson. She got pregnant and refused to get an abortion. He was fine with that and was proud of his baby. With a smile he thought of his six-year-old son and how adorable he was—an intelligent little boy eager to learn and listen.

Geoff sighed, pride filling him as he stared into his drink. He wasn't in love with his son's mother. In all honesty, their affair was short and bitter. Still she clung to him like a wet rag, annoying him, bothering him, harassing him. To make matters worse, she wasn't the most attractive person. She was too tall, too thin, and too plain, and had the personality of a doormat. No, he would never mix work with pleasure on the job again.

"Hi, there," Grear said brightly, coming to stand beside the good-looking weatherman. Since he and Sissi continuously insisted they weren't involved, she decided there was nothing wrong with her striking up a conversation with him.

He glanced at Grear and smiled pleasantly. Grear was a sweet-looking girl. Plump, dimpled cheeks, shoulder-length hair. She looked more like a little girl than a woman. He offered his charming personality in full. He turned to her and said, "Hi, yourself."

She grinned happily. This guy was as fine as Percy and Craig, she thought excitedly.

"I'm Grear. A friend of Sissi's. I saw you by yourself and thought, Lord, he looks lonely. So here I am," she rambled.

He chuckled, leaning forward to whisper, "I'm glad you noticed. I was just thinking of going home."

Her round brown eyes widened, then she blinked, before saying, "Oh, no. Don't do that," she gushed. "I bet you haven't even eaten yet."

"As a matter of fact—"

"Here." She grabbed his arm and started walking toward the buffet table. "Sissi went all out for the party. There is so much food, and hardly anyone has eaten. And look what time is. Oh, but isn't it incredible, this place. It looks like some old southern mansion. Well, it is actually just renovated. I am starved. I had a little salad earlier, but it really didn't do anything for me. I think she brought some more chicken wings out, too. Whoever does the cooking for her is a genius. I wish I wasn't just a secretary," she continued hastily. She was speaking so fast Geoff could hardly understand what she was saying.

"Yeah, it's a lovely place," Geoff managed to respond as she picked up two plates, one for her, one for him and started filling them with food.

"Can you believe it? I graduated with all of them: Sissi, Percy, Nicole, Michelle, Craig . . . uh what's-his-name . . . oh, yeah. Eddie. It was fun back then. Everyone says I look so much younger than Sissi, do you think so?" She actually paused and Geoff looked up in surprise.

"What?" he finally asked, not sure what she had just asked him. She appeared disappointed.

"Nothing really. But how is it that some people get all the luck? I'm saying, Craig and Nicole, sweet as they can be—and yet they do okay. He's a computer technician or something with a company in D.C., and Nicole's starting another boutique soon. I hear she and Sissi may go into business together down here. I guess one of them is going to have to give up her career since she's getting married . . ."

Geoff frowned at that comment. He accepted the plate she offered him with a tight smile then prodded, "So how long have Craig and Nicole been together?'' He walked beside her until they found a comfortable space near the door. Grear paused long enough to try to remember the date.

"I think officially, five years. Everybody knows they've been dating forever, but in the beginning it was Michelle and Craig, you know.''

No, he didn't know.

"Then, of course, they broke up a few years ago, but Craig got with Nicole. And now, oh, wow. Now there's this incident with Nicole and her cousin's husband. I heard they were sleeping together,'' she added in a hushed whisper.

Geoff scowled, remembering Nicole's irritated outburst earlier in the yard. He hadn't expected this sweet girl to be a part of the gossip, but then no one in the room was truly a friend of Nicole's, except perhaps Sissi, he decided. He took a closer look at Grear and wondered if she would be leaving for the evening or if she was on the weekend guest list.

"Of course, I don't believe . . .'' she stammered at his scowl.

Good for her, he thought candidly.

"Nicole's probably never cheated on Craig. She's not like, well, you know, Sissi and Michelle.''

"Oh?'' he probed.

"Well,'' she began, taking a piece of chicken and pulling off the skin. "Everybody knows about Sissi and Percy. And of course there is Michelle and Craig. Do you want something to drink?'' she asked, abruptly switching the conversation, feeling uncomfortable beneath his unsmiling gaze.

"Sure,'' he answered. A moment later she was milling back through the crowd to get their drinks from the bar.

Geoff was torn between annoyance and intrigue. He knew about Sissi's affair with Percy. But that was ancient news, he thought. He had grown irritated with Grear, but he was careful not to hurt her feelings. Her conversation was much too intriguing, if not gossipy, to just walk away like he wanted to, so he allowed his gaze to wander about while waiting for her return.

Unwilling to admit he was looking for Nicole, his eyes burned into the back of Craig. What did she see in that guy? He was obviously cheating or close to it. Even someone as simpleminded as Grear knew there was something going on with the man. But, why should he care? He didn't even know Nicole well enough to be concerned over who she chose to marry. When Grear returned, he was much more amiable, although he kept the conversation trivial and off Nicole Burns.

Tired and ready to call it a night, Craig searched the blur of faces for Nicole. He was going to get her and sneak away from the others before anyone could distract them. But Nicole was nowhere in sight. He wondered if she could have gotten the same idea earlier and gone off to bed without him. That was the type of behavior that he so often complained about. She would isolate him from her activities and then wonder why he didn't know what was going on. He sighed, took another sip from his drink, then set it on the mantel over the fireplace. Without a word, he left Eddie, who was engrossed in deep conversation with some woman and Percy, who had been staring into the fireplace for what seemed hours.

Michelle was in tune to Craig's impatience and immediately ended her conversation with her girlfriends. She was determined to corner him and insist on an apology after the way he had embarrassed her earlier.

"I'll be back," she whispered to them and hastily left the party. He was already on the top stair when Michelle reached the basement door, but he didn't glance back or seem to notice her. The moment she was up the stairs and off the carpeted floor, she slipped out of her high heels and, holding them close to her stomach, tiptoed at a discreet distance behind Craig.

Craig walked back through the main house, remembering the stairs near the front door that most likely led to the bedrooms. Unaware of Michelle close on his heels, he peered around the corner, glancing inside the living room. He didn't see Nicole and quickly left. He was beginning to grow worried and decided he should have asked Sissi to show him to their room. He frowned, hoping that Nicole had not gone somewhere to mope. Sometimes she could be such a wimp, he thought impatiently. It was a part of her character that he did not admire.

He opened a few more doors, glancing inside before hastily moving on. He came to the end of the hall and decided that Nicole must be upstairs. He would have to find Sissi now. He walked out of the room that must serve as a library for Phil's work, with its wood-paneled walls and dark cherry wood desk and bar.

"Craig," Michelle whispered, stepping inside the room before Craig could leave. He turned sharply, staring at Michelle from head to toe, his eyes clearly showing his loathing at the sight of her. She leaned against the door and shut it, oblivious to his disgust.

"What?" he said harshly, hands on hips, his eyes unblinking even as he noted that she had taken off her shoes.

"I was hoping . . . I wanted to talk to you, alone," she said suggestively.

"Fine," he said coldly, "we're alone."

"Craig," she murmured, letting go of the doorknob and allowing her shoes to fall to the floor. She walked slowly, carefully up to him. Oh, he was angry with her, but she hadn't lied about Nicole. She had witnessed Nicole and Keith locked in a kiss as she left his hotel room. Once Craig realized just what kind of woman Nicole truly was, he would come to his senses. She was inches away from him now, and Craig continued to glare down at her. He was trying not to be impressed by her exaggerated swaying hips, her pouting lips, her sensual dark green eyes.

"Yeah?" he asked testily, glancing over her head at the door.

"I'm so sorry," she whispered, the heat from her breath moist against his cheek. "I didn't mean to upset you. I just thought you should know about Nicole."

"So you told every person you knew first?" he berated her.

She hesitated, blinking rapidly as if confused. "It wasn't supposed to happen that way. I openly mentioned it to one person, Grear or Sissi, I think."

"Sissi would never add to a rumor like that, Michelle. We both know this. Why can't you face up to what you did?" he demanded, his annoyance renewed by her blatant attempt to deceive him.

"I know, I know," she said quickly, not wanting him to turn from her. If she could just get him to kiss her. Craig was always weak after a kiss, and she was determined to have her way. She knew Craig. He might act as if he was turned off and disgusted with her, but it wouldn't be the first time he had given in to her while confessing to love Nicole.

"Then stop trying to play this game," he snapped, holding his head high and away from her.

"I'm not," Michelle muttered, for once feeling uncertain about her hold over Craig. "I . . . oh, I don't know, Craig. I'm sorry."

"Yeah, right," he grumbled.

"Craig," Michelle moaned, putting a carefully manicured hand flat against his chest and pressing her body lightly against his. "I miss you so much," she whispered huskily.

He considered her with wavering eyes. Michelle was an attractive woman but he loved Nicole. It wasn't in his plan to hurt Nicole any more than Michelle already had done. He knew the moment he was told about the engagement party that he would have to deal with Michelle. If only she wasn't so beautiful, so sexy. Ignoring the slightly exposed skin that showed off her full cleavage through her dress, he shoved her hand from his chest and took a step away from her.

"Michelle, turn around and leave," Craig said calmly, trying not to lose his patience with her. Michelle's smile was wide and alluring as she ignored his command. Purposely she put her hand to the back of his neck and pulled his head down until his lips met hers. He was stiff and informal yet unresisting. Michelle chose to ignore his indifference and kissed him passionately as she pressed her body against his. With silent delight she could feel his body responding to her and eagerly finished her kiss before whispering, "You see, you didn't want me to leave."

"You're wrong. I want very much for you to go away. Now!" he growled, prying her hand from his neck and shoving her away from him. Michelle gasped, unable to accept his words when his body so obviously desired her. Refusing to give in so easily, she stared into his eyes and slowly began to lift her dress over her head. Craig had to resist the urge to help her. Instead he snarled and said in a cold, indifferent murmur, "It won't work, Michelle. Whatever we had ended a long time ago."

"Really? I seem to recall just a few weeks ago making love to you," she said in a huff, pausing on the last button.

"That was a mistake," Craig said defensively, averting his eyes from her.

"Like hell it was, Craig. You wanted me just as much as I want you now," Michelle cried bitterly, finally realizing that he was sincerely rejecting her. Suddenly conscious of her partially undressed state, she picked up her dress, slipped it back on, and stood watching him in dismay, not believing the words he was saying.

"I was drunk, you were a vulture. Hey, these things happen."

Michelle flinched in disbelief.

"You don't have to be so cold, Craig" she whispered painfully.

"No? You don't have to keep starting confusion between me and Nicole. You think I don't know the hints you threw at Nicole about us?" he shouted. They both tensed at the rise in his voice.

"Donna did that, you said that yourself," Michelle cried, frustration blurring her confidence.

"With your help."

"No. She just cares about you like I do, Craig."

"Yeah? You tell Donna everything, don't you. And she tells Nicole or me. I'll tell you what, Donna's the reason that I realized I don't want you. Your so-called friend helped me figure out that you're not worth the trouble. Tell that to Donna!"

Michelle was dumbfounded. What did he mean? Donna wouldn't come between her and Craig. Donna knew how much Michelle loved Craig and that Michelle would do anything to get him from Nicole. How could she go behind her back?

At Michelle's stunned silence, Craig added, "Michelle, I do not want you! Get that through your thick skull. I'm in love with Nicole, I'm going to marry her, and I tolerate you only because, like any stray dog, I can't seem to shake you." Without giving her a moment to respond, he brushed past her, slammed from the room, and left her alone.

Michelle was devastated. In shock, barely able to stand in the humiliation from his torrent of insults, she shakily sat on the leather chair. Closing her eyes to hold back frustrated tears, Michelle curled up in the chair, too distressed to return to the party anytime soon. Earlier she couldn't wait for Donna to arrive to show Nicole just who was in charge. Now she couldn't wait to confront Donna about Craig. Whatever she said to him, Michelle was determined to find out. Donna was messing with the wrong woman, she thought bitterly as she stared at the closed door.

It was close to one A.M. and most of the others were still partying. It was as if they were back in college. No one wanted the party to end. The music had changed from Motown tunes to hip-hop of the nineties, the odor of a thousand perfumes assaulted Nicole's nostrils, and she was feeling particularly light-headed. She had searched the party for Craig in vain. He was nowhere around. She noticed, too, that Michelle had disappeared. She lowered her eyes, disgusted at the suspicion that ran through her mind. Michelle was good at getting what she wanted, at least where men were concerned, especially Craig. Staring into her drink, not wanting anyone to notice her anxiety, she heaved a deep sigh.

"You all right?" Percy asked from Nicole's side.

Nicole looked up at him with a bright false smile, trying to hide her distress.

"Sure . . . I'm just exhausted. I should be going to bed," she said evenly. Percy nodded, his expression full of concern, but he looked casually around the room searching for Sissi. She was talking with Janice and a few other women and for once didn't look up at his glance.

"Why don't you go upstairs. You are staying for the weekend, right?" he asked, returning his attention to Nicole.

"It seems that way," she murmured.

"You need some direction?" Percy laughed at Nicole's amused smirk. "I can walk you up if you like," he added with a wink and a grin when Nicole made no move to leave the party. Percy seemed so relaxed and confident, and Nicole was proud of him for getting over Sissi and not ruining her best friend's engagement party. She was so engrossed in her own problems, she hadn't felt the tension between the ex-couple, but knowing Percy, Nicole wouldn't have been surprised if he had made a scene. He was always so determined to have his way—and the way he used to love Sissi, it was a wonder he ever let her slip away from him. Nicole smiled and rolled her eyes, knowing he was kidding about being with her, he was too much of a gentlemen. She responded with a dry, "No, thanks. I think I can manage. I should find Sissi though," she added.

"She finally escaped Phil. She's over there with Janice," Percy commented bitingly.

"I know she's tired of Phil standing over her like that," Nicole remarked, her eyes spotting Phil standing like a guard only a few feet away from Sissi.

Percy considered the couple with narrowed eyes. As he stared, Sissi looked across the room and caught his gaze. She blinked but didn't skip a word in her conversation. After witnessing Sissi's and Phil's affectionate exchange earlier, he was determined to avoid Sissi for the rest of the night.

"He's a coward," Percy couldn't help saying.

"What?" Nicole asked, glancing at Percy in surprise.

"A coward. He's so afraid of losing Sissi that he can't

allow her to breathe. Me, personally, I have to have air. Let that woman breathe. How else is she going to miss you?"

"Well, yeah, I see," Nicole drawled. "She's had about three years of breathing room." Nicole laughed.

Percy frowned, not amused. It hadn't been that long. In fact, it had been only two years since they broke up. In all of that time, whenever he saw Sissi, it seemed that she hated him, wanted nothing to do with him. Until tonight. But this time Phil was by her side, and he wasn't going to make a fool of himself by being rejected.

"That's not what I meant," he muttered. Nicole's gaze fell back on Sissi for a moment before glancing around once again for Craig. She agreed with Percy about breathing room, but Craig was taking the concept a little too far.

"So you wanna go up?" Percy asked after a moment of silence fell between them. Nicole grinned again, happy that his gloom had escaped him as suddenly as it had captured him.

"Yes, I do, but I'll get Sissi to show me the way." She laughed.

"Okay, but you don't know what you're missing," Percy called as she walked away to get Sissi. She glanced back at him, saying, "That's what you think."

He chuckled, pleased to see her humor return. He didn't know how true the gossip was and didn't particularly care. He only knew from the day he met Nicole when they were all just freshmen in college, Nicole was the sweetest, most gentle little thing he had ever met. She was nothing like the type of women he desired, but she deserved a good man. Craig, his best friend, was not a good man. Percy used to tell Craig, straighten up or lose her. But Craig proved Percy wrong and without fail managed to slip out with Michelle and still come home to Nicole—both women willing participants in his blatant trysts. One thing was for certain, if Nicole was to ever sleep with another man, Craig had only himself to blame. She was a good girl and, from Percy's point of view, if she had been with Keith, Craig deserved it.

Chapter Ten

"I'm sorry to pull you away from the party, Sissi and Janice. I couldn't find Craig, and I'm so tired," Nicole apologized walking between Sissi and Janice up the stairs to the bedrooms.

"Why are you worrying about it? You know Phil was crowding me," Sissi scolded, easily dismissing Nicole's concern for pulling them from the party.

"I heard that," Janice reiterated.

"Why does he do that? It must be horrible not having a moment's peace," Nicole whispered, glancing around as if Phil was near them.

Sissi scowled, silently agreeing with Nicole. It was as if he was always there. Always watching her like a psychotic warden of love. It was definitely a mistake to agree to play his fiancée under these circumstances. But the damage was done. She wished she had never confided in Phil, that she had never trusted him, and that she had been stronger when Percy abandoned her. If she hadn't been so depressed from losing the baby, and then her grandmother passed away and left her the house, and then Phil was there, like an angel, a true friend, a snake in the grass. She frowned, wishing she could put him in the past. The weekend couldn't end soon enough for her. The only problem was, once it was over with Phil, it would be over with Percy, too. Percy would leave North Carolina and never look back, that was the kind of man he was.

"I guess I'm learning to deal with it," Sissi muttered, leading the trio up the stairs to the second-floor bedrooms. She was tired of carrying the burden of lying to her best friends. They thought she was some kind of a fool to marry Phil. But they didn't understand. He was acting this way only because he knew how seriously he had messed up. On a normal day Phil was kind and considerate and just . . . everything she needed to get over the losses she'd had to endure. If he could have kept his pants on, everything would be all right.

"You shouldn't have to learn. I couldn't deal with that crap," Janice snapped, infuriated that Sissi appeared to be settling for Phil.

"Sure you could if the man was who you love," Sissi commented, referring more to Percy than Phil. Janice, believing Phil was on Sissi's mind, shook her head in disapproval but refrained from commenting, although she completely disagreed with Sissi.

"I hear you, Sissi. In one way or another, we all deal with something or compromise ourselves for the ones we love," Nicole added.

"Humph! I won't myself. Or you, either," Janice added with a friendly squeeze on Nicole's slender shoulder.

"Ditto," Sissi added.

Nicole thought she would burst with pride. Although neither of them had directly mentioned the rumor, it was their way of siding with her, of saying that they believed in her.

"Thanks. I love you both. You know that?" she said in a choked voice.

"Oh, now there you go, trying to get mushy on us." Sissi laughed then gave Nicole a gentle hug.

"I, for one, don't want to ruin my makeup with tears. The night is still young," Janice stated, intending to return to the party after walking Nicole to her room.

"Sissi," Janice complained a moment later. "You need an elevator in this place," she snapped, by the trip from the basement to second floor. Sissi nodded in agreement, although she was breathing evenly as they walked down the hall.

"I'll tell you what, had I known how tiresome these steps could be I would have opted for the city life. Elevators, neighbors. This green acres life is a little dull and harsh, too. You know?"

"Sure do," Janice agreed as they reached Nicole's room at the end of the hall. Sissi opened the door, and Janice let out an appreciative whistle.

"Wow," Janice said, turning in a complete circle to get a full spectrum of the room. Nicole smiled, having seen the room when she'd arrived that morning, still it was impressive and looked slightly larger in its present lighting.

"Isn't it lovely?" Nicole asked Janice.

"It's fabulous?" Janice drawled, nodding her head, impressed, her hands on her hips as she walked around the bed and examined the room.

There were soft gray curtains hanging from the window. The blinds were open, allowing moonlight to spill into the room. To the left of the window was a large ficus plant, to the right a queen-size bed. The comforter and matching sheets were champagne satin, the carpet the same soft gray as the curtains. There was a complete bedroom set of deep cherry wood. The wallpaper was a soft pattern of marble gray. It was classy and shone completely with Sissi's taste.

"I know who's going to get down tonight," Janice teased Nicole, plopping onto the queen-size bed.

"That's right, so get your funky self off my bed." Nicole laughed, playfully pulling Janice from the bed.

"Sissi, if I had known it was going to be this nice, I would have said I was staying," Janice gushed, now leaning against the dresser.

"You can if you like," Sissi offered, resting her arm against the six-drawer chest. Janice smiled, a feline look on her wide lips.

"Nah, I better not. It's already crowded enough."

"No, it's not," Sissi exclaimed. The more guests, the merrier for her. She had no desire to be in Phil's company any more than necessary. "There's only me . . . and Phil, of course," she added hastily. "And Craig and Nicole, Michelle, Eddie, Geoff, and, you know, Percy," she ended, a little flustered at the mention of Percy's name.

"I don't want to get into it with Michelle," Janice said carefully. Sissi smirked, crossing her arms over her chest as she considered Janice.

"Don't let Michelle rule you. Stay and enjoy yourself. We're going shopping before lunchtime, around ten A.M., and then tomorrow night, we're going to sweep the town."

"Oooh, I want to stay." Janice grimaced, but she truly despised Michelle. She couldn't possibly remain civil for yet another day with that woman.

"I wish you would, too," Nicole added softly.

Janice closed her eyes for a moment then glanced from Sissi to Nicole then sighed. "Oh, why not?"

"Good. My home is yours, Janice," Sissi said, pleased at Janice's decision.

"And Michelle's, unfortunately," Janice muttered.

"Michelle's, too . . . she's okay," Sissi said carefully, walking over to the window and moving the curtain slightly to the side to gaze into the parking area. People were leaving, but the muffled noise below indicated that she still had a houseful. She thought she saw Michelle's familiar face when she realized it couldn't be. The girl she saw was driving off with a few other guests. Sissi sighed. She and Michelle had not had a falling out. In fact, from the beginning when Sissi was in her second year of college, Michelle learned not to play with Sissi. And Michelle's tryst with Craig was none of her affair, especially when Nicole chose to stay with the man.

"Sure she is," Nicole retorted as if reading Sissi's thoughts.

Sissi appeared uncomfortable, and Nicole grimaced, contritely saying, "I'm sorry. I shouldn't have—"

"Please. I know where you're coming from. We both do," Sissi added, glancing at Janice. Janice nodded in agreement, and Nicole suddenly grew restless, uneasy at the prospect of discussing Keith and Donna.

They all fell silent until the slight muffle of noise below invaded the quiet.

"Well, I hate to put you two out, but I am sleepy," Nicole said, relieved by the slight distraction. She stretched and yawned and Sissi chuckled.

"Sure you're tired. You don't want to be scolded about Keith," Sissi said bluntly.

"I'm not afraid to discuss Keith or the lies spreading around downstairs. I'm tired and can talk about him tomorrow," Nicole said hotly.

Sissi shrugged, gave Janice a slight nudge toward the door, and said evenly, "My, you can be so testy sometimes."

"I think I earned that right," Nicole responded.

"I suppose if I see Donna I shouldn't send her up now," Sissi teased, trying to lighten Nicole's mood. It didn't work. Nicole didn't smile and her eyes darkened.

"Donna's not going to come. It's way too late," Nicole muttered then demanded in a cranky voice, "Are you going to let me get some rest?"

"Okay. All right. I'm not one to press the issue. It's as good as forgotten. Night now," Sissi added airily before she closed the door behind her.

Donna Harris felt nauseous. During the entire ride she had argued and sworn at her date that he was driving too fast. He was making her sick, the moron, but he had gotten her to North Carolina in one piece. Slightly dizzy, she stepped out of the car, dropping the cigarette she had been puffing to the ground. Even in her discomfort she paused in fascination at the sight of Sissi Adams's home.

"My goodness! Who does she think she is?" she spat out in a disgruntled slur.

Her date, a young man not much older than twenty, peeked out the window at her outburst to glance from Donna to the house. He pursed his lips in appreciation at the mansion and said, "Not bad."

His words caused Donna to whirl around and glare at him. "How the hell . . . how the hell would you know . . . good from bad? You're a boy and a hoodlum to boot!" Donna snapped in a drunken stammer.

He frowned, staring up at the older woman in irritation. Sure she was cute and had a spicy sexy way of talking to him that most girls his age hadn't mastered yet. But he didn't have to put up with her insults all night. From the moment she had taken her second drink, she started flinging insults at him. So she was older than he. So she had a husband and a nice home in the suburbs. So what? He had enough of her attitude. Besides, right now, with her clothes hanging off her body like a wet mop, her breath smelling like she had smoked a pack of cigarettes, her eyes slightly bloodshot from too many drinks, she wasn't attractive enough to talk trash to him.

Feeling empowered by his anger and disgust with her, he got out of the car and caught her by the elbow. "Easy, baby. You don't want to go in there acting stoned. Remember why you're here."

"You remember!" Then yanking her arm free of his support, she snapped, "I can . . . can walk."

The young man looked crestfallen and froze in his tracks. He couldn't control this woman, and he could foresee her embarrassing him the moment they entered the house.

"You need to lay off the booze if you can't handle it," he mumbled, walking behind her with his hands shoved deep in his pockets. Donna halted suddenly and swept around to face him. Her bloodshot eyes were angry and dark, partially from smeared makeup and partially from lack of sleep during the ride.

"Hey, you can leave. Okay? I'm a married woman."

"Then act like it," he snapped, glaring at her in frustration.

Her eyes widened in disbelief at his tone and without warning she balled her fist and punched him with such force that he stumbled backward, his hands flying out of his pockets in a wild attempt to balance himself.

"What's going on?" Geoff shouted, racing up to Donna and quickly grabbing her arms before she could swing at the young man again. Donna yelled in fury and began kicking and struggling until Geoff pinned her against him, his determination fueled by his concern for his own personal welfare.

The young man came to his feet and spat on the ground. Wiping his mouth where a dribble of blood had escaped him from Donna's assault, he glared from her to Geoff and hissed, "She's a crazy drunk! I'm outta here." With that he jumped in his car and backed all the way out of the driveway. A few guests had been en route to their vehicles when the ruckus began and watched in silent curiosity as Geoff tried to calm the furious woman, who could have been Nicole's sister they looked so much alike. When Geoff finally set her free, after the young man's car was out of sight, the others slowly entered their own cars, realizing the scene was over.

"Don't you ever touch me again," Donna gasped, a hiccup escaping her the moment she was free.

"I hope not to," Geoff retorted calmly though his shin was killing him from the blows she had given him during her struggle.

"Who are you anyway?" she demanded testily, adjusting her clothes and running her fingers through her curly hair as she considered him in hostility.

"Geoff Roberts, a friend of Sissi's," he added for clarification, although he was watching her carefully. She was definitely a part of Nicole's family, right down to her suspicious attitude. So she must be the notorious Donna.

"I'll bet you are," she drawled slyly.

Geoff frowned at the implication but was not at all interested in continuing a conversation with her. "If you're all right, I'll see you inside," he offered though careful not to touch her again.

Her upper lip snarled back in a nasty rejection as she responded. "I'll see my own way in," she snarled.

He rolled his eyes in exasperation, not in the mood to be gallant for a strange woman with a vicious attitude. Abiding by her wish, he stepped aside and allowed her to climb the stairs to front door. He wasn't even in the mood to let her know that she could enter the party through the side basement door. Let her find out for herself, he thought, weary of Sissi's unapproachable girlfriends.

Donna didn't give him a second thought as she immediately marched in her drunken glory up the flight of stairs and banged on the front door. She was going to expose Michelle and Nicole for the conniving hussies they were. The truth was going to be told this night—of that, Donna was determined.

Chapter Eleven

The evening should have been coming to a halt, but people were still partying. Phil's friends looked ready to stay until the end, and Sissi's friends were ready to accommodate them. Sissi wondered where they all got the energy. They had been eating and drinking and dancing to loud music for hours.

She sighed, noticing that she had not seen Craig or Michelle around. Janice was on the dance floor, dancing with Eddie, who seemed to be genuinely happy at the moment. Janice had a lot of energy, Sissi thought, and Eddie was experiencing it firsthand as he tried to keep up with Janice's sassy moves.

Since she hadn't seen Percy in over an hour, she assumed he had gone to bed for the night as Nicole had. Sissi's eyes were heavy with disappointment and she wanted to lean her head back, close her eyes, and forget her yearning for Percy. His early departure was just one more way of letting her know his lack of interest.

His rejection was difficult to ignore but deep inside of her, she innately believed that he still had feelings for her. If only she could have a moment alone with him. If only she could dance and be gay and enjoy the music like the others were doing, it would help pass the time of this farcical engagement party. It would help to take her mind off Percy. She sighed again, wondering, as she sat alone watching her friends, if Percy had really gone off to bed. He was going to be here all weekend—there would be time to talk, time to clear the air, she consoled herself.

She tried to relax as she listened to Toni Braxton's plaintive love song "Another Sad Love Song." Trying not to allow the lyrics to sadden her more, she closed her eyes.

Until that moment she had made a conscious effort not to think about tomorrow. She had given her best effort to pretend that she was happy, to fake the engagement, to pretend that she had no feelings for Percy. But she was no actress and her loyalty was all she had, and even that was waning as the night progressed. "Racking my brains like crazy," she whispered to herself.

She had to end the charade now. Phil was acting as if nothing had changed. But it had, drastically. From the moment she saw Percy, she knew that there was no going back to Phil. Even if Percy completely rejected her, if he had nothing to say to her, she knew that she could not marry Phil Richardson under any circumstances. And to fool all of her friends, to pretend that she was happy when she was drowning in misery from Phil's oppressive intimacy, she could no longer bear it. The engagement was off, and it was time that everyone knew it. She made her way through the maze of dancing couples, for the stairs, which would lead her to the end of the masquerade.

At the realization that she was going to announce to everyone that she and Phil were in fact not going to get married, Sissi paused, pensive over what she must do next.

With a sweeping glance about her, she felt a twinge of regret. Her friends, *their* friends, were oblivious to her dilemma. But they would get over it, as would she. It was unfortunate that Phil had ruined it for all of them. That wasn't her fault or her doing. Could she have married him out of gratitude? She wasn't sure anymore. She knew only that at one time his kindness, the effort he put into making her happy, was enough to live on. But after witnessing him in the throes of passion with Nancy, she realized how much she needed true love—the kind of love she had shared with Percy, filled with passion and understanding and devotion. No, she could not settle for Phil, not now, not ever.

She continued up the stairs and opened the basement door.

As if on cue, Phil stepped into her path, drink in hand, his sullen gaze falling directly on her. The sight of Sissi standing forlorn in the doorway gave him pause. He was in an instant panic, sensing that her melancholy was about him. Couldn't she just get past his affair for the evening? Did she have to keep dwelling on it, he thought irritably.

"Phil," Sissi whispered softly. It was in her tone, in her wide-eyed stare, as she gazed on him.

"Sissi," was all he could say in a voice so choked with fear that her name came out muffled.

He took her hands in his. He didn't want her to speak. And as he held her hands, Sissi raised her eyes, feeling first then seeing Percy standing in the foyer. So he was still awake and watching her. Was that hurt she saw on his face? She paused, almost breathless at the sight of him. Feeling the pressure of Phil's hand squeezing hers, she diverted her gaze and attempted to speak calmly.

"I . . ." Sissi began in a barely audible whisper, unable to shake the shame that filled her at not being able to keep her promise. "I can't . . ."

"Where are they?" A piercing shriek interrupted Sissi's impulsive words.

Sissi looked past Phil and watched in surprise as Donna made her presence known. As the front door slammed shut, Sissi was torn between anger at being interrupted from her decision to end the lie now and annoyance at the uncouth manners of Donna. Worse yet, Sissi immediately could see that Donna was inebriated.

"I'm going to straighten this out tonight!" Donna was yelling as she walked toward the stairs. "Michelle! Nicole!" she called, starting up the stairs as if she knew exactly where to find them.

Percy tore his gaze from Sissi, realizing he had been frowning at the exchange between Sissi and Phil, and turned baffled eyes on Donna.

"Hey, Donna, why are you making a scene?" he asked. For a fleeting moment he and Sissi locked eyes as he passed her and she, too, approached Donna. Donna ignored them both as she started to walk around the house in search of Michelle and Nicole.

"Donna," Percy repeated more firmly, though keeping his tone low.

Donna halted her search and whirled around to face him in a huff. "What?" she snapped, rolling her eyes in obvious annoyance at his intrusion.

At her snappy tone Percy folded his arms across his chest in an almost fatherly manner and considered her mock disappointment. Beneath his reproachful gaze, she allowed a wide smile to spread across her mouth that made her appear almost congenial, and she staggered toward him.

"Percy, baby," she gushed before a loud hiccup caught her words. Percy held back a smirk at her shabby attempt to be seductive.

"Making a scene, Donna?" he chided softly, taking in

her disheveled appearance and noting with a pang of sadness her bloodshot eyes. What had she done?

"No, baby, I'm just trying to wake this party up." She laughed then hiccuped several times.

Percy, knowing continued admonishments would only agitate Donna in her state rather than calm her, attempted to laugh lightly. His laughter brought Sissi's sharp eyes on him, but he ignored her and said to Donna, "Too much to drink tonight, huh?"

"I've had a few. But I can handle mine." Then putting her hands on her hips, she gazed up at him beneath her long dark eyelashes and demanded, "And where were you headed?"

"Why? Do you want to go?" Percy asked with another light laugh, feeling confident that he had distracted her, at least for the time being, from causing a scene.

"Are you inviting me?" she prompted gleefully.

"No, I don't take advantage of plastered women," Percy said evenly. Donna scowled and seemed to notice only then that Sissi and Phil were standing right beside her. She glared from Sissi back to Percy and hissed, "I bet you would if I were Sissi!"

Sissi gasped at her words and raised her hand to slap the impudent woman. But Phil intervened and pinned her arms at her side, whispering in an urgent voice, "It's not worth it, Sissi."

Percy caught Donna by her arm and, opening the first door he saw, the coat closet, he pulled her inside. Tossing Sissi an apologetic glance that Sissi could not fathom, he closed himself in the closet with Donna, purposely shutting out any room for her to show off

"What are you trying to do?" he hissed, barely able to contain himself from shaking her. Donna glared up at him, although she could not see his face in the darkness.

"Telling the truth! Did you have to pull me in here? I

want to talk to Nicole," she whined a second later, seeming unaware of the confusion she was causing.

Percy scowled, shook his head in frustration, and snapped, "Be quiet, Donna! You know why I stopped you." But at her words his anger simmered and he grew slightly amused, never thinking he would be sequestered in a closet with a drunken Donna.

"Oh, let me guess, to save you and Sissi from being embarrassed by the truth."

"No, to save you from embarrassing yourself further," Percy answered firmly.

"I'm outta here," Donna fumed, putting her hand on the doorknob to leave. Percy stopped her, holding her hand in a tight grasp. Though it was still dark, they could see each other now, and Donna had no doubt that Percy wasn't going to open the door until he was sure she was calm. But first she had to hear his lecture, she could see it in the determined set of his jaws.

"Sissi shouldn't be the root of your anger, Donna. And I'll be damned if I'll allow you to hurt her!"

"Still loving her, huh?" Donna said slyly. Percy scowled. He had known Donna for years and with each meeting she was worse and worse. To think when they had first met he thought she was one of the sweetest women he knew.

"I care about her," he answered evenly. "But you should know better. Or do you want everyone else's life to be ruined like yours?" Percy asked harshly.

"My life isn't ruined!" Donna screeched.

"Lower your voice," Percy ordered firmly.

"Lower your own," she retorted, but they both fell silent.

Percy stared at Donna and sighed heavily, watching her lower lip tremble. Her eyes were dark, her makeup was smeared. Her hair was in wild disarray, and the odor of gin was strong. She looked like she would crumple before him, and that was the last thing he wanted.

"Are you all right?" he asked slowly.

"Leave me alone," she muttered.

"I can't leave you alone. Not until you get yourself together. And what are you doing, drinking yourself into a stupor?"

"You're not my father," Donna swore, resenting his chiding tone. She was feeling dizzy again and was ready to vomit. He had better release her, she thought with rising anger.

"You're not leaving this closet until you promise to be cool."

"I just . . . Percy, baby . . . I just want to find Nicole." She tried to sound contrite.

Percy scowled, reading through her false meekness and shook his head yet again. "I'm going to let you out, but when I do, you're going to go upstairs, talk to your cousin and act like you have some sense. You two are family, and you can't believe everything that you hear."

"You can't tell me what to do," Donna blurted, trying to squirm free of Percy.

"Yes, I can! Nicole's been moping around all evening, embarrassed by this whole thing. You know she wouldn't sleep with Keith."

"Did I say she did?" Donna hissed in exasperation.

"No, but look at how you came in here. All loud and ready to fight," Percy added solemnly.

"I wasn't ready to fight. I'm sick, you idiot!"

"I'd be sick, too. I can smell the gin all over you," Percy insisted.

"Let me out of this closet . . . now. I will scream and yell and cause a scene that you and your high and mighty friends won't ever forget. Now!" Donna fumed with a determined stamp of her foot. She was fed up with the conversation. Percy was not listening to her. He wanted to be the peacemaker. He had no idea what was on her mind, of that she was sure.

"Okay, but you had better make it your business not to make a scene," Percy threatened.

Donna didn't respond. Believing that she was calm now, Percy cautiously opened the closet door, peered into the foyer and down the hall, then stepped fully from the closet, Donna close behind him. Sissi and Phil were gone, and Percy was relieved—he didn't want to see Sissi again tonight.

"The bathroom's over there. Powder up and let's get ready to shine for the loving crowd," Percy said.

Donna glared at him, annoyed with his jubilance as she slammed the bathroom door shut. He had better be gone when she came out. She had no argument with Percy, it was Nicole and Michelle she wanted to find.

Chapter Twelve

Sissi was furious with that little drunkard.

She wanted to throw Donna out of her house on her backside. Instead she was forced to go back down to the party with Phil. He was concerned that everyone would be suspicious of their absence. At the moment Sissi could care less what their guests thought. She was incensed. However, the moment they were at the party, Sissi managed to ease away from Phil and feign interest in conversation with one of her friends. She spent all of five minutes listening, before she found an excuse to go back upstairs.

Phil tried to become distracted with a conversation with his colleagues, but he could not shake off Donna's comment. He had continued on as if Donna hadn't said a word, but her words were explosive for, and painful to, him because they were probably true. When he had another chance, he would make Sissi see how right he was to insist on their engagement party. He would win her back.

Coming up the stairs, Sissi peeped around the foyer and

saw that no one else was on the floor. She took off her heels and tiptoed to the door, careful not to bump it as she listened to the couple enclosed in her coat closet.

They weren't saying much but Sissi was surprised to hear Percy defend her engagement to Phil. So he didn't care that she was getting married? She wanted to weep but held her chin up as the pair continued to argue back and forth.

The moment they fell silent, Sissi ran into the closet next to them, holding the door slightly ajar to see them leave. She felt a lump in her throat at the sight of Percy, she loved him too much. Cautiously she came out of the closet as Percy headed downstairs and Donna went in the other direction. She debated between following Percy and confronting him or waiting for Donna to come out of the bathroom. The decision was made for her when Donna swept from the powder room like a theatrical actress and stamped into the hall.

"Sissi," Donna called in surprise, her voice only slightly slurred with the help of Percy's sobering conversation.

Sissi's face was livid, and Donna knew that she was not forgiven by Sissi for her remark, even if Percy had given her a break.

"Are you done with your nasty insults?" Sissi demanded, in no mood to be toyed with. She didn't care if Donna had drowned in a gallon of black market moonshine. She wasn't allowing anyone to belittle her in her home.

"I'm sorry . . . I was just so angry when I got here," Donna stammered, trying to maintain her composure, although she was feeling awkward beneath Sissi's forbidding gaze.

"I'm not Percy, that's no excuse. I want to toss you out of my house but Phil asked me to be nice," Sissi said with such deliberate calm that Donna became hesitant.

"Sissi . . . look, Sissi," Donna said, flustered. She had never had a confrontation with Sissi before and wasn't sure what to expect. But she sensed it wouldn't be wise to abuse Sissi's patience. "I apologize . . . excuse me. I'll apologize to Phil if you like, too. I didn't mean what I said. Honest."

Sissi didn't respond, her eyes narrowed as she considered with cool disdain the woman who was the center of Nicole's problems. Sissi was appalled at the sight of Donna, although she tried to keep her surprise out of her eyes. Donna couldn't be much older than twenty-six, but with the dark rings under her eyes and her drawn, haggard appearance, she looked much older. Her hair was unkempt and limp where curls should have been. Her face was thin and drained, and Sissi felt a pang of sympathy for the woman. Sighing heavily, she bent forward and gave the woebegone woman a gentle hug, although she whispered sternly, "Don't let it happen again, no excuses."

Donna nodded and returned Sissi's charitable hug. "No problem," she responded in a choked whisper. For a gauche moment they both fell silent, then Donna said hesitantly, "You have a beautiful home."

"Thank you."

"Hey, would you like a quick tour?" she asked as an idea suddenly came to her. What better time than right now for Donna and Nicole to talk. Everyone was downstairs, and if Donna got loud, no one would hear them.

"I would love to but I'm too tired. Can I see it tomorrow? I would love to go to bed," Donna declined in a lazy slur.

Sissi hesitated. She hadn't invited Donna to spend the night or the weekend. The girl was brassy. At Donna's inquiring gaze Sissi offered an apologetic but tight smile. "Sorry. I spaced off on you. Sure, I can show you to a room."

"Thanks, Sissi. I didn't drive down. Keith has the car, you know. And as you may know, right now we're a little angry with each other," Donna explained slowly, carefully pulling out every word, sensing Sissi's discomfort with her staying the night.

Sissi felt immediately ashamed. If Michelle could stay, Donna most definitely could. She gave Donna a friendly squeeze on her shoulder as they climbed the stairs. "Don't worry about it. I've got room," she said reassuringly, although she was thinking that she had better get a loan soon because with Phil leaving, the house might not be hers much longer.

"Does that happen a lot between you two?" Sissi began with casual interest.

"What?" Donna inquired just as casually, although Sissi believed Donna knew exactly what she was asking. Sissi shrugged, at the moment she wasn't at all concerned with the issues behind Michelle and Nicole. What she wanted to know was, "Does Percy find himself pulling you in closets often?" She shrugged again seeming nonchalant in her inquiries, but Donna was not fooled. She understood where the questions were leading.

"No. I'm not always upset," Donna added with a smirk. So Sissi still loved Percy, too.

"Or drunk, I hope," Sissi included dryly.

"I'm not drunk. I handle my alcohol well," Donna added proudly. "Besides, he didn't do that for me. It was for you, for your sake," she said somewhat slurred. "Even a drunk could see that. Not that I am."

"Right," was all Sissi could say.

They stopped at the top of the stairway, and Donna looked down the long expanse of the hallway. "This is boss, girl," she said. "Where do I sleep?"

"Follow me." Sissi paused in front of the bedroom door. "Donna, I have to tell you, I thought it would be a good idea if you and Nicole talked," Sissi said.

"We'll talk in the morning," Donna responded. She was

tired now, less drunk and in no mood to hear Nicole's whining.

"I think tonight is better. Especially if you plan to spend the night here," Sissi insisted. Donna frowned then with broadening comprehension stared from Sissi to the door. With a defiant smirk she took a step backward and shook her head.

"I should have known you were up to something. This was too easy. I'll just get a ride into town," Donna said evenly, turning from the door and preparing to head back down the stairs.

Sissi smirked in irritation and said with rising impatience, "Donna, you and I know that Nicole never slept with Keith. Everyone knows that Michelle hates her," Sissi said reasonably. Donna shrugged and returned Sissi's sardonic gaze.

"I never said I thought she slept with my husband. Michelle said that."

"Then you need to let Nicole know," Sissi said. Before Donna could respond, the door opened and with sleepy eyes Nicole looked directly into her cousin's face. She instantly perked up and opened the door wider.

"Donna," she whispered in surprise, sounding pleased yet edgy to see Donna. Donna sneered, crossed her arms across her chest then tossed Sissi an irate glance.

"Are you going to stand there and monitor our conversation?" Donna asked rudely, her heightening anger emboldening her words.

Sissi raised her eyebrows in surprise before saying, "I'll be downstairs if you need me." She had a moment of concern that she shouldn't leave the two alone but continued down the stairs without a backward glance.

Donna stepped quietly into the room and watched patiently as Nicole closed the door then sat on the bed. They eyed each other in silent contemplation. Donna's headache was easing up, although she was still nauseous from time to time. She had come down from her high almost completely and, looking at Nicole's forlorn expression, she wasn't sure if she wanted to be sober.

Nicole was watching her cousin with uncertainty. Feeling the tension growing between them she finally whispered, "Donna."

Donna raised her hand sharply to silence her cousin, saying between clenched teeth, "Don't Donna, me. You may have them all fooled, but like Michelle, I know where you're coming from."

"I don't understand how you could believe Michelle's lie. You know how she is," Nicole began with pain-filled eyes at her cousin's rejection.

"I know how you are!"

"Then how could you believe Michelle?" Nicole retorted, unable to restrain her rising temper. Nicole glanced over Donna's shoulder, hinting wordlessly that Donna was growing loud.

"Who said I believe her?" Donna hissed, lowering her voice only slightly. Nicole paused, blinking in uncertainty at Donna's outburst.

"Well, isn't that why you're here?" Nicole stammered with a confused frown creasing her delicate eyebrows.

"Oh, don't even try it. You know why I'm here. You know why I'm angry with you and Michelle. I know she lied about your sleeping with Keith anyway. But you, you're trying to help Keith to divorce me!" Donna accused.

"What?" Nicole stammered. "Where did you come up with a conclusion like that? And why would I do that?"

"You know why!" Donna was screaming now, and Nicole grew more agitated. She didn't want anyone to approach them now. She didn't need for Craig to hear more lies, more ridiculous new gossip. Nicole was furious.

"I did not steal Keith from you. He still loves you. You

and Michelle have twisted this entire situation around to meet your psycho needs," Nicole blurted.

"Michelle has nothing to do with your telling Keith to divorce me. He told me you suggested it."

"Oh, why would he? He's lying," Nicole bit out, balling her fist in frustration.

Donna saw Nicole's balled fist and glowered. "Oh, so now you want to fight me? Well, come on with it, Nicole. Because I know what's going on with you and Keith, and it's dirtier than adultery," Donna spat out as she too balled her fist and kicked off her high heels.

"I'm not fighting you," Nicole groaned, tired and frustrated. "Stop acting like a hoodlum. You know how Michelle is, Donna. You know she wants to tear me down, for a lot of reasons. She must have put Keith up to this. I would think you would know better than to believe anything she says."

Donna was glowering with rage. Did Nicole think that she was a complete imbecile? She ran her fingers through her hair and offered a lopsided smile that did not reach her eyes.

"Nicole, I apologize. Okay?"

"Okay." Nicole smiled brightly, relieved that she was at last able to get Donna to believe her.

"Just tell me one thing. What really happened?" Donna asked barely above a whisper.

"Nothing," Nicole answered. But at Donna's fierce frown she added, "Well, he did say he loved you—that he doesn't understand what's going on with you. I told him"—she paused to collect her thoughts—"I told him I didn't have a clue, of course. I said he's a good man, that he deserved better—"

"Better? Better than what? Me?" Donna demanded.

"Noooo," Nicole dragged out. "He loves you, Donna,

as do I. But you've been pushing him away. He doesn't understand.''

"Like hell he doesn't. And I don't believe you. I know you told him to dump me.''

"I never told him that. But what do you care. You left him,'' Nicole stated, exasperated.

"I was bluffing, okay?''

"Leaving your husband is not a game you should play!'' Nicole chided her cousin.

"Oh, what? You call yourself consoling him by telling him to divorce me? Forget you.'' Donna seethed then flung open the bedroom door. Nicole let out a surprised gasp, and Donna nearly screamed in shock at the sight of Craig standing outside the door. Craig was about to knock when the door was flung open. He took one glance at Nicole's flushed face and Donna's fierce narrowed eyes and asked, "What's going on?''

"Nothing. Excuse me,'' Donna murmured then stormed past him. Fearful that Donna would make her accusation in front of everyone, Nicole raced out of the room behind her, calling, "Donna, wait—''

"Did she believe you?'' Craig asked, grabbing hold of Nicole's arm as she dashed by. Nicole nearly tripped from the sudden halt and in irritation yanked herself free.

"I'll be back,'' she called. "Donna,'' she begged as she caught hold of Donna's hands. Donna wrenched free and kept walking.

A few people were standing near the bottom of the stairway, saying their good-byes to Phil and Sissi. They paused as Nicole sped down the stairs to catch up with her cousin. They were on the bottom step when Donna stumbled, and Nicole grabbed her hand to steady her.

"Let me go!'' Donna bawled, pulling free so fiercely from Nicole that she bumped against the wall from the force.

"Don't do this to us, Donna. Don't let Michelle hurt us like this," Nicole pleaded softly, humiliated that everyone was listening to her.

"What a joke. You're no better than Michelle. Get lost, Nicole, and take Craig with you!" Donna added as Craig approached them.

"Calm down, baby," Craig said soothingly, hoping to end the embarrassing scene before it got worse.

"I'm not your baby," Donna fumed between clenched teeth then brushed past two of the guests and left the house. Nicole moved to follow her, but this time Craig didn't let her brush him off so easily

"Let me go after her," Nicole cried, trying to release herself from Craig's determined hold.

"No," Craig said firmly. "Let her cool off. She'll be all right. Come on, you need to rest," he said evenly, ignoring the remaining guests who watched them as they went back up the stairway. Nicole gave in, frustrated by Donna's refusal to be rational. She would deal with Donna later, but right now she needed to get some sleep.

"I have a headache," Nicole moaned, wrapping her arm about Craig's waist and leaning her head against his shoulder.

"I'll find some Tylenol."

"This whole week, especially tonight, has been one long nightmare. I just hope Donna is all right out there," Nicole whispered.

"It's no biggie, Nicole. Donna's just tripping right now. I don't know where Percy went off to but Eddie was still down at the party. I'm going to get some Tylenol from Sissi, and then Eddie and I will go find Donna," Craig offered, trying to calm Nicole's worries.

She nodded and paused in front of their bedroom door. "Look for Donna first. I'm exhausted. I just want to lie in the dark to help ease my headache," Nicole insisted.

Craig frowned then nodded slowly. "Do you think I need to pull out the car?"

"No. Besides in the morning you'll need to go fill it up with gas. No, just take a look outside. She couldn't have gone that far, Craig," Nicole added in a tired murmur.

"All right. But just for you, baby. Not Donna." He kissed her on the forehead. "Try and get some sleep, it's late." Then he left her, heading back down the stairs as Nicole closed the door and lay down once more.

Craig hurried down the stairs, his temper in check even as he determined he was going to put an end to Donna's foolishness once and for all. He just had to find her.

Chapter Thirteen

Michelle held her breath and waited in strained patience until the ruckus ended and Donna finished her tirade. She stood just inside the room where Craig had so coldly left her. When Craig left her side, she had fallen in a tearful heap on the floor and, smothering her voice with a pillow that was in Phil's chair, wept profoundly. She loved Craig. She had prayed for him. She had given him everything he wanted. And all he had ever given her in return was heartache and a cold shoulder, except when he wanted a warm body to lie next to him, she thought resentfully. Hearing Craig come to Nicole's rescue again and again all night was more than she could bear.

At hearing the front door slam, Michelle crept softly down the hall and peered around the stairway into the foyer. It was empty. She could hear the murmur of Craig's voice, though, just before an upstairs door closed. Guessing that Craig had gone to bed with Nicole, Michelle became enraged with jealousy. Nicole was not going to get Craig, of that she was determined. Stealing another swift glance around her, she hurried for the front door and determined she was going to find Donna and win her favor. She had to prove to Craig that Nicole was not the woman she pretended to be—and Donna was the key to her success. Michelle scanned the lawn, calling out Donna's name in repeated fervent whispers.

Donna watched Michelle with suspicious eyes. She had no doubt that Michelle was up to something again. As Michelle circled the lawn, Donna slowly came out of the shadows, her eyes narrowed with obvious impatience, her arms folded across her chest, and she asked in a exasperated sigh, "What do you want, Michelle?"

Michelle paused, catching her breath after her slight exertion. "Donna," she gasped, a broad grin bursting forth as she spoke.

Donna did not return the smile and repeated, "Why are you following me, Michelle?"

Michelle hesitated, considered Donna, and tried to formulate her words with caution. "I wanted to make sure you were all right. I couldn't help but overhear you in the hall."

"I'm fine," Donna said stiffly, her eyes never straying from Michelle's face.

"Good. I know Nicole can be such a witch at times," Michelle said heatedly, trying to show Donna that she had her support.

"So can other women I know," Donna retorted. Since arriving at Sissi's house, she had been repeatedly harassed. There was no end to the torrent of questions and lack of privacy. Her head was pounding, and she just wanted to lie down and rest.

"I know you're tired," Michelle said, sensing Donna's

impatience with her. "But I just wanted to make sure you know that I was not lying about Nicole and Keith. I saw them with my own eyes, Donna," Michelle insisted, her forehead creasing in a frustrated scowl at the thought of not being believed by her last possible ally.

"No, you didn't, Michelle. You saw Nicole giving Keith a hug," Donna snapped, her eyes daring Michelle to exaggerate anymore. Michelle blinked in surprise, upset by Donna's smug comment. Until that moment Michelle had chosen to ignore Donna's obvious drunken state, believing that she was able to think coherently, that she had her wits about her. But obviously not.

"No. No," Michelle insisted, scowling in utter frustration. "They were all over each other. Nicole and Keith are lovers. I saw them right there in the hall. You weren't there. I know you don't want to believe it—"

"Michelle, shut up!" Donna snapped then started walking toward the woman with deadly purpose.

"What . . ." Michelle sputtered.

"Just stop lying. I was there. I saw when Nicole arrived," Donna began dryly. Ignoring Michelle's disbelieving gaze, she continued. "I saw when Nicole left not even twenty minutes later. And they were not kissing. In fact, as I recall, Nicole barely gave Keith a hug and he had to beg that from her. Remember?" Donna inquired.

Michelle gulped, uncertain how to respond. Finally, beneath Donna's condescending gaze, Michelle asked in a tight voice, "You were there? But why did you let me think you had no idea what was going on between them?"

Donna chuckled, pleased at Michelle's dismayed expression. "It was none of your business."

Michelle grew weary. Feeling that she had nothing to lose, she stated, "I don't believe you were there, Donna.

I believe you're repeating the sorry excuse Nicole gave you because she's your cousin.''

"I couldn't care less if she were my sister. The fact is, Nicole is a good-for-nothing, two-faced liar just like you."

Michelle gasped then glared at Donna with open hostility. "I am nothing like Nicole. I don't know what you're getting at, but I'm beginning to think you're crazy," Michelle seethed.

"I'm not crazy. I know exactly why you want to ruin Nicole, but I'm not helping you. No, Michelle, honey, come first thing in the morning, I'm telling all."

Michelle was livid. From the moment she approached Donna, she had been bombarded with insults. If Donna wasn't going to believe her, fine. So she had exaggerated a bit—it wasn't as if anyone could prove what happened once Keith closed the door with Nicole inside his room. Frustrated with Donna's disagreeable attitude toward her and even more confounding hatred of Nicole, given that she didn't believe that Keith and Nicole had made love, Michelle rolled her eyes.

"Fine, Donna. But may I ask why you let me believe you believed me? Why you let it go this far if you didn't have any doubts about your husband and Nicole?" Michelle demanded, insulted by Donna's superior gaze.

"Because Nicole deserved it. In one instance you were right, Michelle. Nicole is not the innocent Craig makes her out to be. But then," Donna added with a derisive appraisal of her, "neither are you. So thanks for your help and good-bye. I'll be sure to talk with Craig in the morning." Donna turned her back before Michelle could speak and headed back toward the house. She was on the stairs when a smug grin spread across her mouth. She could feel more than see Michelle's angry eyes on her and was enjoying every minute of it. Michelle's lie had only given Keith fuel to demand a divorce. He wanted to leave

her at any cost now, and Donna was completely baffled—
at least until she discovered Nicole's role in his decision.
Well, she would have the last word.

"I know what I saw, Donna!" Michelle called out one
last time running up the stairs and standing in front of
Donna. Donna stopped, waited patiently for Michelle to
move aside then with a mocking shaking of her head
walked quietly around Michelle.

Fuming with frustration and despair, Michelle raced
inside the house and ran to her room on the first floor.
Without Donna's support she was unable to get Craig to
side with her. She was going to make Donna pay for the
mess she was causing. She heard the front door close and
scowled. She could just envision Donna's glee.

Hearing footsteps entering the hall, she paused and
stared at the bedroom door. Someone was likely lost. Sissi
had purposely put Michelle on the first floor and Craig
on the second, as if she thought she could keep her and
Craig apart. Michelle scoffed in resentment. If it wasn't
Sissi interfering, then it was Donna. Who did they think
they were? Hot with animosity, Michelle stood and slipped
out of her dress. As she tossed the dress on the bed, she
heard a muffled sound outside her door. This time she
was sure someone was there. Frowning with impatience,
convinced that it was Donna come to harass her more,
Michelle walked to the door and flung it open.

"What do you want?" she exclaimed harshly before her
voice faded away in stunned disbelief.

Standing at her door was Craig, his hand paused in
midair as he was about to sip from his drink. At the sight
of Michelle, his eyes widened at her unexpected attire.
Her body was barely covered behind the flimsy white demi-
bra, panties, garter, and stockings she sported. She still
wore her high heels, not having had the opportunity to
kick them off before Craig's knock on the door. She

couldn't have planned the moment better, she thought, savoring his appreciative gaze. Beneath his flattering exploration of her unveiled body, Michelle didn't flinch, nor did she shy away. She knew one thing from the mesmerized gleam in his eyes—if she didn't have him before in the library, she certainly had him now.

Craig had come in search of Donna, certain she and Michelle were together conspiring to soil Nicole's character even further. He was going to set Donna straight and, if Michelle tried to interfere, he had something for her, too. The last thing he had expected to find was Michelle standing brazenly in the doorway, her body as glorious as the last time he had seen it.

"Waiting for someone?" he inquired in a rasping murmur, bringing his drink down to his side.

Michelle didn't respond. Earlier he had scorned her, left her alone and tearful in the wake of his rejection. Now he was here, unable to pull his gaze from her. She didn't want to break the spell of his unfettered yearning for her. She reached behind him and with a gentle nudge against the small of his back, she steered him inside the room. Craig didn't resist, too entranced with risque thoughts at the sight of Michelle to recall that Nicole was waiting upstairs for his return.

Leaning against the door in provocative patience, she gradually closed it, all the while keeping her misty green eyes on the man she loved. Oh, he might think he wanted Nicole, but she knew better. Why else would he keep finding his way back into her arms?

"I knew you would come," she murmured.

Craig didn't respond. He set his drink on the chest of drawers beside the bed. With a swift click, Michelle locked the door behind her and watched as Craig began unbuttoning his shirt and stepped out of his shoes.

She walked purposely toward him. Standing fully in front

of him, she unsnapped her bra. Craig watched as the bra
slipped from her shoulders, down her arms and fell to the
floor, releasing her swelling breasts and taut nipples for
his eyes to consume.

Captivated by their fullness, he reached up and fondled
them before darting his cool wet tongue around her nipples. Michelle flung her head back in silent bliss. The very
feel of his hands against her body sent shivers of ecstasy
through her, but when his mouth greedily began suckling
her breast and his gentle teeth nibbling at her nipple, she
quivered in weak delight. It had been over a month since
last she had made love to him. His affection was so scarce
and far in between that each time was like the first when
they came together.

He came to his feet and slightly bent her body back so
that he could more freely suckle her breast as his hand
found the warm flesh between her thighs. Feeling the heat
of her wanton desire for him, his mouth freed her breast
and he sat down again, this time tugging her panties free
of her body. He pulled them down until she stood with
only her garter and stockings between them.

Knowing she was ready, feeling the warm moisture
between her thighs, he desperately wanted her, just as she
was, standing vulnerable and bare before him. He began
devouring the flesh of her abdomen with wild, forceful
thrusts of his tongue. Michelle gasped and held on to
Craig's shoulders for support as her knees weakened in
languid delight.

He grasped her buttocks in an insatiable clutch as his
mouth moved down toward the hidden slope of her inner
thighs and continued to ravish her.

Michelle moaned, her body quivering from his lustful
embrace. She bent over, bringing her mouth to his as he
looked up at her. He met her kiss, his tongue searching

the depth of her willing mouth, and Michelle could taste the brandy he had been drinking.

She squealed lightly when he scooted her from the floor and flung her on the bed. Pinned beneath him, she could feel his erection. As he explored her body with his mouth, Michelle lifted her head and planted wild, fervent kisses on the flesh of his shoulders, over his muscular chest, and along the tip of his flat hard nipples.

Her lustful submission aroused him. Hastily he shoved out of his slacks, his eyes never leaving her yielding body. He swore with impatience when his leg tangled in his underwear as he tugged free of them. The moment he was free, he reached for Michelle and once more devoured her with inflamed kisses and eager caresses. When she spread her legs and lifted her hips in silent invitation for him to take her, he hastily grabbed her hands, entwined his fingers with hers and deliberately, amorously penetrated her yielding flesh.

Michelle gasped with pleasure, and repeatedly raised her hips to meet his demanding thrust. Panting, squirming beneath his pounding flesh, Michelle groaned and gasped with each plunge. She lifted her knees, her feet flat on the bed and spread her thighs as far as she could, silently inviting him to fully probe her body. She was his, and she wanted him to know it indubitably.

His body, saturated with sweat, pulsated with unrestrained passion as the feel of her smooth breast crushed against his chest and her soft body was laid bare for him. No longer able to control his excitement, with a deep ineffable groan, he released himself within her then crashed in exhaustion against her hot, pliant body.

Michelle lay in bliss and stared at the ceiling, the weight of Craig's body a pleasure as she ran her fingers along his hair. Within a few minutes she heard him snore, and a smile curved her lips. He was hers now. This time she was sure of it. Her only problem was Donna. She sighed. She would worry about Donna's claim tomorrow. Everyone would think everything she said was developed from her drunken haze anyway.

Feeling full and satisfied, she closed her eyes in fatigue, content to be in Craig's arms, even if he had fallen into a heavy, inebriated sleep.

Chapter Fourteen

Sissi was tired but she kept on smiling. If Phil hadn't messed up, it would have been her night to shine, to show off. But it didn't matter now. There was no reason to shine. Phil didn't truly love her, regardless of what he claimed. And Percy had long since disappeared. After his conversation with Donna, he came downstairs but only for a moment. When she arrived back at the party, Percy was gone. Likely to bed, she decided with a final glance around the room. She wanted to escape, too, but those few diehards had to offer their congratulations again and in the process, they wanted to waste her time talking. Couldn't they see that she barely knew who they were, could barely remember their names? She just needed to be alone. Spotting Eddie in deep conversation with Maryl, she went to him and whispered, "Do me a favor, check on Nicole. Donna's here now and Craig's up there, too. I want to make sure she's all right. Thanks, honey," Sissi added when Eddie immediately set his drink down, nodded with a slight hint of inebriation, and immediately left the party.

"Sissi, I'm so proud of you," Maryl whispered the moment Eddie stepped away. Sissi paused only for a moment to toss a strained smile Maryl's way, but her eyes narrowed and she wondered what in the world had she done for Maryl to be proud of her. She was supposed to be getting married, not starting a new job, she thought with caustic dislike for the older woman.

"Well, thank you, Maryl. Coming from you, I know it means a lot," Sissi responded with such testiness that Maryl was taken aback. Before Maryl could respond, Sissi walked away. The moment she was outside of the house, she felt better. She leaned against the cool post, staring out into the darkness of the North Carolina night before walking slowly down the stairs. She needed to be completely alone, without a chance encounter with anyone, especially Phil.

No destination in mind except isolation from her guests, Sissi headed toward the small guest home she had insisted Phil begin renovating. There was no electricity there, no running water, it wasn't fit for anyone to stay in, but she was determined to make it livable. She opened the door and at once knew she was not alone. Instinct and hope against hope brought Percy instantly to mind.

"Percy?" she whispered, walking fully into the small house.

Percy didn't move a muscle at the sound of her voice. When the door first opened, he promptly hoped it was Sissi. All of his instincts told him to stay away, to find a ride into town but he couldn't leave. Now she stood in the doorway, barely a shadow on the darkness of the night. The slight breeze caused her thin dress to blow up against her slender thighs, and he took a sharp intake of breath before answering gruffly, "Yeah. It's me."

It took a moment for her eyes to adjust to the darkness,

but she could see his form, she could sense his presence, and within moments she was able to clearly see his dark, brooding eyes. With the practiced ease of a graceful swan, she closed the door and walked boldly toward him. The light from the moon filtered through the curtained windows, trickling along the lighted path like a silent barrier between the two.

"What are you doing in here?" she asked huskily.

He stared down at her, his eyes devouring in a hungry gaze. Trying to still his uncontrollable desire, he said in a sharp voice, "I wanted to be alone."

"Are you sure? I would bet a million bucks you were hoping I would come out here," she said egotistically.

Her smile was provocative, and it was as if she knew his innermost secrets. He had said he wanted to talk earlier, that he had some explaining to do. But that was before he had to endure watching Phil and Sissi exchange intimate gazes and Phil constantly touching her. That was before he realized that he had lost her forever.

"You flatter yourself, Sissi," he said roughly, averting his gaze from her keen brown eyes. He couldn't help but recall how Phil caressed her all evening and then announced their passion for each other. But when he saw them come up from the basement right as Donna arrived, he suspected they had been sharing intimate moments together. He knew love when he saw it, and it had been all over their faces. Why Sissi was playing games with him was what he couldn't understand.

Sissi pursed her full lips into a pouting tease. "I would much rather have you do that, Percy," she whispered, stepping even closer to allow her body to brush against his ever so slightly.

Percy remained frigid even at the shock his body felt from the brief touch of her pert breast against his skin. Through his heavily starched white shirt, he could feel her softness, remember her warm and willing embrace, her poignant kisses.

"I had better get back," he said abruptly, stepping around her as if she carried a plague.

Sissi paused in uncertainty, not expecting his abrupt response. Was he really immune to her now? she wondered Conjuring all of her resolve and feminine wiles, she whispered in his ear, surprising herself even as she challenged him. "You can't honestly say you don't still love me, Percy Duvall?"

Impulsively she nibbled his earlobe then nuzzled his ear with her sensuous pouting mouth, Phil forgotten in the unexpected moment with Percy.

Percy had to still himself from fidgeting or weakening. It was what she wanted to, to make a complete idiot out of him for her own self-esteem. That was last thing he needed to do was give her a sign that he still desired her, let alone loved her. Strengthened by his distrust, he pulled away from Sissi and with a direct gaze into her radiant brown eyes, he responded coolly. "I am *not* in love with you, Sissi Adams." He couldn't be sure if he sounded convincing, the words rang so falsely in his ears. But it must have been real enough for Sissi. Her expression was immediately downcast, her dark seductive eyes suddenly fragile in the gaze that fell painfully away from him. He instantly regretted his words, knowing the lie was his only defense against Sissi.

"Then I guess . . . I guess I had better go back to the party," she whispered in a pained, small voice.

Percy stiffened his shoulders, narrowed his eyes and again speaking bluntly, agreed. "Yeah. You should get back."

Staring into his dark determined eyes, Sissi knew he meant every word he spoke. His rejection was painful, but he had hurt her before. She could handle anything he

dished out. Gaining a semblance of dignity, she lifted her
proud chin and, with a rigid back, headed for the door.
As she turned from him, she wanted to declare that she
was a free woman and that she loved him. But she wouldn't
do it. He hadn't changed, and he didn't deserve a confession from her.

Watching her as she walked towards the door brought
a panic to Percy that he had never felt before. It was as if
she was walking out of his life for good. It was as if he
knew that if she walked out that door, she would be lost
to him forever.

In a voice unfamiliar to him, he called her name: "Sissi."

She paused, her back to him in hopeful agony.

"Yes," she responded coolly, somehow able to maintain
her composure and keep the tremble out of her voice. But
she could not turn around to face him yet, even when
his hands lightly touched her shoulders. With a surge of
excitement, she felt his warm mouth press against her
neck. When his caress left her neck and found her earlobe,
she gasped. Slowly his arms encircled her, and he turned
her around to face him.

Her eyes squeezed shut lest she open them and find
him gone. She waited for his familiar and sorely missed
sensuous mouth to possess hers. He did not disappoint
her. His kiss was hungry, full of longing as he pressed her
body to his with a passionate need she longed to fulfill.

Sissi was drunk with pleasure and held on to Percy as
if her life depended on his very breath. Her heart was
hammering wildly against her chest as his passion inflamed
her aching soul. She moaned in languid bliss, and Percy
could feel her eager body molding softly against his. Her
sigh pierced Percy's muddled thoughts, and he was
instantly furious with himself.

He shouldn't be kissing her. He shouldn't be alone with
her. She was marrying someone else. He couldn't get lost

in Sissi. He couldn't risk that pain again. Just as suddenly as he had held her, as he had kissed her with the pent-up passion that haunted him, he released her, leaving her defenseless in the abrupt isolation.

"What . . . ?" she said, flustered, her mouth pleasantly swollen from his kiss.

"You don't change a bit. Always have to have your way. But I won't be your toy."

"Oh, come on. That's my line," Sissi scoffed, exasperated with him. He had kissed *her*. He had held *her*. She didn't force herself on him. How dare he kiss her with such ardent affection and then complain as if she had attacked him?

"I'm leaving," Percy grunted, more irate with himself than Sissi. He wanted to talk to her, but he couldn't get the words out. He wanted to hold her but knew it was wrong to love a woman who was soon to be married. How could he confess his emotions when she would only laugh at him? And why did she have to be so sweet in his arms?

Having no idea of the tumultuous emotions he was hiding, Sissi was enraged. "Then go!" she scorned him, although her haste to stand in front of his path to the door was in direct contradiction to her words.

He halted, exasperated with her. Staring at her behind a shield of angry eyes, he wanted to shake some sense into her. Had she no idea why he had to leave? Didn't she know that if he stayed he would be unable to resist her exquisite charm and find himself making love to her? She was practically a married woman, the last thing he wanted to do was leave her feeling guilty as she started her new marriage. No matter what he thought of Phil Richardson, he had to honor Sissi's wishes. Why couldn't she understand that?

"Move, Sissi," he demanded as calmly as he could muster. He had done her enough harm when she miscarried their baby. He would not bring any more burdens on her.

"I will move, Percy, but only after you tell me why you kissed me. Why?" she demanded in fierce whisper.

"Because you were there. Now let me past," he snapped, his eyes dark with fury.

Sissi gasped, unable to believe how cruel he could be. With a fierceness she hadn't expected, Sissi hissed. "Don't you *ever* kiss me again. Ever!"

How she could have misjudged him so thoroughly? How could she have believed for even an instant that he still had feelings for her? She didn't know. In that instant she was sure that he still blamed her for losing the baby. He hadn't changed at all. Humiliated with her futile attempt to seduce him, Sissi moved from his path.

"Good night, Percy Duvall," she added in barely contained fury.

Percy was shocked by the vehemence of her anger. He stood, stunned. He had to explain, he realized, but it was too late. She had already stormed away and raced from the cottage, leaving him alone to wallow in frustration.

Chapter Fifteen

Phil watched in sullen observation as Sissi entered the house, her usually smooth stroll burdened by the weight of her drawn shoulders. Head bowed, expression disappointed, she went directly upstairs. It was almost three A.M. and he was tired. With quiet ease he returned to the party that was by now nearly abandoned. With the dexterity of a polished political figure, he set about the task of letting the last few guests know kindly but firmly that the party was over. Sissi wasn't feeling well, he claimed, and he needed to see to his fiancée's needs. But he and Sissi appreciated everyone's support for coming and wanted those who were leaving to drive safely back home.

Percy watched from the cottage as the cars pulled off the grounds that marked Sissi's home. Phil must have tired of his guests and wanted to be alone with his wife-to-be, Percy thought with displeasure. He wanted to slap himself for being a silly fool to turn away from Sissi. It wasn't as if Phil was her husband yet. He could have changed her mind, stopped the wedding, confessed his love to her. But he was afraid that she would laugh at him. And that, he couldn't bear.

Like a panther biding his time, he waited until most of the cars were gone before he slipped back into the main house. The front door was still unlocked, and a few stragglers were in the main hall. They were laughing and drinking, holding on until the very last moment. Percy quickly hurried down the hall and went back into the basement, noting without delay that Sissi was not present.

Craig and Nicole were gone, too. But Janice and Eddie were still hanging around. And like the odd ball out, Phil was talking to them, his half-empty glass in hand. Percy was disappointed to see Phil, but he was tired and wanted to know where he was sleeping.

"Hey, man," Percy inquired approaching the small group. "Do I have a designated room or should I find my own way?" he asked in a tired drawl.

"I'll show you, give me a moment," Phil said gruffly after looking at Percy with haughty disapproval.

Percy caught the snub but maintained his composure. It had been a long evening, the last thing he was in the mood for was another confrontation with Phil.

Phil felt drained, too. He was under stress, especially after witnessing Sissi's return from the cottage. Was Percy there with her? Had *he* rejected Sissi? Why was she so sad? He just couldn't imagine Percy Duvall or any man rejecting Sissi's affection.

Percy nodded then leaned against the wall, observing the last of the guests down their liquor like it was going out of style.

"Hey, Percy, Percy!" one of the men yelled from across the room.

At hearing his name, Percy looked up with a frown. He stared at the short, slightly balding man, not recognizing him. The man appeared disappointed as he spread his arms in an approaching gesture of a hug.

"Man, Tyek Jones? Remember me? Percy, little Tyek?" he insisted.

Percy couldn't place him but forced a smile to his face and nodded. "Hey, Tyek, how are you?"

"Good, Percy. My business has taken off with a giant leap. Into entertainment, my friend. And doing well, not to mention never short of a date," he added with a hard, exaggerated laugh.

Percy gave a short clipped laugh but swore inwardly, wanting the stranger that he still couldn't place to get lost. "That's good," he said, unable to come up with a more interesting remark.

Obviously smashed and oblivious to Percy's disinterest, Tyek grabbed Percy and gave him a hearty hug. "It's good to see you again, man," Tyek said with a choked voice, as if he and Percy had been the best of friends.

Percy all but shoved the man off of him in an attempt to get away. "Yeah, you, too," he said as he finally freed himself from the overzealous hug. "I guess I'll see you around. Oh, good, Phil, I'm tired," he continued when Phil approached them.

"Tyek, I suppose you're tired, too? I can show you to your rooms since I'm going up."

"You're staying the weekend, too?" Percy asked Tyek, surprised. He had thought he knew everyone who was staying.

Tyek laughed heartily, giving Percy a hearty pat on the back as he responded, "Nah, man. I'm leaving at the break of dawn. I got a flight to catch and meetings to attend, you know what I mean. But I'll catch you later," Tyek responded as if Percy was pressed to engage in conversation with him. Percy smirked, holding back a laugh at the little man's conceit.

"So you ready, Percy?" Phil asked impatiently, wanting to spend no more time than necessary with Percy.

"Yeah," Percy responded, anxious to get away from the annoying man and the whole scene.

"See you at breakfast, Eddie," Percy called as he followed Phil from the basement. He just wanted a good night's rest. He only hoped that he was able to rest without visions of Sissi invading his sleep as she had been doing so often in the last year.

Comfortable that everyone had gone to bed, Phil checked the doors and locked the windows before finding his way upstairs. Just outside of Sissi's bedroom, he hesitated. He was tired and knew she would likely be asleep. He probably should sleep elsewhere but if he did, wouldn't everyone know? Sighing, confident that he was making the right decision, gingerly, he pulled off his jacket and opened the bedroom door.

The lights were out and the room silent, but he could hear Sissi's gentle breathing. He approached the bed and stared down at her with torn emotions. He had given everything he had to Sissi Adams, including his heart.

He had always wanted Sissi. And though he knew that he couldn't have her while she was in love with Percy, he bided his time, knowing that nothing lasted forever. It was his good fortune that the egotistical Percy couldn't see beyond his own conceit to appreciate that Sissi was the best thing that had happened to him. When Sissi fell into his arms, he had been so careful, planning every word, every action to the minute until he had her convinced that he was the only man that truly loved her the way that she needed to be loved. Of course, then he ruined it all by falling into his old habits.

Nancy was just too luscious to resist. She was one of his

students and, from the day she started the course, she let him know that she was interested in him. At first he hadn't considered her, because he was so involved with Sissi. But once Sissi accepted his proposal, he became cocky and slipped with the young girl. She was constantly asking for his help, wanting to be tutored by him, and she made it clear that it wasn't just the books that she needed help with.

The first time she leaned over and kissed him, her full pink breast exposed in his face, left him totally flustered and unable to resist her. He had made love to her several times and, had he not been so greedy, Sissi would never have found out.

He sighed, tossing his jacket on the chair. Sissi hadn't stirred. He leaned over the bed and whispered, "Sissi?"

She didn't move. Her breathing was steady, the slight rise and fall of her chest confirming that she was asleep. He was disappointed. He had hoped to talk to her before the morning. He undressed then lay beside her, his nude body warming up against hers. He put his hand on the flatness of her stomach and pressed his body against hers until they were molded together, her back in the crook of his body. He lay holding her, cuddling his cheek against her back, and placed warm, small kisses on her flesh. His hand began caressing her abdomen until slowly it ran up her body and cupped her firm breast.

The warm body cuddling up to her awakened her from her exhausted sleep. For a moment she imagined that Percy had slipped into bed with her, but then she recognized Phil's gruff hands. She flinched then became enraged.

"Phil!" she hissed sharply, snatching his hand from her body and jumping from the bed, pulling the sheet with her.

Phil leaned up on his elbows, frowning in feigned innocence at her reaction.

"I didn't mean to wake you, baby," he said softly.

"Wake me? You have no business in here!" she snapped, securing the sheet around her in a fury.

"Sissi, calm down—"

"I will not calm down!" she hissed. "You think because I had a few drinks and faked a few smiles for your evening that I had forgiven you? Are you out of your mind?"

"I know you haven't forgiven me. I just thought . . . I missed you, honey—"

"I am not your *honey!*" she snapped. "Now get dressed and get out of here!"

"Sissi, just think about it. If I don't sleep in here, everyone will know something's wrong."

"I don't care what they think. The party's over, and I kept my promise. Now if you don't get up, get dressed and leave, I will walk out of here screaming at the top of my lungs that I am *not* engaged to you." Her breathing was fierce, her chest heaving up and down in a fury that she could not control.

Phil stared at her a moment longer, then pinching his mouth in an attempt to maintain his composure, he slowly left the bed and pulled on his robe. Impatient for him to leave, Sissi stormed to the door and flung it open, waiting with barely contained fury for him to leave the room.

"If Percy wasn't here, Sissi, would you still want me out?" Phil couldn't help but ask.

Sissi became incensed. He was the one who slept with Nancy. He had no room to question her. "Get out!" she bit out with such vehemence, Phil took a step back.

"And where do you suggest I sleep tonight, Sissi?" he asked in a sour voice as he stepped outside of the room.

"I don't care. Why don't you try Nancy's dorm room?" Before he could answer, she shut the door in his face.

Chapter Sixteen

Phil stood staring out the window. He had lain awake all night, torn from the knowledge that Sissi had no intention of forgiving him. Had it just been them, the incident with Nancy would not have been so easy to kill their relationship. But the moment Percy walked through her doors, Sissi was lost to him.

The hour was early, and he had slipped back into Sissi's bedroom, more from necessity than a desire to ignore her wishes. His clothing was still in the room, and he needed to dress. But once he was dressed, he was unable to leave. She was sleeping so peacefully. With a tinge of regret, his eyes scanned the length of her body and fell on her long brown limbs that peeped from beneath the coverlets, her arm hung over the edge of the bed.

At that moment he wished he knew the secret desires that possessed Sissi whenever Percy was near. He wished that he had the power that Percy had to conjure up a love in Sissi that could cause her to shed all of her inhibitions, all of her desires, to give all of her love to him. He sighed sadly, shrugging his shoulders. He was hungry and needed a cup of coffee. He would need his strength if he was going to win back Sissi's love. Pulling on his jeans, he left the room.

The hall was silent, everyone was still asleep. Putting a firm hand on the bannister, he headed for the kitchen. The dawn light was just beginning to filter through the windows. Walking to the curtained window, he opened the curtains to allow the light to more fully fill the room. Then he opened the refrigerator and considered its contents for a few minutes. He decided he might as well cook breakfast for everyone rather than have a medley of cooks wrecking his kitchen.

Nicole stretched, smiled, then rolled over, reaching out to hold Craig. She found his pillow but no body. She blinked, opening her eyes in surprise. The pillow was just as fluffy and full as it was when she had lain down. She propped herself up on one elbow, a curious frown creasing her delicate forehead. Had Craig slept there last night? She pursed her lips then shrugged. Of course he had. But Craig was an early riser. He must be downstairs.

He could be out jogging or anything, she thought calmly, wanting to believe that she had not slept alone. She lay back on the pillow, trying to fall back to sleep. She moved the blankets, then replaced them, then removed the pillow, then replaced it before recognizing her restless state would not allow her to fall back asleep. Tossing the covers aside, she got up, found her suitcase, and began searching for something to wear.

Pulling out a pair of jeans and gray sweatshirt, she found her way down the hall to the bathroom. The door was closed. She hugged her clothes to her then knocked on the door. When no one answered, she gingerly tried the knob and pushed it open.

"Hello?" she called softly. The room was steaming, the glass doors of the shower were filmed with mist, but no one was there. Perhaps she had just missed Craig. But she would have certainly seen him in passing down the hall. She put her clothing on the sink counter, dropped her shoes on the floor, and ran the hot water for her shower.

Craig groaned and gingerly sat up. He had a brutal headache, the backs of his eyes were throbbing and appeared bloodshot. He searched the room in a hazy blur and scowled. Where was he? He rolled cautiously from the bed and walked to the window. He was on the first floor, he realized with a swift glance over the lawn and parking area.

The early morning light filtered through the room. He glanced around him with a baffled frown. The blanket was on the floor, and his clothes were entwined with it. Suddenly he panicked—in a sudden flash he recalled making love to Michelle. How could he get that drunk? His gaze landed on the empty space beside him on the bed.

Michelle was gone. He felt a moment's panic. If Michelle was gone, knowing her, she could be taking advantage of the moment and telling Nicole everything right now. In fact, she could be planning to bring Nicole back to the room to prove they were having an affair.

Cursing himself for being a fool, he grabbed his slacks and clumsily pulled them on even as he glanced at his watch. It was well after six in the morning. Rushing, he fell on the floor, one leg in his pants.

He swore before kicking and struggling into the slacks. It took him a moment to get it together but once he was fully dressed, he made sure that he had his wallet, his watch, and anything else that was his before racing from the room.

He prayed that Nicole was still in bed, that her headache had given way to exhaustion, and that she had slept the night away. Please let her be asleep, he begged silently. On the stairway he paused, glanced down the hall, then quietly entered his bedroom. His worst fears had come true. Nicole was gone.

He stood in the middle of the room, looking lost as he wondered where she could be. Was she out looking for him? Were she and Michelle discussing last night? He ran to the window, saw that her truck was still parked on the lot. Another glance around the room and he reasoned that she was likely in the bathroom. Hoping against hope, he undressed, opened his suitcase, found his sweat suit and pulled it on, cursing Michelle's wanton charm the entire time.

Not wanting Nicole to return and find him changing his clothes, he hurried from the room and went outside. A rushed half-hour run would get him sweating enough to say he had gone out jogging. The only problem was, had she gone looking for him? Frowning, worried, he raced down the path that led to the main road. A good run would help him solve his problem.

Geoff pulled on his jeans. As he pulled on his T-shirt, he caught a glimpse of the figure leaving the front of the house. Geoff paused and considered the man about to jog from the house, recognizing him as Craig Williams. Curious, he watched as Craig jolted from the house and raced down the road as if he were being haunted. Geoff smirked, sure that if Craig had that much energy he probably didn't make love to Nicole last night.

Turning from the window, he zipped his jeans and then

left his room. Sissi's friends were the most interesting bunch of riffraff he had ever seen, he thought scathingly, except for Nicole. She had appeal, class, and a strong spirit, something her cousin Donna was sorely lacking. He walked into the kitchen, not surprised to see Phil was already moving about like a chef from frying pan to the boiling pot of water.

"Good morning, Phil," he greeted him.

Phil glanced at Geoff and nodded. "Early for you, isn't it?" Phil asked, turning back to his bacon and sausages.

Geoff poured himself a mug of black coffee before responding. "Sure is. But you know how it is when you're not home."

"Yeah," was Phil's short reply.

Geoff took a seat, drank his coffee, and flipped open the newspaper that was lying on the edge of the table.

"Umm, it smells good in here," came a bright voice.

Geoff and Phil looked up, recognizing Janice. "Good morning," they said in unison.

"Ditto. Oh, I would love some of that. Is it ready?" she gushed, standing over Phil as he started picking up sausages and putting them on a plate.

"Whenever you are," he responded.

"First I need some coffee. Did Sissi tell you how beautiful I think her house is? I love it here. I couldn't live in the country like this, but it is peaceful. I know I'll be visiting often. Well, as often as you two would let me, of course—"

"I'll be right back," Geoff interrupted, coming to his feet as Janice sat down with her coffee.

"Okay, I'll just talk to old Phil until you get back," Janice said brightly. Geoff smiled at her, thinking how annoying it was to have someone so talkative in the morning. If it weren't for Nicole, he would make his polite excuses and exit the premises altogether. But even with her rejection,

Geoff couldn't wait to see Nicole, to talk to her again and maybe even make her forget all about her lover, Craig Williams.

Nicole entered her bedroom wrapped in a terry-cloth robe with a towel thrown over her shoulders. She dabbed a drop of water from her eyes as she dropped her clothes on the bed. It was muggy in the room, and gingerly she walked around the bed to open the window. She glanced at the clock on the nightstand and whistled softly. It was almost seven A.M. Time was flying by, and she had spent too much time in the bathroom.

As she stepped in front of the window, she noticed that Craig's clothes were tossed on the floor. She paused, staring down at them in confusion. She didn't recall his clothes being there before she went to shower. She knew when she woke he was gone, but so were his clothes. She gingerly circled the room. Then she noticed Craig's suitcase sitting on the chair beside the bed, and that it was open as well. Now she was sure that his suitcase was not open before she got in the shower!

First she was annoyed, wondering where he had been, then she relaxed, sure that this was a reasonable answer for his behavior. There was no way he would be so bold as to find his way into Michelle's arms while she was under the same roof with him. No way.

She sighed, refusing to worry about Michelle now. She was disappointed that Donna could not be convinced that she and Keith were not lovers. Donna made her plans so complicated now. She pulled the towel from her shoulders and tossed it in the pile of dirty clothes in the corner before leaving the room.

She was at the bottom of the stairs when Geoff entered the foyer. His handsome face broke into a gracious smile at seeing her. She felt instantly self-conscious, not at all comforted by his appreciative grin. Immediately she realized that she had not put on any makeup and that her hair was pulled back in a plain ponytail.

"Good morning, Nicole," he said evenly.

"Good morning, Geoff, was it?" she inquired hesitantly, as if his name had escaped her memory. He grinned, confident that she hadn't forgotten his name.

"That's right."

"You're up early," Nicole commented, glancing about to see if anyone else was around.

"As is most everyone else," Geoff responded.

"Really? Have you seen everyone else," she quizzed him.

"Not everyone," he drawled. "But your friend Craig is out jogging, Phil is in the kitchen prepping breakfast, Janice is in there chatting up a storm, and who knows who else is lying awake in the privacy of their rooms," he added, walking around her until he had one foot on the bottom step and was peering down at her with compelling brown eyes. Nicole gaped up at him and felt oddly vulnerable beneath his gaze. She tensed slightly at the intensity of his perusal of her and wondered how he saw her.

"That was very informative," she managed to say with an air of mockery in her voice.

"I'm a weatherman, it's my job to be informative," he remarked, refusing to lower his gaze and release the tension between them.

"I thought it was the newsmen who had to be informative," Nicole murmured.

Geoff chuckled and after considering her in more detail, queried, "I take it you don't think the weather is news?"

Nicole laughed, rolled her eyes in defeat, and responded, "I didn't mean that."

"Then what did you mean?" he probed, his voice lowering in a husky baritone as he found himself lost in her warm brown eyes.

"I meant that weather is ordinary and happens every day. It's not news it's . . . it just is." She shrugged weakly.

"Ordinary? There's nothing ordinary about the weather," he said, then lowering his voice to a provocative murmur, he added, "The weather can be hot and burning, causing your body to bead with sweat and weaken with exhaustion or," he continued, his face within inches of hers as he spoke in slow deliberate phrases, "it can chill your flesh like a melting ice cube, dripping its cool waters down your back, your collarbone, your—"

"I think I get the point," Nicole murmured quickly, cutting him short. He smiled, considered her with his bold eyes. Then without weighing the consequences, he brushed her slightly parted lips with his own.

Nicole didn't resist, although she was caught off guard by his daring move to kiss her. His mouth was barely touching hers, but gradually he applied pressure until, like a panicked kitten, she squirmed free of him and stepped to the side, gazing up at him in wide-eyed fascination.

"You have a lot of nerve," she said with a slight tremble in her voice.

Geoff narrowed his gaze, gave her a cocky smile, then shrugged. "That's how I got to be the weatherman." His words were full of insinuation and double meaning.

Nicole felt flushed with embarrassment and decided she could no longer play his game. "I had better go," she said, though she continued to stare into his bold brown eyes with almost childlike awe. He was nothing like Craig, she decided. She found him attractive, she had to admit, but he need not know it, she thought fiercely, moving to leave him.

"I'll see you later," she said, walking around him, careful not to brush against him.

He grinned again, nodding his head, and said, "I'm sure you will," then he continued from the house. Nicole hesitated at his comment but refused to glance back at him.

"Nicole, good morning. You look so refreshed. Headache all gone?" Janice chirped the moment Nicole entered the kitchen.

Nicole smiled, bent over, and gave Janice a warm hug.

"It's all gone. And you're up early, too, Phil," she added, taking a seat beside Janice and smiling up at Phil.

He nodded, his usually somber expression not changing as he set a plate in front of Janice. "Can't help it when a group of strangers are in your presence," he said.

Nicole hesitated, glancing at him in surprise. Was there a tinge of bitterness in his words or was he unaware of the hostility he was exhibiting? She could only murmur an uncomfortable, "Oh."

"Well, I for one get up early every morning. Sleep is far overemphasized by everyone, especially on the weekends," Janice said, unaware of the undertones in Phil's words.

"Care for something?" Phil asked Nicole.

"I'm not really hungry. Where is Sissi?" she asked with a quick glance around the kitchen.

"Sissi? She's still asleep. You can expect to see her about eleven or noon." Phil's answer was dry, uninterested, but Nicole caught the bitterness in his voice and wondered what had happened last night after she went to bed.

Sissi sat up slowly, feeling the emptiness of the room and instantly thought of Phil. She was relieved that he had not made another attempt to come to her. Where he got his audacity, she had no idea. His attempt to make love to her last night had left her drained with outrage. Was he so arrogant that he thought after only a few days since she caught him in the arms of another woman she would make love to him?

She yawned and stretched, hating the idea of getting up to face everyone. She had gotten less than three hours of sleep, and even that was restless. She got up and took a quick glance out the window. Craig's blue Nova was still parked outside, and Sissi wondered if Percy was up yet. Could he have slept in the barren cottage? She wouldn't be surprised if he had with his stubborn ways.

Percy paused on the stairway at the sound of the bedroom door opening. He was on his way to the kitchen where he smelled breakfast cooking and the aroma of coffee. Sissi came into the hall and he paused, the breakfast forgotten. It was as if the very thought of her brought her into his presence. She had been the first person he thought of when he awoke, the last person he thought of before he drifted off to sleep in his lonely room. As she headed for the bathroom, she didn't even notice him and, when the bathroom door shut behind her, he felt shut out.

Recalling her stinging words in the cottage, he licked his teeth and squared his jaw. She needn't worry about him coming near her, he thought fiercely. Of course, he should let her know it. He started toward the bathroom door. He was going to stay for another day or so—Craig needed him by his side right now, he reasoned—and in the meantime Sissi needed to be reassured that he would not bother her and would give her no cause to feel hounded by him.

His coming to her now had nothing to do with a desire to see her, he just needed to clear the air before they saw anyone else. He paused just outside of the bathroom door, wondering for a sparing moment where Phil was. Then shrugging, he put his hand on the doorknob and was surprised to discover it wasn't locked. That was just like Sissi, foolishly trusting everyone.

He listened for a moment and was about to fling the door open without knocking when Eddie and Michelle stepped into the hall. Michelle paused, crossed her arms across her chest, and gave Percy a feline smile.

"You might want to knock first," she suggested with a sly grin, noting Percy's surprised expression.

Hearing the shower running, Eddie frowned at Percy and asked, "What's going on?"

Percy was irritated at their intrusion. It was early in the morning, and the entire house was awake. Gritting his teeth and dropping his hands to his side, he said evenly, "Nothing. I was just heading downstairs."

"Yeah?" Michelle said. "It looked as if you were heading into the bathroom to me. Didn't it appear that way to you, Eddie?" she asked for support.

Eddie eyed Michelle in annoyance that she was putting him in her little sick game. He gazed at Percy and responded with a cool, "No. It looked as if he were heading for the kitchen."

"Oh, you're such a wimp with Percy and Craig," Michelle complained, giving Eddie an irritated nudge. Eddie ignored her comment, sensing a long day of sensitive attitudes.

Percy tossed Eddie an appreciative nod before stepping up to Michelle with furrowed eyebrows. "Michelle, sweetie. Don't get into my business. I don't get into yours," he said, but Michelle could hear the veiled threat.

She cowered beneath his anger and whined, "I'm not getting in your business, Percy. As a matter of fact, I came up here to find you and Eddie to come have breakfast with me," she said, slightly flustered beneath his dark gaze. Paranoid, feeling vulnerable, she wondered if he knew about last night with Craig. Reason said he knew nothing.

No one was there when Craig came to her, and no one saw her leave. When she last checked, Craig was gone from the room and probably consoling Nicole's broken heart right now. Certain of Nicole's shock when she discovered Craig had spent the night away from her gave Michelle cause to smile.

Percy narrowed his eyes at her obvious glee and was about to scold Michelle further when the shower shut off and the bathroom fell silent. All three of them looked at the door before Percy immediately broke the silence. "You wanted to have breakfast, then let's have breakfast." Leading the way down the stairs, Percy practically was running from the floor. His was wired with aggravation. It was like being in college again. Everyone was in his business, watching him, scoping out his relationship with Sissi. It was none of their business. Entering the kitchen, he tried to shake his frustrations with a large helping of eggs, bacon, biscuit, and a scoop of grits—the entire time pointedly having no conversation for Phil.

Sissi and Craig entered the foyer at the same time. Sissi paused on the stairs when the front door opened and Craig entered, sweating hard from his morning run.

"Hey, Sissi," he huffed, out of breath.

Sissi looked him up and down before saying, "Good morning. Good run?"

"It was okay. I ran too long, over an hour."

"Hope it was worth the effort."

"What do you mean?" Craig asked hastily, uncomfortable with her comment. Could she know about last night?

Sissi shrugged, not hearing his agitation, assuming his breathless speech was due to his morning run. "Nothing. You've got to be hungry. Come on, join me in the kitchen," she said, tucking her arm in his. Craig hesitated then feeling comfortable that Sissi meant nothing by her comment, he obliged her wish and together they entered the kitchen.

The breakfast table was full, to Sissi's surprise. After the way everyone was drinking last night, she just knew she wouldn't see anyone before ten A.M. And here it was half past seven and everyone was up and chatting away. The only persons missing were Donna and Geoff. Sissi wondered idly if they were together, then thought it was not likely—Geoff was much too sophisticated for a woman like Donna.

". . . you know it's going to be big," Janice was babbling, the eggs on her fork dangling just in front of her mouth as she paused to talk. All eyes fell on Sissi and Craig at their grand entrance, Sissi sparkling fresh from her morning shower and Craig weighed down with a sweaty sweat suit.

"Good morning, all." She laughed then releasing Craig walked over to Phil, who was leaning against the kitchen counter with a cup of coffee in hand, watching her in his usual brooding manner.

Phil considered her with sour eyes, still resenting being put out of the room. Sissi ignored him and sat beside Janice and Nicole.

At the table Michelle sat between Eddie and Percy, her eyes darting curiously from Craig to Nicole. Nicole stared at her plate, trying not to show that she hadn't seen Craig since he left her to find Donna. Just for a moment her eyes caught Michelle's and, in that instant, she knew that Craig had been with that woman—it was written all over Michelle's smug expression.

"Phil, *dear,* be a sweetheart and pile my plate high, I'm starved," Sissi said brightly, her gaze on Phil filled with false appreciation. Phil hesitated, glancing at her in surprise. One moment she was hating him, the next she was giving him her brightest smile. He wasn't sure what she was up to, but he was glad to see that she had lightened up.

"Janice, I can't believe you're up this early, too. So, what's going to be big?" Sissi asked.

"Your wedding of course," Janice responded, her voice loud with excitement.

"Oh, enough about the wedding," Sissi proclaimed, animating her voice for both Percy's and Phil's sake. "I want to talk about the boutique Nicole and I are thinking of opening. It's going to be so adorable. Isn't it, Nicole?"

"I've heard enough already," Craig muttered.

"I want to hear but not right now," Eddie said as he wolfed down bacon. "Besides, aren't all boutiques the same?" he asked jokingly.

"No, they are not," Sissi stated. "Our shop will be different. It will cater to all women of all flavors. We'll have American wear, Eurocentric wear, African wear. We'll even have a little something for gentlemen. But you wouldn't know about that," Sissi added with a teasing wink at Nicole and Janice.

"Hey, what do you mean? I'm a perfect gentleman," Eddie said, pretending that he was wounded by her words.

"Yes, you are," Sissi said. "And that's more than I can say for some."

"Good morning, everyone," Geoff said, coming into the kitchen as Sissi was speaking. "Good morning, Nicole." He gave her an appreciative smile, and Craig frowned at the gesture. Where did Geoff get off smiling all cozy at his woman? Nicole was so caught up in her suspicions about Michelle and Craig that she hadn't really been listening to the exchange, or paying that much attention to what Geoff said. But Sissi's quick reply saved her from having to respond.

"Nicole's so busy thinking about our boutique, she probably didn't even hear you. I was just telling everyone about it."

"That's right," Janice easily responded.

"Hey, Nicole, where's Donna?" Eddie blurted, trying to divert everyone's attention from the increasingly uncomfortable scene.

"She's still in bed probably," Geoff answered, recalling Donna's lewd behavior when she arrived.

At the mention of Donna and Geoff's easy response to the question, Nicole instantly looked up, suspicious of how Geoff would know where Donna was unless he had been with her the night before.

Michelle observed the jealous glance from Nicole and considered Nicole with a haughty smirk as if to say, "Ah-ha!"

Nicole allowed her gaze to casually glance away from Geoff and landed squarely on Michelle's knowing eyes. She sucked in her cheeks and stared at her plate. She hated Michelle more and more.

Craig's forehead was creased in a baffled scowl. The exchange between Nicole and Geoff hadn't escaped his notice. Had she been with him while he was out? Is that why she wasn't kicking and screaming when he walked into the kitchen? Incensed at the thought that Geoff could have slept with his woman, and conveniently forgetting that he had been with Michelle last night, Craig scowled at Nicole and spoke with icy resolve. "I had better jump into the shower."

"Yeah, man. You're ruining my breakfast." Eddie laughed.

Nicole barely looked his way as she continued to sip her coffee, her eyes lowered in thought. Huffing in irritation at her lack of response, he asked, "Are you coming up, Nicole?"

"I already showered," was her automatic reply.

Craig paused, coming to his feet slowly, his eyes roving over Geoff in suspicion. The only thing that kept him from believing Nicole had stepped out on him was her timid nature. She didn't have the nerve to creep on him. Feeling a little more secure at the thought, he shoved past Geoff and hurried up to the room that he should have shared with Nicole.

The moment Craig left, Sissi glanced at her watch and snapped her fingers. "Oh, ladies, I'm heading to town for a quick shopping spree first thing this morning. I promised to take everyone to the club tonight, and I can't do that without a new outfit."

"You have a dozen things to wear tonight, Sissi. Why do you need anything else?" Phil demanded, rinsing the dishes and setting them in the dishwasher.

"Because tonight I'm going out with *my* friends. I want to look good for them," she answered easily. "Come on Nicole, Janice."

"And me. I'm going, too," Michelle said brazenly, refusing to be left behind as if she were a wet rag. It was as if Sissi couldn't remember that Michelle was there, and Michelle was losing her patience. She was Sissi's friend, too—and she was genuinely happy for her.

"Of course, you didn't give me a chance to finish," Sissi replied calmly.

"It's just past eight and we're in the South. What store opens this early?" Percy asked incredulously, coming to his feet. He wanted Sissi to stay, to talk to her and let her know he was going to stay out of her way. That was all he wanted to do. If she left now, he wouldn't likely see her again until they went tonight, and then everyone would be in his business again.

"None at this hour but by the time we reach the mall, everything will be opening," Sissi answered shortly, trying to sound natural when she answered his question. "We can do a little sightseeing along the way while we're at it." She wanted to add that it was no concern of his what she did anyway.

"Here, Sissi, take my car," Phil said, pulling out his car keys. She stared at the keys as if they were taboo. With the mood Phil was in when she put him out of her room, he could be setting her up. She doubted he could be that in love with her, but she wasn't taking any chances. Hastily she declined, saying, "We can take Nicole's truck. It's more fun, don't you think so, girls?"

"I agree," Janice chirped, compliant with any decision they made as long as she didn't have to drive.

"No, no. I really don't feel like driving," Nicole said hastily.

"Oh, come on, Nicole. Give us a ride in your Sidekick, girl," Janice insisted.

"I'm too tired to drive," Nicole complained, trying to get out of taking the ride. She wanted to go back to bed, to ease her mind, to gather her strength to confront Craig.

"Then I'll drive for you," Sissi offered.

"You don't have to do that. It's not really that comfortable in the truck," Nicole insisted.

"You just don't want to give us a ride." Janice pouted.

"Please, I'll drive. I have my car," Michelle snapped, losing patience with their begging Nicole to drive. They were acting like Nicole had a Rolls-Royce and was the goddess of the road.

At Michelle's offer Nicole recanted her rejection, immediately repelled at the idea of riding in Michelle's car. There was no telling how many times Craig had screwed her in the backseat of the Intrepid, she thought sulkily.

"Don't worry about it, Michelle. I'll go ahead and drive," Nicole said firmly.

"Oh, now you want to drive," Michelle muttered.

"Here, at least take the cellular, in case something happens," Phil added, rushing from the kitchen and coming back with his cellular phone.

"Like what?" Janice asked.

"Anything," Phil said.

"Next he'll have a pager, a video camera, and a police siren set up for me. See you all later. Come on, Nicole," Sissi sighed, tucking Nicole's arm in hers much as she had done with Craig earlier that morning.

"What about Donna? We should wake her," Michelle suggested, pausing at the kitchen door. Sissi and Nicole looked at each other, but it was Janice who quickly said, "Oh, please let that woman sleep it off. Besides, it's crowded enough as it is."

"I just thought I would ask." Michelle shrugged.

"I agree, let her rest," Sissi added.

"Have a safe trip," Phil muttered as they scattered to get their purses. They said their good-byes, waved, and a moment later the house was void of their feminine chatter.

Chapter Seventeen

Nicole's truck was spotless, so spotless that Janice was about to tease Nicole the moment they climbed into the truck. Had it not been for Sissi's interruption on how nice the local boutiques were, Janice would have pointed out the oil stain that was an eyesore in comparison to the clean state of the white truck. It looked drastically close to a fingerprint on the side of the hood. But as it was, she was distracted by the speed of the vehicle and couldn't remember anything except her fear of Nicole's driving.

"I can't believe I insisted that you drive," Janice complained.

"I can handle my Sidekick," Nicole said coolly, keeping her eyes on the road as she spoke.

Sissi had taken the front seat with Nicole. Janice sat in the back beside Michelle, who sat behind Sissi. Nicole was whipping around corners and speeding down the road at breakneck speed. At first Sissi and Michelle had laughed at Janice's whining pleas for Nicole to slow down. But then

Sissi fell silent, glancing at her friend with concern, and Michelle chimed in with Janice's whining.

"Slow down, Nicole. We'll get there," Michelle complained in the backseat. "What's the hurry? The stores don't close for hours," she snapped.

"I can't . . . I can't seem to stop. I think the brakes are going," Nicole said in as calm a voice as she could muster. They all fell silent, holding on to their seats after tightening their seat belts as Nicole tried to keep the truck steady on the road.

"Oh, my God. Oh, no," Janice moaned over and over.

"Shut up," Michelle snapped, fear gripping her to her seat. "Pull the emergency brake, Nicole," she yelled out. "Do something!"

"Ahead is a sharp corner, Nicole. Be careful. Please be careful. Try and slow down," Sissi whispered, keeping her cool, her hand gripping hold of her seat belt. Nicole kept quiet, concentrating on the road.

"Did you hear me, Nicole?" Sissi hissed, leaning back in her seat, pressing her feet to the floor as if she were driving and could brake the vehicle.

"I . . . heard . . . you!" Nicole snapped between clenched teeth as the sharp curve Sissi warned her about approached.

"Oh, God," Janice cried just as Michelle screamed out again, "Pull the emergency brake!"

The truck slowed as the sound of metal against the pavement reverberated throughout the car. It skidded out of control for several feet before coming to an abrupt stop in a shallow ditch.

Nicole moaned and tried to lift herself.

"No, ma'am, don't try to move," a blond female paramedic warned her.

"What happened?" Nicole whispered, her whole body aching.

"Your truck ran off the road, ma'am," the paramedic answered as she continued to check Nicole. Nicole slowly looked around, the accident still not sinking into her memory. She remembered only that Sissi wanted to go shopping.

"Where's Sissi?" she asked in a sudden panic.

"I'm not sure who Sissi is, ma'am," the paramedic answered. There had been four women in the truck. They were lucky, these women, the paramedic thought. It could have been a lot worse.

"Your friend Sissi is there in the ambulance. She had a few bruises, but she'll be fine. The other one," the other male paramedic responded—he glanced at his notes—"Michelle, she's sitting in the police car talking with the officer. And Janice, I believe, has some pretty severe bruises. A fractured leg, I think."

"Is she . . . all right?" she asked fearfully.

"We believe so, but we want to get her to the hospital right away. There could be some internal injuries."

"Oh, God," Nicole groaned.

"And you're Nicole, correct?" he continued to ask.

"Yes."

"Michelle was able to give us information on who to notify. We called Mr. Richardson and Mr. Williams, they should be here soon. How is she?" he asked the other paramedics in a whisper that Nicole clearly heard.

"A few bruises, but I think she'll be fine. Of course, we can't be sure until she's seen by a doctor," the female paramedic responded, stepping away from Nicole. Nicole sat up, looking around the accident scene as her memory slowly came back to her.

"Janice? Where is she?" she asked loudly and immediately cringed from the pain that shot through her head.

The paramedic had come back to take care of her, and the other paramedics glanced at her. Fear instantly shot through her, especially when they hesitated to respond. The male paramedic walked over to the police officers who were checking out the wrecked truck. She watched as they interacted, glancing at her and Sissi, who sat in the ambulance.

Nicole sat up, recalling the accident, and began to fidget with worry. She wrung her hands and darted her gaze from the police officers to the paramedics back to the ground. She was about to yell for Janice in a hysterical panic. They had said she was fine, that they were taking her to the hospital. But where was she! In a panic her mouth opened as she prepared to call Janice's name. Before she cried out, the sound of Craig's powerful motor stopped her.

The Nova came to a screeching halt. Behind his car was Phil's burgundy Buick. The car doors slammed, and Craig and Eddie came rushing to the women's side. Phil wasn't far behind them. But Percy slowly got out of Craig's car, keeping his fear in check as he searched for Sissi. It wasn't until he saw her sitting in the ambulance, looking fully alert and alive, that he was able to ask questions about the accident.

"Craig," Nicole whispered in relief.

Craig carefully held Nicole in his arms. "Are you all right?" he asked gently.

"Yes. I think so," Nicole responded though still in pain, his affair with Michelle momentarily forgotten.

"Careful," the paramedic warned and Craig hastily released Nicole. He flashed a shocked glance over the accident scene, spotting the skid marks reaching from the road onto the grassy mound where the women had been found.

"What happened?" Percy demanded, walking directly to Nicole, knowing now was not the time to invade Phil's privacy with Sissi. But even as Nicole answered him, Percy's worried gaze fell on Sissi. She was talking softly with Phil, and he felt isolated from her. He wanted to hold her, to console her, and make sure she was safe—but he had to step aside, at least for the moment.

"My truck . . . the brakes went out. I . . . it all happened so fast," Nicole stammered out an explanation.

"Are you all right? Nothing's broken, is it?" Percy asked in a muffed, choked voice.

"I'm fine. But I think Janice may have been seriously injured."

"Shouldn't she be sitting or lying down?" Eddie asked the paramedic, concerned at how mobile Nicole was after so serious an accident.

"We checked her, nothing that's obvious is wrong. But she should go to the hospital. She seems a little confused," the blond paramedic responded.

"They were all banged around in the truck," the other paramedic explained to Phil just a few feet away. Phil was holding Sissi's hand. Sissi sat in a dazed state inside the ambulance.

". . . had there been impact, they would have died instantly . . ."

"Who, who died?" Sissi grimaced in pain, looking up sharply at the paramedic's words. Until that moment she had barely listened to a word the man was saying. Everyone stopped talking at Sissi's outburst. Percy moved to come to Sissi's side, but Eddie grabbed his arms and silently shook his head, warning Percy to let Phil handle Sissi's grief. Percy hesitated then stood still, burning internally at not being able to console Sissi—yet again he wasn't going to be there for her.

She shoved Phil aside, got out of the ambulance, and demanded in a frail voice, "Who's dead? I . . . have to know. Just tell me."

"If you would just give me a chance," he sighed

"No one's dead," the paramedic said hastily in an attempt to calm Sissi.

"Oh, thank God," Sissi groaned then weakly dropped to her knees, exhausted and distraught. Before Eddie could stop him again, Percy raced to her side, and on his knees with her, he held her close to his muscular chest. She buried her face in his chest, her eyes dry from shock.

Phil put a firm hand on Percy's shoulder. "Do you mind?" he asked in as calm a voice as he could muster.

Percy looked up at Phil, wanting to say, "Yeah I mind!" but he didn't want to upset Sissi even more. Gingerly he brought Sissi to her feet and, with a final glance at Phil, he stepped aside to allow her fiancé to finish consoling her. Sissi didn't look up. She knew she was being given to Phil and wondered if Percy despised her so much that even in the wake of her traumatic experience that he put aside their differences. Sighing, she whispered to Phil that she needed to sit down for a moment.

"I've never had an accident in my life," Nicole moaned, feeling humiliated by the accident and fearful for her best friend's well-being.

"No one blames you, Nicole," Eddie said hastily.

"I blame myself. I could have . . . I could have killed us all," she blurted, near tears.

"But you didn't. Everyone's going to be all right, including Janice," Eddie insisted. Craig didn't respond, too embarrassed at the scene before him. Was Nicole so caught up in her shame about Keith that she couldn't even keep the vehicle on the road? He was starting to think she must be more depressed than he had first realized.

They were taken to the hospital with a few police officers remaining behind to inspect the scene and have Nicole's truck towed. After being probed again by doctors, Michelle, Sissi, and Nicole were treated for minor wounds but were deemed all right. Janice's wounds were more serious, but her doctor admitted he expected she would pull through just fine. She was at least conscious and before they left, Nicole, Sissi, and Percy came to her bedside. The others waited outside, all too tired to speak.

Nicole sat in the chair beside the bed, and Sissi gingerly sat on the mattress beside Janice.

Nicole was heartbroken after taking one look at Janice. She felt the accident was all her fault. Her wide eyes clearly spoke how she felt, and Janice managed to offer Nicole a weak smile.

"It's okay, Nicole, sweety. I'll be fine," she whispered softly.

Nicole sighed, closing her eyes in a pain-filled moment, saying, "I know . . . I just feel so bad. I could have . . . you could have been killed," she ended, her voice choking on a sob.

Sissi blinked back tears at the thought, happy to be able to hold Janice's hand. Her lively Janice, her spirited Janice. Sissi was finding it hard to feel comfort in the fact the drugs the doctor had given her were causing her to respond in such a lethargic manner.

"But I'm alive. I'll be fine," Janice repeated, closing her eyes in exhaustion.

"We should let her rest," Percy whispered, putting a comforting hand on Sissi and helping her to her feet. Sissi stood up and, before she followed Percy's lead, she bent over Janice and gave her a kiss on her forehead. Janice's eyes slowly opened, and she smiled up at Sissi.

"Don't worry, I'll be . . . I'll be back to normal before the wedding. I promise," she added as she closed her eyes again.

Sissi was moved to tears. She had not gotten a chance to confess her false engagement to Janice. She hesitated, wanting to tell Janice then and there that she wasn't marrying Phil, but Percy's patient gaze on her silenced her. Another glance at Janice and Sissi decided the truth could wait. The shock could very well cause her to worry, Sissi reasoned, as she followed Nicole and Percy from the room.

It was late in the afternoon, and the house was enshrouded in silence. Donna groaned, rolling onto her stomach in discomfort. She felt sick as a dog and heavy, like something was manipulating her movements, holding her down. She coughed, turning her face away from the pillow. She was nauseous and gagged, her stomach turning from the alcohol she had consumed the night before. Trying to lift herself from the bed, she gagged again and grabbed her stomach. She was having the worst hangover of her life.

Dragging her feet from the bed, she walked gingerly to the door. She felt wretched and before she could open the door, her body released the foul sickness that was gagging her. Vomiting uncontrollably, she stared at the nasty mess at the foot of the door and groaned. Sissi would have a fit if she left it there. Glancing around the room, she didn't see anything to clean it up with. With an aching head she left the room and gingerly found her way to the bathroom. Finding it, she wet a towel and took it back to her room.

Moving in slow motion, she wiped up the stain and returned the towel to the bathroom. She tied it in a plastic trash bag and tossed it in the trash can, too exhausted to try and clean it. The house was so quiet as she left the bathroom, she stood for a moment in the hall and considered the closed doors. Nicole had to be behind one of those, probably lying down with another headache. She would confront Nicole again about Keith, of that she was certain. But first she needed a cigarette. She went back into her room, grabbed her purse, and happened to glance out the window. One car was parked in the driveway, and she vaguely wondered where everyone had gone.

She spotted the cottage in the distance and decided that it was an alluring prospect. It was exactly what she needed, some fresh air and isolation from her cousin. She didn't want to see Nicole until much later. She slipped on her shoes, deciding she would go to the cottage. She stuck the cigarettes in her back pocket, peeked in her purse, and smiled. Her bottle of gin was still there. Hastily she tucked her purse under her arm and crept from the house.

Chapter Eighteen

It was late afternoon when they started to leave the hospital. They had visited Janice for a little while but they knew she needed her rest. As they were preparing to exit, the police returned to question them again. At the sight of them, Percy sighed. Hadn't they gotten their answers at the accident scene? When they were finally released from answering questions, it was nearly the supper hour, and they were all exhausted. It had been a trying day, and no one felt like talking.

"I thought they would never stop asking the same questions over and over and over," Sissi said in fatigue as she and Eddie got into Phil's car. Nicole, Percy, and Michelle rode with Craig. Sissi could only guess at the tension in their car.

"It wasn't your fault, Nicole. Everyone's okay," Percy whispered to Nicole, consoling hands massaging her tense shoulders.

"Janice isn't. She had to be hospitalized, I'm surprised they didn't lock me up," Nicole whined.

"Oh, girl, please. They knew it was an accident," Michelle snapped impatiently. Percy tossed Michelle a curt glance, silencing her with his furious look.

Nicole sat in the front seat, closing her eyes in silent frustration. Craig had barely said two words to her since they were taken to the hospital. She didn't know if he was angry with her or confused about what he should say. Either way, it hurt her that Percy was able to find the right words and Craig couldn't.

It was bad enough that Craig continued to flaunt his affair with Michelle but to shut her out at a moment like this—when she most needed him—left her feeling utterly rejected. She couldn't wait to call Keith. She needed that money, and then she was through with the lot of them! She just wished that Janice hadn't been hurt. It would have been poetic justice if Michelle had been in Janice's place or had befallen an even worse fate.

"I called Janice's mom," Craig said softly to Nicole a few minutes later. Nicole nodded, dreading seeing Janice's mother. To have to come face to face with Mrs. Leer was the last thing she wanted.

As if reading her thoughts, Percy patted her on the shoulder. "Don't worry, Nicole. She knows it was an accident," Percy consoled her.

"As if that matters. I nearly killed her daughter. I know she'll want to prosecute me for that alone," Nicole moaned.

"Oh, come on, Nicole. She's not going to prosecute you. It was an accident—a freak accident. And no one, not you or anyone else, is to blame," Percy insisted.

Percy's words, meant to ease Nicole, only haunted him. No one to blame indeed. It was strange that Nicole had driven all the way from Virginia with no problem with her car and suddenly, the first morning at Sissi's house, and her brakes went bad. If it was an accident, it was extremely odd. With suspicion planted in his mind, he glanced at Michelle with a weary examination. As he watched her, he realized that she was not capable of such a scheme, no matter how much she was in love with Craig. In Percy's view, Michelle would have done something like that a long time ago if it were in her nature. Besides, why would she willingly get in a vehicle whose brakes she knew were bad? It didn't make sense and, as he recalled, Michelle had insisted on riding with the women. No, it was just a very unfortunate accident.

"What are you looking at?" Michelle snapped as she caught Percy looking at her. She slumped in her seat and stared out the window, unshed tears stinging her eyes during the ride back to Sissi's house.

When they approached the house, Geoff was pacing the porch, waiting for them with a frown deeply etched in his forehead. His eyes were dark with concern for the women, and it had taken all the energy he had to remain patient until they arrived back at the house.

When he first heard about the accident, he wanted to ride out with them. Eddie had called him to let him know everyone was all right. Janice had to be hospitalized for her more serious injuries, but they didn't appear to be life-threatening. So Geoff, feeling out of place, a stranger among old friends, stayed behind.

It was late in the evening, and he was starting to think perhaps Nicole had been seriously hurt, contrary to what Eddie reported. He watched the cars, waiting with controlled impatience to see for himself that Nicole was all right.

Nicole sat in stoic silence, refusing to leave the car. She

kept thinking of the accident and, as she dwelled on it, she became more and more suspicious. Michelle had done something to her brakes, she was sure of it. Why else would Michelle offer to drive?

Craig waited only for a moment for Nicole to get out of the car. When she just sat there staring at her hands, he huffed impatiently and left her there, Michelle immediately on his heels.

Sissi's eyes narrowed as she watched Craig and Michelle enter the house with barely a hello to Geoff. Her eyes narrowed in disappointment that Craig would allow Michelle to trail behind him while Nicole was left in the car with Percy. Curiously she approached the Nova and peeped her head inside the car.

Percy was still sitting in the backseat, not willing to leave until Nicole got out of the car. At Sissi's approach he waved his hands in the air as if to say he was defeated. "I can't get her to leave the car," he said.

Sissi sighed then stroking Nicole's hair said softly, "Nicole, honey, you can't sit here all night. Come inside. I'll make you tea, and everything will be all right."

"Will it? Are you so sure, Sissi?" Nicole questioned, pulling away from Sissi. Sissi hesitated, not sure what Nicole meant. Sissi was surprised by Nicole's rejection but didn't give up. She opened the car door.

"Yes, I am," Sissi said firmly. "At least, I know I'm your friend. An accident isn't going to come between you and me, and it shouldn't come between you and Janice. She's going to be fine," Sissi whispered. Nicole sighed then, her petite body heavy with grief, and she finally left the car.

"Where's Craig?" Percy fumed the moment he got out of the car. He was furious with Craig for not waiting until Nicole got out with him. He hadn't even tried to console Nicole. What was wrong with the man?

* * *

Craig couldn't wait to escape the morbid scene in the car. He was sick and tired of Nicole's mishaps. And now the accident. Was there no end to her suffering? He had to get away from her and the moment the car was parked, he left her, almost relieved when she refused to leave the vehicle.

He was sitting at the dining room table, a rum and Coke in his hand, his eyes half closed as he pondered over the last few days. He couldn't understand what had happened. It was supposed to be a weekend of fun, of dancing and partying, of celebration. But from the moment he arrived, even before they got there, there was confusion.

Now everyone was upset, and Nicole was depressed. Michelle was his shadow since he had made love to her, and poor Janice was stranded at the hospital for the remainder of the weekend. What next?

Agitated with the confusion he was feeling, he took another sip from his drink before he felt the presence of Percy in the room. He didn't look up.

Percy stood in the doorway a moment, watching Craig. The lights were all on and gave the room a bright cheery appearance that didn't fit the mood of the two men. Finding Craig alone was somewhat surprising for Percy. He had expected to find Michelle with him.

He felt sorry for little Nicole. A cousin-in-law that wasn't worth the time of day, a cousin that was a drunkard, and a fiancé that was a dog. And now she felt she was the blame for an accident that ruined her best friend's engagement weekend.

"I can't believe you left her out there alone," Percy hissed, striding into the dining room with an angry face.

"I can't believe she was driving like a maniac," Craig retorted, gulping down the burning fluid as if it were water.

"You heard the story. Her brakes went out. She was trying to maintain control of the car," Percy snapped, coming to stand in front of his longtime friend. It occurred to Percy that this was a side of his friend that he had rarely seen. Not only was he cheating on poor Nicole, but he had also grown heartless and insensitive to the woman's plight.

"I know what happened, Percy. It's just . . . it's upsetting, man."

"How do you think she must feel then?" Percy chastised.

"She must feel like crap. I know I would," Craig raged, jumping to his feet and putting his hands to his temple as if he could stop the pain that suddenly raged within him.

"I'm sure she does. And with Michelle in the car, too. I don't know how she puts up with you."

"The same way Sissi puts up with Phil! She loves me," Craig finished, his tone resentful as he lowered his voice. Percy flinched, resenting Craig's using Sissi to explain away his wrongs with Nicole.

Craig rolled his eyes, then sat back down and slammed his drink onto the hardwood floor, giving no heed to the damage the liquid would do to the freshly polished floors.

"Leave Sissi out of this, Craig," Percy whispered, his voice full with disbelief at his longtime friend's behavior. "I can't believe that you're acting this way. I had no idea you were so self-centered."

"And you're not?" Craig scoffed. "At least my girl didn't lose our baby. She had an accident that caused a serious scare. But you, you left Sissi after a miscarriage, bro. A miscarriage, so back off me. I'm trying to handle this the best I can."

Percy was hurt by Craig's words and wanted to explain his leaving Sissi. But he decided against it. Craig wouldn't understand, he never had, and it didn't matter. What mattered was that Nicole needed him. "Let's just leave me and Sissi out of this one. I know what I did, and maybe you should listen to experience."

"Yeah? And what am I supposed to say to her now? I don't know how to console her anymore. You don't get it, Percy. Even after Sissi lost your kid, she wasn't always depressed and sad and just plain needy. But with Nicole, it's always something, and I'm sick and tired of consoling that woman. If it isn't one thing, it's another."

"I can't believe what I'm hearing," Percy muttered, turning to stare at the brightly decorated beige and lilac wallpaper as if the walls would answer him.

"I knew you wouldn't understand," Craig snapped, resenting Percy's condescending tone. He didn't press Percy about Sissi when she had the miscarriage, now did he? He was smart enough to mind his own business and let Percy deal with Sissi his way. So why couldn't Percy give him the same respect?

"Your woman nearly died out there today—a woman you claim to love. She's in a state of shock, and you're talking about you're tired!" Percy snorted in disgust.

"Yeah, I'm tired. This whole thing, I just wish it wasn't real."

Percy shook his head, staring at his friend as if he were a stranger.

"It is real. You need to recognize that as a fact," Percy said in a fierce whisper. "You had better get a grip on reality before you lose Nicole."

"Lose Nicole?" Craig scoffed, downing the last of his rum. "Where is she going to go? She loves me too much. I won't lose her," he said as if he was exhausted and wished he could lose her.

"You wanna bet," Nicole shrieked from just outside the door, her eyes filled with disbelief at Craig's cruel words. She had been searching for him, hoping to find consoling arms. Instead she heard him speak of her as if she were some kind of a loser who couldn't live without him. She'd show him!

Craig turned sharply at her words, shocked to see her. He swore under his breath, coming to his feet slowly. For a moment his gaze rested on Sissi, then Geoff, who had come into the dining room with her. They were watching him as if he were a monster.

"Baby," he whispered, opening his arms as if she would come to him. She stared at him, loathing him. Slowly she walked up to him and watched as a smile played across his mouth.

"Craig," Nicole whispered then she slapped him, the sting ringing against his ears as she turned just as coolly away and left the room.

He was shocked, utterly at a loss as to what to do. He didn't move as he listened to the heels of Nicole's shoes clang against the floor as she ran up the stairs.

"Man," was all he could say as he sat back down, heavy with defeat.

Watching him wring his hands irritated her and with a fierce scowl, she walked up to him and stood in front of him until her shins grazed his knees. Craig looked up at Sissi, his face bland as she glared down at him.

"You are the most gutless man I know. I can't believe . . . I thought you were so much better than this, Craig," Sissi murmured in utter disappointment.

"Sissi, you don't understand—" Before Craig could finish his statement, Sissi slapped him with such intensity the blow seemed to echo in the room.

"Whoa," Geoff whistled from the doorway,.

Craig was shocked, never expecting such a reaction from Sissi.

Percy immediately intervened, grabbing Sissi by the wrist before she could swing at Craig again. "No, Sissi, hold on.

We've all had a long day, but you can't get violent with the man just because you don't like what he's feeling."

"Don't you tell me what I can or can't do. You're no better than Craig. I wish you had never come here," she bit out, snatching her arm free and racing from the room as well.

Percy stared at the floor in shame. He knew immediately that Sissi was talking about her miscarriage, and it burdened his heart that she still carried the pain.

"I'll tell you what, Craig. If my woman had just had a serious car accident, I'd be so grateful for her safety, I wouldn't leave her side, not for a moment. I'll see you guys later," Geoff said evenly, his gaze clearly showing his disapproval of Craig.

Craig rolled his eyes. Who cared what that stranger thought, Craig thought in irritation.

"I suggest you get it together, Craig. Put the drink down, forget the slap, and go to Nicole. I just wish I had the opportunity you have right now, to save your relationship before someone else steps in."

Having said his peace and subdued by Sissi's outburst, Percy fell silent and plopped into the chair beside Craig's.

Chapter Nineteen

"Nicole, please, let me in," Sissi pleaded. Sissi was fearful, mindful of how distraught and high-strung Nicole could be. She had been through a lot in the past couple of days and the stress, Sissi realized, could tear her down, especially at the elevated levels it had already reached. Fearful that Nicole could even be depressed enough to consider suicide crept into Sissi's mind, and she began to panic.

"Nicole, if you don't open up . . ."

"Come in," Nicole whispered, opening the door barely a crack before walking back to the bed and sitting wearily on it. She wrapped her arms about herself as if she were cold. Sissi walked toward her, the darkness hiding Nicole's tear-streaked face from her view.

"I could have killed her," Nicole said softly.

Sissi sat on the bed next to her, placed her hands in her lap, and sighed heavily. "But you didn't. You have got to shake this. You can visit her tomorrow. And her mom will be in Monday. So don't worry. It was the truck, not you, that lost control. I know, I was there," Sissi insisted.

"Sure and I was driving the truck that was on the road with bad brakes. That was me, not the vehicle."

"Accidents happen, Nicole. That's why they call them accidents. I know you're upset. You have a right to be but promise, promise that you will shake off this depression. It's not good for you. Everyone is fine and Janice is, too," Sissi added, grabbing Nicole's cool hands and squeezing them for reassurance.

Nicole stared at her for a long moment. "I promise," she said distantly, but Sissi didn't believe her.

"It's late, Sissi. I'm tired and I've had a long day. I just want . . . I want to lie down." Nicole's eyes filled with unshed tears, not for Janice, who she was confident would be all right, but for Craig. He had broken her heart, and she couldn't bear it.

Sissi couldn't contain her need to comfort her. She reached over, hugged her best friend as she had never hugged her before, and whispered in a desperate voice, "It's going to be all right, Nicole. I promise," she added with emphasis.

With a heavy heart, Sissi slowly released Nicole, got up, then paused in the middle of the floor before leaving. Her head was lowered, her eyes unseeing, as she walked mechanically from Nicole's room. She didn't want to go to her bedroom, it was too lonely and isolated from the rest of her friends. What she needed was a breath of fresh air and soon found herself heading out the back door. Her hand was on the doorknob, her thoughts elsewhere, when suddenly she was seized from behind, a cloth gently placed over her nose and mouth. She barely took a second breath before her body succumbed and she fell unconscious.

Sissi awoke with a pounding headache. She lay still for

a moment, uncertain of where she was or how she got there. Then she remembered Nicole and leaving the room. She sat up and flinched in pain, her hand gingerly touching the back of her neck. With a confused frown, she recalled her last conscious moment and realized someone had hit her, knocked her out, and left her in her room. But why?

She scooted to her feet and tried to make sense of her surroundings, realizing as she looked around the murky small space that she was not in her room but in the cottage that she was renovating into a guest house. She took a shaky step and nearly fell, her body still weak and shaken from the blow. Holding on to the wall for support, she was standing with her back to the door when it squeaked open and Percy stood in the moonlight, staring at her.

"Percy." She breathed a sigh of relief. He had entered just as a sense of panic enveloped her.

"Why did you call me down here, Sissi? Now is not the time to have another argument," he grumbled immediately, closing the door shut behind him as he fully entered the cottage. He stood with his hands on his hips, his eyes slightly narrowed with burning frustration. Had she no idea how cruel her words were as she last parted from him? He guessed she didn't. He guessed she simply didn't care.

He wanted to shake her, to hold her, to release tears, to make love to her, to forget that he was a fool and had left her when she needed him most. Angry with himself, resenting her for bringing him such pain, he impatiently stared at her.

Sissi frowned, confused. She hadn't called him. She had no idea what he was babbling about. She started to approach him then fell weakly to her knees, feeling slightly dizzy from the movement. Percy took an anxious step toward her then narrowed his eyes suspiciously. Was she playing some kind of game with him? he wondered and sighed in exasperation. Of all times to play on his emotions. How could she stoop to such a low trick after the frightful experience they all had?

"Percy," she whispered, shaken, "I'm . . . I don't feel . . . right. I don't know what you're talking about but—"

"Like hell you don't," he hissed, walking up to her and offering her his hand even as his frown increased. Her dark brown eyes were large in the darkness, confused by his attitude as she began to fully comprehend what he was saying. He believed that she had called him to the cottage. Immediately she thought of Phil and became suspicious. She had to tell Percy what was going on.

"Percy, I . . . I didn't call you down here," she started tiredly, coming gingerly to her feet, afraid to move for fear that she would faint again.

Percy scowled, starting to wonder if she was in fact feigning illness. Swiftly he pulled her to him, holding her in a firm grasp as he bit out, "No? I'll tell you what," he said between clenched teeth. "I'm tired of this mind game you've been playing."

"I haven't been playing a mind game with you, Percy. Phil has," Sissi murmured, stunned by his sudden closeness.

Percy hesitated, his scowl slowly faded as he lift his eyebrows. "Phil? Why would he want us together?" Percy demanded.

Sissi sighed, slightly embarrassed to admit that Phil had cheated on her, but she slowly explained. "I . . . I caught him with another woman," she muttered. Percy blinked but remained silent. Sissi kept her eyes lowered as she continued. "I broke off the engagement a few days . . ."

"Then why the party? Why the game, Sissi?" Percy asked, torn between annoyance that Sissi had allowed him to believe she was going to marry Philip Richardson and relief that the whole engagement was a lie.

"Phil begged me. He has a reputation, a career, and I couldn't just see him ruined."

"So you sacrificed your dignity for a man who cheated on you," Percy scolded softly. Sissi glanced up at him, her brown eyes sad and humiliated beneath Percy's smug expression.

"I suppose sometimes giving someone a chance is better than turning a cold shoulder when you're most needed," she responded pointedly. Percy felt as if he had just been slapped. He knew exactly what she meant when she spoke of a cold shoulder.

"I never meant to be cold, Sissi," Percy groaned, his regret trembling his voice.

Sissi stared at him and in a loving motion, she gently lifted her hand and traced his cheek. "I believe you, Percy Duvall," she murmured softly.

Percy stared down at Sissi and caught her hand. Unable to tear her gaze from his, Sissi sighed when Percy planted a kiss in the palm of her hand then brought her hand to his chest and whispered, "You've always had my heart, Sissi. Always." Then he bent over and gently kissed her slightly parted mouth. Sissi felt weak with pleasure at the feel of his full mouth against hers. She didn't protest or move as he released her hand and pulled her to his broad chest. His kiss deepened as he held her in a longing embrace. She barely had a moment to regain her senses before he swiftly lifted her from her feet and carried her to the bedroom of the small cottage.

"Percy," she managed to gasp as he flung her on the bed. "Are you sure . . ."

"I'm sure, Sissi. Are you?" Percy groaned, cutting off any answer she may have had with another passionate kiss.

She had come to the cottage by no means of her own and so had Percy. And he had flung some accusation at her that she could not help but ponder. She hadn't called him to the cottage. She had no idea how she had gotten there herself. But her concerns were being dismissed with every caress, every moment that passed as his hands found her blouse and quickly released her buttons. She had gone braless and was instantly exposed to his hungry eyes. With an insatiable hunger, he found the dark sweet nipples that had grown tart from the sudden exposure to the humid air and teased them with the coolness of his tongue, suckling hungrily against them until Sissi squirmed with passion. She gasped at the tender fondling of her flesh, all sense of time gone. She allowed her body to be ravished by the enigmatic charms that Percy, and Percy alone, possessed.

Unable to focus, Sissi was torn with her love for Percy and her fear of losing him again. She knew only that she had longed for this moment, for him to take her in his arms, and together they would forget their sad loss and start fresh.

"Yes," she murmured, arching her body to allow his mouth full access to her tingling flesh.

Percy caressed her silken skin with firm hands, wanting to feel, to possess, to remember every inch of her smooth, soft body. She was his. This night if never again he would make love to Sissi. The word *love* paused him for a moment. He stared down at her in open amazement. Her slender body was aroused and desirous of him, and he was awed by her response. Yes, he loved Sissi Adams and wanted her like no other woman he had ever known—he had always wanted her.

Passion and love for this woman tore at his soul. An entanglement of mixed emotions rippled through his veins, causing his desire for Sissi to swell to an unbearable height. She had broken off her engagement to Phil, and Percy was elated. He groaned, dipped his head in a sweet agonized love for her. He kissed her neck, savored her lips with hot kisses, and inflamed her delicate bare shoulders with small, tender loving nips. His hands fondled her petite supple breasts before sliding down her sleek stomach and stroked the small curve of her waist.

Sissi writhed beneath his hungry sampling of her flesh. She reveled in his passion for her, feeling the depth of his desire pressing against her thigh through the rough material of his jeans. His ardor left her breathless. His breathing was heavy as his hands deftly removed her blouse completely from her, his hunger to feel her completely nude peaking. He unzipped her jeans then a moment later, her tennis shoes were tossed across the room. She lifted her hips and on cue, he tugged her jeans free from her. He struggled impatiently out of his pants until the only blockade between the two of them were her panties and his briefs. Within moments those barriers were tossed to the side, and they lay nude.

Sissi shivered though it wasn't cold. Percy's body was still beautiful and had been so missed by her body that it sent chills through her, even as his gaze inflamed her inner soul. The moistness between her legs spread through her veins, and she sighed deeply. Never taking his eyes from her gently writhing form, Percy pulled her into his firm hold and found her mouth in a deep, lustful kiss. They lay enclosed in each other's arms, their hands exploring each other's bodies as if it were for the first time.

Sissi was swept up in the fog of Percy's passion and, with a gasp, she was suddenly pulled up under him, pinned between him and the bed. He lifted her hands above her head and continued to kiss her deeply, his body rubbing slowly, deliberately against her. She gasped, aching with desire for him. Without inhibitions she spread her legs, his manhood pressed tantalizingly close to her warm moistness, and they both panted with anticipation as he continued to prolong their passionate union. His kiss left her lips, and he began to explore the rest of her.

"Take me, Percy. Please," she panted, arching her body provocatively to his. Percy groaned, ignoring her pleading as his tongue explored her nipples again, encircling them in the prison of her passion. He allowed her arms to be released as he trailed his tongue down the center of stomach, pausing at her navel where again he circled it boldly before, with light nibbles that tickled and caused her to writhe even more, he nipped at the flesh of her inner thighs until his tongue found her craving of him and possessed her fully. Sissi gasped, shocked. Percy had never explored her so boldly, so possessively, so lovingly. She could have melted into the bed so delightful was the feel of his tongue. She moved with him, encouraging him to press on.

"Percy," she panted, parting her lips in excitement. "I . . ."

Aroused by her approval, he stroked and pressed against her flesh until he felt the trembling of her thighs. "Not yet, baby," he grunted, suddenly lifting his head and crawling back up to her until his body straddled hers completely.

Gracefully she wrapped her hand about his neck and brought his mouth once more to her. Her tongue was hot and sweet, and she kissed him deeply while her hand found his erected evidence and began stroking the already hard muscle that demanded attention. His kisses were sweet, deep, and tasted of her. Her strokes increased, tenderly, urgently, until he gently removed her hand and then swiftly maneuvered to enter her fully. Sissi arched, gasping in sheer pleasure, her eyes half closed as if she were drugged. Percy melted into the hot moistness that greeted him. Repeatedly he stroked: even, deliberate, purposeful strokes. He wanted her to know his love, to feel his love, to forever remember his love. He suddenly pulled from her. Sissi gasped, pressed her hands against his buttocks, trying to encourage him to reenter her.

"Open your legs," Percy coaxed swinging his hips left and right until her legs fluttered apart. Swept into delirious pleasure, he grabbed Sissi's buttocks, sat up on his knees and pulled Sissi up to a sitting position. She grabbed hold of his shoulders and together they met repeatedly. Percy squeezed her soft buttocks, grunting and panting as she met him stroke for stroke.

"I love you Percy!" Sissi suddenly cried.

Her words stunned him, causing him to miss a beat as his eyes popped open. She was writhing wildly against him. Her head was tossed back, and the sheer passion that she exhibited excited him. He groaned, shoving deeper into her until he thought he would explode.

"Sissi, Sissi!" he shouted, his passion beyond control when suddenly he stiffened, squeezed her so fiercely that she flinched in pain, even as his stiff erect muscle gave her a final pleasure.

Exhausted with the pleasure of her body, Percy fell back, lying sidelong over the bed, Sissi beside him. He lay with his arm lazily straddled over her back, his eyes wide open. The words she blurted riveted him with shock. She loved him. Could it have been passion or being caught up in the moment? He frowned. No, Sissi was passionate but fully in control even when she was out of control.

A smile spread on his face, and he felt a thrill of pleasure rush through him. She loved him. And he knew that he loved her. They had to talk—there was no way he could sit back and allow her to marry Phil now. He sat up, leaning on his elbow, prepared to admit his love to Sissi. He stared down at her with adoring eyes, and she smiled. He put a gentle hand on her cheek and bent over to kiss her.

Sissi slowly began to close her eyes when they suddenly widened and she jumped up, shocking Percy.

"You smell that?" Sissi whispered, grabbing her shirt and holding it in front of her. Before Percy could react, she left the room and cautiously looked around the small cottage. Percy caught up with her, his expression confused as he watched her.

"What?" he asked, pulling on his pants. Sissi blinked, scowling up at him as the odor filled the air.

"Smoke? You can't say you don't! Look!" she gasped, pointing at the window. Percy blinked in surprise then ran to the window.

Flames were licking their way up to the window. The cottage was on fire! The smoke was ominous and clear now. Crackling flames were crawling up the walls, and now he could hear what was the crackling of burning wood.

"Get your clothes! Get out of here!" he commanded instantly, rushing Sissi back into the bedroom. She didn't need much prompting as she wasted no time in grabbing her jeans, but she had barely pulled them on when Percy grabbed her arm.

"Dress outside," he hissed, rushing her to the door, his own pants unzipped. He put his hand on the cottage door and yelled in pain, instantly released the knob. The door was burning hot. The fire had already caught hold of the entire outside and like a taunting child, dared them to try to exit. A window shattered, and they both jumped and turned around. They didn't see any glass.

"That was the bedroom window. It must be all around the house, Sissi." He paused, considering her, his eyes filled with worry and concern for her safety. Sissi cringed at his gaze, wondering what he was thinking. "You're going to have to run through that fire. That's the only way out. Or we'll both burn to death. You understand?" He wanted to be blunt, to shock her into taking any chance necessary to get out of the cottage.

A lump of fear constricted her throat, but she managed to nod. Run through a fire! Her heart leapt with dread, but she kept a semblance of calm as the fire grazed the house like a greedy set of flaming hands. She pulled on her jeans and blouse and wished that she had on shoes, but there was no time. Percy ran back into the bedroom. By now the house was filled with smoke, and barely anything was visible.

"Percy!" she cried, the blaze loudly crumpling the defenses of the wood. She was afraid that the room or wall would tumble on them at any moment. Percy raced back from the room, carrying the only sheet that was on the bed, the sheet that marked their lovemaking.

"I saw something like this in the movies. Wrap this around you, and run like hell, Sissi. Then toss it. You'll be okay, I promise," he added softly at her look of disbelief.

"Shouldn't it be wet?" she asked just as softly, the panic in her tamed by a sense of hopelessness.

"There's no time for that, Sissi. Just run!" he cried, shoving her toward the door.

"I can't, I can't. Not alone." She finally wept, all semblance of composure gone.

"You won't be alone, silly. I'm with you. It'll slow you down if I hold you. I want you safe, please, Sissi. Go," Percy added, trying to be patient and calm.

Sissi swallowed her fear, wrapped the thin sheet about her, covering her head and then with as much speed as she could muster, she ran through the flames that led her to the grassy mound of safety several feet away, the entire time screaming and crying Percy's name.

"Sissi, thank God! Oh, my God, Where's Percy?" Eddie asked, grabbing Sissi, who kept running even after she had conquered a safe distance from the flames and smoke. Eddie had seen the flames from the house. After yelling a warning upstairs, he ran from the house, praying. His worse fears came to light when he saw only Sissi screaming like a madwoman, running toward him.

"He should be right behind me," she wailed, glancing

with a worried frown at the burning building. Percy was not in sight. "Oh, my God—"

The fire ate at the wood cottage until the logs began to tumble. Sissi thought she would faint when the wood began to crumple and still Percy had not come out. Had he been hit by a burning wood panel, or perhaps he had frozen up after forcing her to run through the flames? Her thoughts were wild, scary, and she tried to shake them off. She couldn't imagine Percy weakening in the face of danger. Something must have happened to him.

"Percy—" she screamed. "Eddie, you have to get to him. You have to help him," Sissi sobbed between coughs, only slightly mindful of Phil and the others racing toward them. When the back of the cottage completely collapsed, Sissi screamed and fell to her knees, watching the fire burn the cottage in utter dismay. Her eyes were full of fretful tears when Percy suddenly burst through the flames. Through the blur she saw the flames try to whip him before he, staggering toward them, coughing and choking on fumes, dropped to his knees holding something large and unwieldy in his singed arms.

"Thank you, God," Eddie whispered silently.

Chapter Twenty

Sissi couldn't believe her eyes. She had shed the sheet Percy had given her, and stunned, knelt on the grass with him.

"Donna!" Nicole screamed.

"No, Donna! No," Nicole moaned.

"Is she . . . is she dead?" Nicole asked, leaning over Percy, who was miraculously not seriously injured. His face and arms were smudged, and he was winded. But he had not been burned. Donna on the other hand had not survived the fire. Sissi was sickened at the sight of Donna and was thankful that Percy had escaped such a fate. She averted her gaze.

Nicole came to her feet, staring at the burning house, her expression horrified. Percy coughed repeatedly, trying to clear his lungs of the smoke.

"What kind of weekend is this?" Eddie bit out, turning his back at the sight of Donna's burned body.

Sissi chanced a glance at Phil, who hadn't said a word

upon arriving. Looking into his eyes, Sissi felt a thread of apprehension. It occurred to her that something was definitely wrong. Donna hadn't been in the guest house . . . or had she? Sissi was so confused when she woke up, she couldn't be sure. And Percy had been so angry, so blinded by his rage that perhaps he hadn't noticed her, either.

But it didn't make sense.

Sissi had the oddest feeling that just as she had been hit and placed in the cottage, just as Percy had been lied to and sent to the cottage, someone had sent Donna to the cottage as well. Or worse, they killed Donna and tried to cover it up in the fire. But then why send her Percy there?

She held back another suspicious scrutiny of Phil, suddenly very afraid of him. She had to talk to Percy. Let him know what was going on in her mind. Phil was up to something, she just couldn't prove it. Panic filled her but she kept her calm, slowly lowering her eyes from Phil's watchful gaze as she tried to hide her suspicion about him.

"It's been some kind of a weekend, thanks, Phil," Craig grumbled.

Phil glanced up at Craig's complaint. He would never have expected Craig to be so crass in the face of the trauma that Nicole had faced. The woman had been through a lot over the last few days, and all Craig could do was drink himself into a stupor.

Nicole had fainted within minutes of seeing Donna. Geoff, not Craig, had taken her into the family room. Phil had always considered Craig the easygoing one, the most reliable—even if the younger man was completely unfaithful to Nicole, Phil knew he couldn't be one to judge. Regardless, he was completely surprised by Craig's total inability to deal with the pressure of the last few hours. Phil allowed his gaze to trail over the room until he settled on the clock. It was almost midnight.

Sissi and Percy were still sitting with the ambulance and answering questions for the police. It was the second time in one day that Sissi had been forced to endure a policeman's probing of her. Phil had just finished talking with the fire department and was exhausted. It had been a long day.

Phil stared out his window, watching Sissi as she sat in the ambulance, her face still ashen from the smoke. Someone had placed a gray blanket around her slender shoulders, and as natural as a newlywed, she was gently rubbing Percy's forehead.

So considerate of Sissi to make sure her lover was safe, Phil thought. He had no doubt that his suspicions were right. The fact that Sissi's blouse had been completely undone and Percy had worn no shirt when he escaped the fire was all the evidence that Phil needed. And she called *him* a cheat. Ha!

Phil frowned, his thoughts raging from wondering what had started the fire to how Percy and Sissi managed to slip by him without his knowing they were gone from the house. Then he thought of Donna and was saddened by her death.

Phil decided that Donna was the only one who could have started the fire. She was the only one who smoked cigarettes and, if her attitude the night before was any indication, she was out of control. He turned from the window and sat back in his leather chair. He was tired. He wanted Sissi's friends gone. All of them. He wanted time alone with her to end their fight and be friends again.

"Mind if I get another drink?" Craig asked Phil.

Phil shrugged and watched as Craig walked to the bar and began pouring himself another rum and Coke. He sat back and considered Craig with apathy, answering with a sarcastic, "Feel free."

Again silence fell between them as Craig downed the liquor in a few gulps. Phil stared at him, watching the younger man pace the room like a caged panther. Something was wrong with Craig not being able to handle the situation that had come up. Something was strange about the way that Craig allowed Nicole to deal with her problems alone and even allowed Geoff, a stranger obviously interested in the young woman, to console her, to support her, to comfort her. Phil frowned then sighed. It wasn't any of his business, but he thought again about how much he wanted Sissi's friends gone.

"I knew it was a bad idea, coming down here," Craig began, holding his near empty glass in a tight grip. "Something's not right. Nicole . . . I . . ."

Phil stared at the floor, his eyes following the rugged lines that patterned the oak floors and remained quiet as Craig rambled on.

"I can't handle this kind of crap. I know what you're thinking, Phil," Craig rushed on, giving Phil a sidelong glance.

"I doubt if you do, Craig," Phil scoffed.

"Well, it doesn't matter anyway. I'm tired. I'll catch you later," Craig said with another hesitant glance at Phil.

"Later," Phil muttered, Craig already forgotten as he recalled again the image of Sissi half dressed and distraught with concern over Percy's supposed demise in the fire. He wished Percy had died in that fire!

He snarled, came to his feet, and was determined to kick Percy out of his home. And it *was* still his home, regardless of what had occurred between him and Sissi.

Sissi had not asked him to leave yet, at least not before Monday. So Sissi had fallen, so she had slipped up. It didn't matter. Hadn't he done the same thing only a few days earlier? He could forgive her. He loved her, and no one was going to change that or stop him from marrying her.

Chapter
Twenty-One

It seemed the police would never leave, but when they finally did, it was nearly three-thirty in the morning, and Sissi couldn't be sure if she was more exhausted from her pent-up suspicions or lack of sleep. She closed the bedroom door and lay on her back, staring up at the skylight in the spare bedroom. She couldn't believe that it was only two days ago that she anticipated seeing Percy. Now she anticipated being as far from Phil as she could. She didn't trust him and was wary of sleeping under the same roof with him.

Perhaps he was so jealous of Percy that he had tried to kill him and her, and Donna had caught him and . . . she sighed. It was a wild thought brought about from exhaustion and an overload of traumatic events.

The stars were shining brightly in the clear, peaceful night sky. It was a beautiful night. The air was gentle and softly breezed over the grounds. It was all so mellow and calm. If only Donna hadn't died. She closed her eyes only to open them quickly at the tap on the door. She scooted up on her elbows and watched the door suspiciously.

"Who is it?" she called, praying that Phil had not come to her again.

"Percy," came the unexpected response.

Sissi hesitated, too excited to move, then she jumped from the bed and raced to the door. Her heart pounding wildly against her breast, she swung open the door and stared with wide-eyed joy and relief at the man she loved.

Percy looked at Sissi with a compassion he had thought lost to him. She appeared so vulnerable in that moment, so adorable and lovable. Impulsively he pulled her into his arms, wanting to protect her, to keep her safe from any further accidents. And Sissi felt safe in his arms. It was natural, loving him.

"I thought I was going to die from agony when you didn't come out of the cottage," Sissi whispered, still distressed from the whole episode.

"When I saw Donna, I thought . . ." He paused, unable to put the anguish he felt into words.

"It's okay, Percy, we don't have to discuss it now. It's all over, you know." Her voice caught on a sob, and Percy squeezed her even closer to him. They stood there, holding each other amidst the open doorway, finding comfort in each other's arms. Their despair and newfound love isolated them from the world, from the occupants of the house, from the sixth sense that would have warned them of Phil's presence. He stared at them from the hallway, his beady eyes and twitching lips a clear signal of the rage he felt at their embrace.

"You lying whore!" Phil swore, his words so harsh it was like a bomb exploding in the hall.

Sissi jumped, more from the sudden yell than from being caught in Percy's arms. As his outburst became clear to her exhausted senses, Sissi's eyes narrowed in an instant dark rage, and she stood brazenly in front of Percy, putting her hand on his hip as she scoffed, "I'm a lying whore? How dare you call me that after what you did?"

"Is that it, Sissi? You're using Nancy as an excuse to sleep with your old flame?" Phil demanded, walking with such deadly purpose that Percy cautiously stepped around Sissi to shield her from any sudden movements Phil could make.

"I was not sleeping with him," Sissi denied, although it was just hours earlier that she had been caught up in the rapture of Percy's loving embrace.

"Do I look like a fool?" He was standing with his fist balled against his hips, glaring upon them with a rage that Sissi had never witnessed.

"You're acting like one," Percy commented.

At Percy's calm statement, Phil was momentarily distracted from his rage with Sissi and directed his wrath at Percy. "You don't have anything to say," Phil snapped.

"Take it easy. I was just comforting her. She's been through a lot," Percy tried to exclaim, feeling slightly guilty that he had made love to Sissi. But Phil's anger was misplaced as far as Percy was concerned. He didn't care what Phil thought, he wouldn't allow the professor to come near Sissi until he was completely sure that Phil had calmed down.

At Percy's explanation, Phil's rage increased, his eyebrows furrowed with the jealousy he was never able to conquer toward Percy, and he sneered, "Comfort her how, like you comforted her earlier in the guest house?"— balling his fist as if preparing for battle. "You don't fool me a bit. I know you two made love in the cottage, and you want to make love to her again. You want to steal her away—"

"Percy can't steal what was never yours!" Sissi cried, incensed that Phil had the audacity to be angry with her for hugging Percy after she had caught him having sex with another woman. Where did he get his nerve?

Percy glanced at Sissi in surprise, wondering if she meant her words in the literal sense, but a movement from Phil caused his eyes to snap back on the professor in wary guard.

"You say all that, but you don't deny making love to him?" Phil demanded.

Sissi frowned, rolled her eyes, and murmured bitterly, "It was over between us before Percy got here, so that's none of your business."

"So you told him? I knew it!" Phil blurted in such a fit of rage that Percy grabbed Sissi and moved her to the side.

"You need to calm down, now," Percy warned.

Phil glared from Percy to Sissi and then back to Percy. The two men were face to face and obviously sizing each up. Sissi cringed with dread, certain that they were about to come into a full-blown brawl. She wanted to cry out for Craig or Geoff. She didn't need either of them proving a point for her or themselves. She just wanted Phil out of her life. Despising Phil for creating the malady of a weekend, she looked at him in ire.

"I'll calm down after I kick you out of here," Phil retorted, his eyes settling on Sissi.

Sissi flinched beneath his loathsome gaze, instantly recalling his murderous expression when first he saw her outside the burning house. She averted her gaze, disgusted by the whole scene he was creating, as if he had any room to make a fuss about anything she did. She looked at Percy, prepared to ask him to leave but to take her with him. She would kick Phil out later, but for now she just needed to get away. But her impulsive decision was dampened when she saw the expression on Percy's face. She recognized his stoic calculating square jaw and knew in that moment that she would not be able to convince him to turn from Phil and leave the mansion. A weekend already fretted with dark interludes, Sissi had no desire to be in the middle of yet another dangerous encounter. But she couldn't up and leave Percy's side. Her face was marked with dread. She gasped when Percy responded to Phil's threat in a cold, low retort, "I'd like to see you do that." His tone was daring, smug, and incensed Phil beyond reason.

Phil snapped, what little composure he had slipped completely from him. He lunged at Percy, his large hands fierce as he attacked his rival. Foolishly Sissi tried to come between them and was instantly knocked aside by Percy's unwitting move from Phil's grasp. Sissi slammed against the wall and slid to the floor in a daze. Her body still sore from the earlier bouts, she cried out in pain.

Her cry distracted Percy, and he bent toward her to help her to her feet. As he bent, Phil clasped his hands together, snarled back his upper lip and, bringing all of his weight in his elbow, sent a fierce blow into the small of Percy's back with the edge of his elbow.

Percy let out a pain-filled yell, nearly dropping to his knees from the pain, his hand against the wall keeping him upright. But before he could gather his strength, Phil let loose another blow in Percy's back so fierce that Sissi screamed in fear.

She scrambled to her feet and grabbed Phil's arm as she shouted for Craig and Eddie to come help her. Percy was just coming to his feet, his face twisted with rage as Craig came running down the hall. Phil was preparing to send another blow Percy's way, Sissi's determined hold on him the only thing keeping him from a full-blown encounter with Percy.

"Stop it. You don't have to do this, Phil," Sissi pleaded.

Percy was irritated with her pleading to Phil. He didn't need her help, he could handle the professor.

"Help me! They're going to kill each other!" Sissi cried

as Phil finally shook free of her desperate hold and caused her once again to stumble backward.

The moment Sissi was out of the way, Percy swung, landing his fist square against Phil's jaw. Phil's head snapped back, the blow catching him off guard. Percy swung again and again until Phil fell to his knees.

Within moments the floor was full with the other guests as they raced down to the hall on hearing Sissi's cries. Craig was the first to arrive and, ever cautious of Nicole's sullen face, he kept his gaze on the scene of the two men. He was hesitant, not sure how to intercede. With an impatient and disgusted grunt, Geoff brushed past Craig and the two women and hurried toward Percy and Phil before either man could attack the other again.

"Are you two crazy? Haven't we had enough drama for a day? What are you fighting about?" Geoff demanded, glaring at the two men in unveiled disgust.

Geoff was slightly taller than both men, if not as stocky, but he could hold his own. There was no loyalty for him with either man. Had it been Craig fighting and on his knees, Geoff wondered if he would have even bothered to help. He dismissed the question, the pained expression on Sissi's face causing him to frown at the two men. From his glance at Michelle and Nicole, who stood on the stairway watching in wide-eyed shock at the scene before them, he knew he had better break up the fighting men because no one else seemed capable of doing it.

"Get . . . get out of my way," Phil groaned, struggling to come to his feet.

He was red with fury and bruises from Percy's fierce blows. But he was determined to even the battle with the punk, he thought bitterly. Geoff looked at Phil with pity. The man was beaten, there was no doubt about it.

"I'm not going to let you fight," Geoff said calmly. As

he spoke, Eddie came running up the stairs, out of breath after hurrying from the basement on hearing the noise.

"What's happening now?" he asked, panting.

"Your boys are fighting," Geoff answered, never taking his eyes off Percy and Phil.

Eddie took in the scene and scowled. What had happened to his friends? Had they all gone crazy while he was doing his internship? Was he that out of touch with them? He felt as if he didn't know them anymore.

Percy snorted mockingly, his hands still balled by his side, and he eyed Phil then Geoff. Geoff gave him a sidelong glance, noting Percy's bull-like stance, his flaring nostrils in the heat of his passion.

"Now, cut this crap out," Eddie interceded, his boyish voice deeper than usual in his frustration.

Percy ignored him, not blinking an eye as he watched Phil get himself together. As Geoff stood watching Percy, Phil rushed past Eddie and attempted to tackle Percy to the floor. Percy was prepared. Before Phil could ram his shoulder into Percy's chest, Percy swung, causing Phil to stumble backward momentarily. Sissi screamed, and Percy tossed her another annoyed glance. Was she in love with that foul-mouthed jerk?

With a beastly growl, Phil charged again, only this time Craig had come forward as well, with a little nudging from Nicole, and quickly grabbed the determined professor.

"Get off me!" Phil stormed, his breathing fast and fierce as he struggled to free himself.

"Keep still, man. Calm down," Craig hissed in Phil's ear, holding the man's brutish arms behind his back with all of his strength.

Phil snarled, took a deep breath then suddenly relaxed, causing both Sissi and Craig to relax. Craig was sure that the steam had died from Phil, and slowly he released him.

The moment Phil was free, Sissi ran to his side. He

remained on his knees as he struggled to capture his breath. His face was swollen, and the gashes made from Percy's fist were bleeding.

"Oh, Phil, what were you thinking?" she murmured so softly that he could barely hear her.

"Go away," he huffed gruffly.

"You're hurt. I can help you," Sissi insisted, feeling pity for him. She reached out to help him to his feet, but Phil ignored her hand. He snarled back his upper lip and with a bitter glare on Sissi managed to come to his feet. Still breathing heavily, he looked her up and down with such insolence that Sissi was tempted to slap his face. But she stood her ground, unflinching, although her heart beat wildly like a panicked bird beneath the hostile glare he landed on her.

"I'm leaving tonight. Tonight! You and your heathen friends can rot here! I don't need this!" he spat out, then with another threatening glance at Percy, he shoved past Sissi, down the stairs and a moment later, the front door was heard to slam shut.

"Percy." Sissi finally turned to him, coming to his side and forgetting that everyone was still there.

Percy frowned at her, feeling foolish that he had allowed himself to get lost in her sweet gaze again, feeling like an imbecile that he had allowed himself to lose his cool over her just because she had recently broken off her engagement. Her only concern a moment ago was Phil. She may have been pretending to be engaged to Phil, but it was obvious that if Phil hadn't walked away, Sissi would have stayed at his side. It was in her loving attempt to help the man, after what he had called her. How could he have been so blind as to think that Sissi cared about him?

"Just leave me alone, Sissi," he hissed and turned away from her.

"Why? What's wrong now?" Sissi demanded, instantly frustrated by his reaction.

"What's wrong? Why don't you think about it, Sissi—how you run to Phil like a puppet. He attacked me, remember? Never mind, I'm out of here at first light. I'll make my statement to the police from my hotel in town." Without another word, without a backward glance to see Sissi's startled face, he walked briskly away. He didn't dare look at her, so hurt was he by her devotion to Phil.

Sissi was shattered. How easy it was for him to make a cold decision and just leave her. And after he had vowed his love to her? One moment he was warm and loving, holding on to her as if he loved her endlessly, the next he was a cold unfeeling jerk who cared only about his feelings.

"If that's what you think, then why not leave tonight?" Sissi snapped, her eyes were misted with tears even as the words escaped her. "It's always been on me, hasn't it, Percy? You're never at fault, you're never to blame for anything that happens with us. Everything that we lost, that I lost, it was my fault. Always my fault. Just like tonight. I forced you to make love to me tonight, didn't I?" She laughed harshly, almost hysterical, and Michelle tossed a shocked glance at Percy.

"Oh, my," Michelle snickered, looking from Percy to Sissi with open glee at the lovers' quarrel.

"Sissi . . ." Percy sighed, regretting his harsh judgment as hastily as it had come.

"No, Percy. Go on and run," Sissi cried. Her lower lip quivered, and she thought she would faint, but she managed to stand and face Percy.

"I'm not running, Sissi. I'm . . . I'm confused," he admitted grudgingly.

"And I'm not?" Sissi demanded.

"I didn't say that, Sissi. I'm . . . a lot has happened," Percy responded hastily. A swift glance around him and he felt the overwhelming presence of Craig and Eddie as they watched him. Sissi saw his discomfort and grew even more disappointed.

"You can't even say you love me. It's always about Percy. Percy's pride. Percy's love. Never me. Why I thought you had changed . . ." She paused in utter frustration. "All that has ever mattered with you, Percy, is you. So go on and run away again. But don't you dare come back. Don't you dare think I'll be a fool for you again. You don't deserve my love, you egotistical, arrogant jerk!"

Her words were thrown at him like a doubled-edged sword and tore at Percy's soul. Before he could respond, Sissi turned from him and ran back into her room, slamming the door and locking it shut behind her. Tears spilled from her eyes, and she thought her heart would burst from the pain she was feeling. She couldn't bear to see him a moment longer. She didn't want to hear any of his snide remarks and to know his rejection again was more than she could bear. Especially with all of her friends standing there, watching as Percy once again destroyed her faith in love.

Percy felt like a complete imbecile as he stood amid his peers. Sissi had held nothing back this time. And she was right, he realized instantly. He glanced at Nicole, then Michelle, then lowered his eyes in guilt. He had misjudged Sissi, he knew that now. Sissi was a compassionate woman and he should have understood. He couldn't blame her for being angry with him. When was he going to learn? He wished everything she said wasn't true. But he knew it was. She hadn't done anything, except proclaim her love to him. So now what? She wasn't going to keep forgiving him for the same crimes of passion, she had just said so herself. He could have kicked himself for being a rash fool.

"You should go to her," Eddie whispered after a few

moments of uncomfortable silence fell between all of them.

Percy looked up at Eddie in surprise. Eddie usually stayed neutral, rarely giving an opinion on matters of the heart. Percy saw him as a kid, incapable of dealing with serious emotions. But tonight Eddie looked, acted, and sounded like a man his age. And perhaps Eddie was right.

"I agree. Sounds like a now-or-never deal to me," Geoff Roberts added. He was leaning on the banister, watching Percy with sympathy, their earlier confrontation forgotten.

"You heard her for yourself. She wants me to leave," Percy mumbled, his ego not allowing him to share his feelings with them.

Eddie rolled his eyes, shook his head, and waved his hands in the air, signaling defeat.

"You are too much, Percy. Well, I'm going to get some rest. I'm going to the basement, I'm turning on some tunes, and I'm shutting this crazy night out of my mind. I'm outta here," he said before leaving them behind on the stairs. If Percy couldn't see that Sissi had already chosen him, he was a fool, and Eddie was too tired to care anymore. He had done his part in bringing them together by arranging their meeting at the cottage.

In exasperation at Percy's attitude, Nicole rolled her eyes and closed the few steps that distanced them to confront Percy, her petite frame blocking his path. Michelle had silently walked away, hoping in the confusion that Craig would find his way to her side again. But Craig didn't notice so intent was he on observing Percy's scandal unravel. And Percy had the nerve to scold him about Michelle. The hypocrite, he chided with an uncontrollable smirk.

Percy sighed and crossed his arms across his chest, knowing by her stance that he was about to be lectured.

"She doesn't want you to go, Percy. She's been through

a lot. All of us have. But that doesn't give you or Phil the right to talk to her as if she's at fault. You two have been acting like a couple of high school boys battling it out for the girl next door. Besides, Percy, if ever Sissi loved a man, you're the one. If you're too blind to recognize love when you see it, maybe you don't deserve her, just like she said."

"Yeah," was all Percy could mutter. He stared at the floor as if he was a reprimanded boy. Shamed by Nicole's admonishment, he slowly allowed his arms to drop in dismay at her words. Nicole was right of course and, like a love-starved puppy, he stared down the hall and went over Sissi's passionate words. As if lightning had struck him, he straightened his shoulders then ran back up the stairs. He was determined to hear it from her, without the wild throes of passion inciting the claim. If she loved him, then he was willing to do anything she demanded. He was hers. Forever.

"Come on, Nicole, let's go to bed. It's late," Craig said in a testy murmur as Percy raced past him. Craig took hold of Nicole's arm partially to guide her back to their room and partially to maintain his balance. His head was killing him and he felt sluggish, exhausted. He wanted to lay his head on a soft pillow, close his eyes, and forget the events of the past two days. And he definitely did not want another drink, that was what had gotten him sick in the first place.

With a barely contained hiss, Nicole shook her arm free, causing Craig to almost tumble forward before grimly raising her eyes to him.

"You go to bed, Craig."

"But, baby, I don't want to leave you like this," Craig pleaded, although he was already taking backward steps up the stairs.

Nicole smirked, giving him a doubtful look before saying in a deceitfully calm voice, "I'm sure you don't, baby, but I'm not tired."

Craig paused at her tone and considered her with uncertainty. Was that sarcasm he heard in her voice? He wondered then shrugged with impatience. He was tired, and that was all that mattered to him right now.

"Okay, Nicole," he relented with a heavy sigh. "I hear you. And I know where you're going with your comments to Percy and how it related to us. So I'm sorry. Just come on to bed." He was pleading now.

Nicole was not at all moved by his poor admittance of understanding or guilt. His words were as solid as air, and she had no interest in pretending that she believed in him.

"Craig," she sighed. "A lot has happened tonight. Any meaning you may have assumed was for us is null and void at this moment. Sissi needs a friend right now, and I plan to make her some tea. Okay? So go ahead upstairs, lay your head down, and I'll be there in a little while."

A little surprised by her firm tone, he was too tired to argue any further. He shrugged and nonchalantly accepted her rejection. She would eventually come around, he decided. He was somewhat glad to escape the responsibility of having to be the doting lover.

"Okay. If you're sure." Then without a second glance behind him he left her.

Geoff considered Craig's retreating back with a derisive grin. When he first met Craig, he had expected a lot more strength of character from the brother, but now he was sure that Craig Williams was the weakest man he had ever met. Considering Nicole's obvious lack of interest in Craig just now, he allowed his flirtatious brown eyes to fall on her. She was adorable, he thought. Her short terry-cloth robe exaggerated her petite stature, exhibiting her slender glorious legs. With a half-raised eyebrow, Nicole considered Geoff thoughtfully and waited in an almost serene silence for him to speak.

"Still in love?" he asked with a sardonic grin tugging his handsome mouth.

"Not with Craig," was her cool response.

"Perhaps you'll find another soon," Geoff suggested, following her as she started to slowly leave the stairs. Nicole shrugged then glanced over her shoulder to eyeball him.

"Perhaps I already have," she easily replied. Geoff's grin broadened, and he hastened his pace to fall into step beside her.

"I feel the same way," he murmured, watching her in admiration. Nicole allowed a sedate smile to peep forth as she led Geoff to the kitchen. A casual glance about the kitchen assured Nicole that they were alone.

"Can you close the door?" Nicole asked casually as she ran the water and filled the teakettle. Geoff obliged her then came to stand by her side.

"Making tea?" he asked, watching as she put herbal tea bags into four small teacups.

Nicole peered up at him with a pacifying smile. "Something like that."

"How can I help?" he asked, leaning on one elbow against the counter as he watched her with adoring eyes.

"By making me forget Craig," she whispered so softly that Geoff was not sure he had heard her correctly. He froze and stared at her. Nicole paused over the tea and returned his gaze.

"Are you sure you want that?" Geoff asked carefully.

"Yes," Nicole murmured then hastily lowered her eyes.

"How can I make you forget Craig?" Geoff queried, folding his arms across his chest as he leaned against the sink.

In a move that was more courageous than any Nicole had ever made, she raised her eyes and said softly, "By taking off your clothes."

Stunned by her brazen request, Geoff dropped his arms

to his side. She had not paused or even glanced at him while she filled the sugar bowl, pulled out two small trays, and placed the teacups on them. He stood up straight, a slight frown creasing his forehead at the possibility that she was playing him for a fool.

"Uh-huh. Are you toying with me, Nicole? Because if you are . . ."

"No. I'm serious. I like you a lot. I . . . there's no future with me and Craig. I know that now. I just thought . . . tomorrow I'm leaving and I . . . for once in my life I wanted to be . . . daring." Nicole stopped talking, feeling suddenly foolish and unattractive. He was considering her in silence, and she felt as awkward as a child.

"Making love in the kitchen is daring?" he finally asked, his tone edged with a hint of amusement.

Nicole raised her eyes at his comment and with a half-smile replied softly, "Yeah, it is."

"And what happens afterward, Nicole?" Geoff asked, his tone suddenly serious.

"We wake up," Nicole responded, then feeling brave again she pushed the trays aside and walked up to him until they were standing toe to toe.

"Am I asking too much?" she murmured, her eyes raised to stare into his.

Geoff got a heady whiff of the subtle perfume she had sprayed in her hair. He was surprised, truly, that the reserved Nicole could be so . . . so spontaneous. But who was he to turn down a beautiful woman's offer. And he could see a future with Nicole. He reveled in the sweetness of her hair then slowly lifted it in his hand and gently rubbed it against his cheek. Nicole smiled up at him and stepped closer, pressing her body to his as he bent his head and caught her mouth in a tender kiss.

The teakettle whistled, and they both jumped apart. Nicole laughed, a little flustered from the piercing cry.

Geoff gave the pot an injurious glare then with a deliberate snap, turned off the fire.

He barely had turned off the flame when Nicole wrapped her slim arms about him and, staring up at him, whispered, "Kiss me again."

He graciously obeyed, cradling her slender body against his as if she were a precious jewel. Their kiss deepened, both demanding more and more of each other. Encouraged by her immodesty, Geoff effortlessly hoisted her from her feet and sat her on the heavy oak kitchen table. She murmured in delight and wrapped her legs around the small of his back.

"Take me now," she breathed heavily, her nimble fingers expertly relieving him of his shirt before hastily unbuckling his pants. Geoff hesitated only a moment, shaking off his uncertainty at blatantly making love to Nicole on the table before following Nicole's lead. In a moment he had removed her robe and gently laid her back against the table.

"You want me, Geoff?"

"I want you," Geoff groaned.

"For how long?" she whispered, the pain in her voice causing him to look up and, without hesitation, he responded. "Until you no longer want me." Then putting a firm hand against the small of her back, he leaned her over and devoured her nude flesh with a lustful hot tongue.

Nicole kicked off her slippers then rubbed the soles of her soft feet against his lower back, over his firm buttocks, and down his thighs. Excited by her featherlike strokes against his skin, he caught her legs with a firm grasp, causing her to fall back, and began to lavishly taste her silky smooth flesh.

She gasped in a flurry of excitement when his tongue trailed from her thighs, up her abdomen, and found her breasts. Finding her nipples, he hungrily suckled them, savoring their pert firmness against his teasing tongue.

She ran her fingernails lightly down the length of his arms, then his chest, before grasping hold of his shoulders and lightly pinching his firm muscles. Squirming from the slight pain, he seized her groping hands and pinned them at her side as his mouth continued to explore her flesh.

He kissed her eyes, her lips, her chin, then her neck until she groaned with impatient desire. His tongue trailed the length of her slender neck, her shoulders, her collarbone, then again found her pert jutting breasts and licked against them in rapid succession. He grazed his cheek against her nipples then found her navel with his tongue and circled her flat abdomen.

Feverish with desire for Geoff and unwilling to wait any longer, Nicole lifted her hips and rubbed her moist, soft body against the flat of his stomach. Geoff shoved her away, pushing her farther up the table, then dipped his head between her thighs and with lascivious delight sampled the pleasures of her eager flesh. Nicole squirmed beneath his expert tongue. Geoff covered her mouth, trying to muffle her shrill cry as he continued to ravish her.

As he tasted her sweet, moist flesh, Nicole dug her fingers into Geoff's shoulders, arched her body, and moved with him until Geoff lifted his head and, through passion-filled eyes, admired her beauty.

With his pants tangled at his ankles, he positioned himself between her knees. Her face was distorted with unbridled passion, and he deliberately allowed his erect muscle to hit against her inner thigh. She ran the tip of her tongue over her lower lip, a slight smile teasing him as he spread her legs and grasped hold of her hips. He took a sharp intake of breath at the moist, soft warmth that greeted him a moment later. Excited by her welcoming embrace, he thrust slowly, languorously within her, savoring every moment.

Nicole began to pursue him, her feverish movement urging him onward. He complied, sensing her urgent desire and with calculated timing, he quickened his pace to meet her demand.

He grunted and groaned above her, trying to match his energy with hers. She opened her eyes, enjoying his passionate grimaces as he tried in vain to conquer her petite body. She was far more woman than he had expected and she knew that it excited him.

Caught up in the throes of passion, neither heard the kitchen door open, neither felt the stoic presence watching them. It was only when they came to a passionate climax, and the room fell silent, that she saw Craig.

Enraged at the sight of their entangled bodies, Craig could only watch his woman as she thrashed and bated Geoff onward. He was frozen with disbelief, noting in an instant that she had never made love to him that way. The woman that he loved, the woman that he had planned to eventually give everything up for, including Michelle, had betrayed him. Forgetting his own continuous betrayal with Michelle, he scowled at the pair.

"Craig," was all Nicole could murmur as she hastily pulled on her robe, her face hot with humiliation. Geoff pulled up his pants then began buttoning his shirt, cautious of Craig's every move.

"You witch!" Craig finally bit out, barely able to speak he was so incensed with rage. Nicole's eyes filled with tears at his words but collecting her pride, she glared at him and snapped, "I'm no more of a witch than Michelle."

"Michelle's different," Craig stammered, unable to believe she had the nerve to bring up Michelle at a time like this.

"How so? Because you're in love with her?" Nicole demanded.

"Nicole . . ." Geoff started softly, walking up to them to intervene.

"Stay out of this!" Craig yelled, his bitter eyes daring Geoff to take another step. Geoff hesitated, then backed up, deciding to let the pair argue without his input, but he was prepared to defend Nicole if Craig attempted to harm her.

"How could you do this to me?" Craig demanded, his gaze falling back on Nicole in despair.

"I learned it from you," she whispered, the hurt in her voice choking her comment to a barely audible whisper. Craig was not moved. He shook his head, staring at her in disgust.

"No, baby, you didn't learn this tacky shit from me," he muttered.

Incensed, hearing the scorn in his voice, Nicole slapped him. Craig stumbled then catching his balance, he looked with contempt from Nicole to Geoff then back to Nicole. The look he gave her made her skin crawl with shame.

"It's over, Nicole."

"It has been for a long time," she retorted though torn by his harsh rebuff.

"Then it won't make a difference if I ask you to stay away from me from now on," Craig hissed, so furious with Nicole he could have shaken her. But he balled his fist to his side, tossed Geoff a threatening glance, then stiffly left the kitchen. It was all he could do not to attack Geoff Roberts. He was determined he wasn't going to stoop to that level.

"I ask the same of you," Nicole shouted near tears as Craig's body disappeared behind the closed kitchen door. Stunned by the encounter, Nicole turned in a daze and sat heavily at the kitchen table. Geoff watched Nicole in sympathy. She was a beautiful woman and deserved more. He just wished he wasn't a rebound for her. But at this stage, he decided, it didn't matter. He would help Nicole get over Craig and in the end, she would love him.

"Nicole," he whispered, coming to kneel beside her. He took her hands which were firmly grasped together as she stared at the floor. At his touch she looked at him, the tears in her eyes threatening to spill onto her cheeks.

"I'm okay," Nicole whispered.

"I don't think you are. You don't have to be okay. Like I said, Nicole, I'll help you forget him. He doesn't deserve you."

"But how could he be so cold . . . after all he's done to me," Nicole murmured as if he hadn't spoken.

"Sometimes, when we know we're the cause of a problem, we're cold to hide our guilt or shame. He knows he ruined your relationship. I promise you, Nicole, I will never hurt you like he has," Geoff added, caught up in his pity for her. Nicole gulped and blinked back her tears before giving Geoff a winsome smile.

"I believe you, Geoff. I just need a moment. I'm . . . I'm going to freshen up then . . . I don't know. I just need to think for a moment," Nicole stammered.

Geoff nodded and came slowly to his feet, still holding her hand. "I'll give you room but remember, Nicole, he doesn't deserve you. Let him go in his misery." He walked to the door and crept it open.

"Where are you going?" Nicole asked with such urgency that Geoff hesitated. She had come to her feet and was staring at him in consternation.

"I thought you wanted to be alone. Do you want me to stay?" Geoff asked in uncertainty.

Nicole frowned then wrung her hands and shrugged. "No. No. I'll be all right. I . . . go ahead. I'll see you later?" she asked.

"Come to me whenever you want. I'll be there," Geoff whispered then quietly left the kitchen.

Nicole paced the kitchen, frustration brewing into anger with Craig. He could so easily turn away from her—be so angry with her. After all he had done to her, he should be begging for her forgiveness, not the other way around. Her face hot with anger, she stared at the teakettle as if mesmerized. Then with a quick glance around the kitchen, she quickly finished preparing the tea on the trays that she had started earlier. Nibbling at her lower lip in agitation, she scurried around the kitchen, searching for something she could add to the tea. She would end her relationship with Craig all right, she thought bitterly, as the impulsive decision to poison the tea came to her.

It was a truce, she thought frantically as she found a container under of the sink. Having no idea what it could be she poured a bit into two of the teacups. Then she heated the teakettle again. She would give Percy and Sissi the tea and offer Craig and herself one as a truce. Of course Craig would have no idea that together, they would be drinking their last toast, ever.

She had forgiven Craig repeatedly for his indiscretions—and one mistake she made, just one, and he was ready to give up on her. Well, it wasn't going to be that easy. It didn't matter that she knew the moment she approached Geoff that she and Craig were finished.

Her decision firmly made, she pushed the trays to the back of the kitchen counter and ran back to her room. As she had expected, there was no sign of Craig. Hastily she tossed aside her robe and pulled on a sweatshirt and jeans then raced back to the kitchen.

The teakettle was whistling loudly. She shut off the fire and hastily filled the four mugs with hot water.

Carefully she lifted the small trays, one in each of her hands. Taking care not to spill the tea or drop the near full cups, she left the kitchen. She paused for a moment and considered the poisoned tea before heading upstairs, determined to put a stop to Craig's heartless treatment of women for good.

Chapter
Twenty-Two

Craig was appalled with Nicole. After leaving her in the kitchen with Geoff, he stormed outside then realized he didn't have his car keys. And at four o'clock in the morning, he wasn't in the right state of mind to be driving. But he couldn't believe what he had seen. She barely knew that guy! He sat in the car, fuming with anger. It was nearly a half hour before he finally left the car. Refusing to dwell on her, not willing to think about the whole sordid affair, he went back to his room, staring at Nicole's open suitcase in disgust. In a fit of anger, he pulled out her clothing and threw it about the room, slamming the clothing onto the floor and kicking it about in a rage. She had hurt him, more than he could bear.

He was stamping on a pair of Nicole's jeans, grinding the heel of his shoe into the clothing, when the door crept open. He turned to it, prepared to curse and swear at Nicole, to demand an explanation. But when his fierce eyes fell on the door, Michelle was who he saw. He immediately calmed down, his entire mood shifting from anger to feigned patience.

"What?" he asked briefly. Michelle looked at the clothes strung about the room then back at Craig in curiosity. She stepped fully inside and, walking up to him, asked, "What's going on?"

"Nothing," was his coarse reply. He had no desire to let Michelle know what had just happened.

Michelle inspected the room again then whistled softly. "Well, you must be taking Sissi's and Phil's breakup mighty hard," she commented dryly.

Craig glared at her, knowing full well that she knew his frustration was about Nicole. "Yeah, that's it. Now I want you to leave."

Michelle smiled at him, his words meaningless for her. "Do you, really? Are you sure about that, Craig? I don't think you are," she continued, standing so close to him that he could smell the light scent of her perfume. She had fully dressed, although it wasn't morning yet. No one seemed to be able to sleep. And for Craig, Michelle was the last distraction he needed. It amazed him that Nicole hadn't come up yet. But when she came, he wanted Michelle gone. They had a lot of talking to do.

"Yeah, I really want you to leave," he finally said.

"And let you suffer in grief over Sissi and Phil alone? No way." Michelle laughed.

"Why don't you leave Sissi and Phil out of this?" he asked tiredly, sitting on the edge of the bed in defeat. He was in no state of mind to struggle with Michelle. Besides, what did it matter. He and Nicole were over, finished. He wasn't going to let any woman make a fool of him, no matter what the reason.

"I thought that's what this was about. You're throwing a tantrum for your best friends? Or is it, oh, let me guess, could it be Nicole? Have you finally figured it out?"

Michelle whispered, her voice full of glee at the idea that Craig was finally believing that Nicole had slept with Keith.

Craig rolled his eyes at Michelle, came back to his feet, and then shut the door.

"What I figured out, Michelle, is that I don't love you. I don't love Nicole, and I don't want to be here with either of you. It's over," Craig muttered then turned to open the door and leave her standing there. Michelle gasped, afraid that for once he had meant what he said. Before he could leave, she ran to him, wrapped her arms about his waist so fiercely that he had to loosen them to keep from being squeezed too tightly.

"Craig, please don't leave me like this. I can love you. Let me love you. I won't burden you like Nicole. Just give me a chance," Michelle moaned.

Craig didn't respond, but slowly he turned to her, looked into her eyes, and returned her desperate embrace. He might never be able to love Michelle the way she wanted him to, but one thing was for certain: in all of the years he had known her, with her all of her devious lies about Nicole, she never lied to him about her love for him. He could stay with her, even if it was just for a little while until he got himself together. At least he knew which way Michelle was coming.

Sighing, he silently consented to her pleas, for now.

Chapter
Twenty-Three

Sissi stared at Percy, her eyes filled with hurt. He had the nerve to come back to her. And for what? To insult her again, she thought grimly.

Percy, deciding it was better to be in command of the situation and not allow Sissi's cold gaze to affect him, demanded the moment he was in the room to know. "Do you still love Phil? I just want to know the truth."

Sissi gave him scornful scanning, annoyed that he even had to ask the question. She put her hand on the door and said in a sharp hiss, "I told you the truth yesterday. It's your problem if you don't believe me. Now get out," she added before attempting to close the door. Percy shoved the door open, forcing his way fully into the room. Sissi stepped back, surprised by his unexpected boldness.

"Like hell it is!" he swore. "You either love him or you don't. Why did you go to him? You said he cheated, that the engagement is a sham. Why do you care?"

"I thought he was hurt. I didn't go to him the way you're implying," Sissi stammered in aggravation.

"Hurt? He wasn't hurt, Sissi. I have to know, do you plan to still marry him, after all of this?" His voice choked in frustration as a great lump of emotion overtook him.

Sissi paused, unfamiliar with signs of weakness coming from Percy. Slowly she responded, "If I planned to marry Phil, I wouldn't have made love to you, Percy. Would I have even told you about the fact that he and I broke up? Come on!"

Percy hesitated but still doubtful, he said, "Why did you make love to me?"

"Oh, you're so conceited."

"It's not conceit. I just need to know. I need to make this clear and somehow understand what's going on. I—"

"I, I, I," Sissi snapped, interrupting him in a frenzy of agitation. So now he wanted a confession of love from her after he was so easily going to abandon her to Phil.

"It has always been I with you, Percy Duvall! Why don't you just leave like you said you would. Huh? Aren't you supposed to be running away? Just like you did when I lost our baby. Remember that, Percy? Even then you were about you and never us. Why I thought you had changed is beyond me. When I got pregnant, when I carried your child, I was proud—proud to be able to give you that final glory. And even then . . ." She sniffed, trying to regain her composure. "But you could not trust me. I never wanted to lose our baby, Percy. I never wanted to lose you," she sobbed. "Let me tell you something—"

"You told me enough," Percy swore before closing the door. Before she could protest, he swept her to him in an impassioned embrace, furious with himself for hurting her, for not trusting her.

"I don't need to hear anymore," he whispered huskily before he kissed her pouting mouth with a passion that denied pride. Sissi was instantly flustered. For a moment she struggled in his arms. She didn't want to kiss him, to succumb to his passion. She didn't want to be a fool again.

"No, Percy," she groaned, hating him for holding her so passionately, despising her weak flesh for desiring him even as he stood there accusing her of loving Phil. At her protest, Percy became even more impassioned.

"I love you," he groaned huskily, his mouth tasting the sweetness of her mouth. Sissi gasped, shocked by his heart-wrenching statement, impassioned with her uncontrollable desire to be in his arms.

"Wait, how can I trust you, Percy? How?" she hesitated. "How can I believe that you'll be here in the morning after you so easily were about to leave me again?"

Percy considered her with loving eyes. As he gazed into her eyes, she had the earth-shattering discovery that he was sincere. It was a tender moment filled with all of the love and passion he had been withholding for two years. She was convinced before he even spoke that he would be by her side come the dawn.

His eyes devoured her, his mouth slightly parted with the passion he was forced to hold back as he took her soft slender hands in his and stated softly, "I was a fool out there, Sissi. I didn't think about anything other than myself, like you said. But I love you and swear, I hope you can forgive me. I hope you can give me a chance to show you the kind of love you deserve. Okay, it's not a moment's passion, it's a lifetime passion I feel for you. I want you safe and warm and loved by me. I want to give you another baby. I'll cherish you this time, I promise. I want you to love me," he added in a deep, husky voice.

Sissi blinked up at him in astonishment. Her eyes told him her secret desires, her longing for him, her loss of the last two years they had been parted. Sissi's heart was singing, his words music to her ears.

"Percy," she whispered then, unflinching, holding his gaze in that bold way he always admired about her. She came to him, wrapped her hand at the nape of his neck and pulled him to her until their lips caught in a passionate kiss.

They made love slowly, languidly, leisurely enjoying one another. Percy caressed and fondled Sissi as if she were his first love and cradled her with loving gentleness in his arms. His touch was almost fearful as if she would disappear at any moment.

Afterward, they lay locked in each other's arms, the past few days and hours forgotten in the glory of at least admitting to each other's love. A knock on the door froze Sissi, and she looked up at Percy with worried brown eyes.

"What if that's Phil?" she whispered in a panic, recalling her earlier suspicion that he could be a murderer.

"I doubt if he would have come back. But don't worry about him, Sissi. I'm not going to let him harm you," Percy promised, gently unclasping her arms from him as he prepared to leave the bed. If Phil was in the same state of mind he was in when he stormed from the house, he might have another fight on his hands. He sighed tiredly even as he reached for his pants. The rap on the door repeated itself timidly, then the soft voice asked, "Sissi? Are you awake?"

"Oh, thank God. It's Nicole," Sissi sighed, breathing easier as she sat up in the bed and pulled the covers up to her chin.

"Just a second," Percy called before swinging the door open and staring down at Nicole with a bright smile.

"I thought you might want some tea, but I see now you're all right." Nicole smiled genuinely pleased to see Percy and Sissi together.

Percy glanced at Sissi with a bright smile before taking the tea tray from Nicole. "Thank you, Nicole. Good night,

Nicole," he added in a mild voice. Nicole grinned, nodded and slowly backed out of the room.

Sissi waved at her from the bed. "Bye."

"Just be sure to drink your tea. You be sure to have some, too, Percy. It's real good. I added just a hint of honey and lemon," Nicole whispered before she helped Percy close the door.

The instant the door closed, Nicole's smile faded and she stared down the hall as if she could see into her room. She had no doubt that Craig was there now. At that moment she hesitated. Could she go through with it? Shaken at the prospect of facing Craig, of watching him drink the tea, she headed for her room, convincing herself that she hated him enough to hurt him, to see him forever regret his humiliating philandering with Michelle.

Percy set the tray of tea on the chest beside the bed. Smiling like a well-fed kitten, Sissi scooted closer to the edge of the bed, enjoying the sweet aroma of honey and tea that wafted from the cups. It was the perfect fragrance to go with her mellow mood.

Catching sight of her peaceful look as he sat on the edge of the bed beside her, Percy smiled as well, happy to see she had no regrets at being with him. He lifted the cup of tea to hand to Sissi, the silence between them underlined with a mutual joy of each other. Ignoring the tea, Sissi reached up and ran the ball of her thumb down the length of his muscular arm, then she paused and scooted to her knees, wrapped her arms over Percy's chest, and laid her head on his shoulder. Percy glanced down at her with adoring eyes, appreciating her affection, loving her compassion At his gaze, she planted tender kisses on his shoulders, then his back, and Percy started to squirm a bit, the feel of her warm mouth against his flesh teasing him.

Sissi laughed, pleased with his reaction. Her kisses increased from soft petals to passionate fondling of his skin. Percy sighed, giving in to Sissi's passion. He set the teacup back on the tray and turned hastily to pull Sissi in his arms, ready to make love to her yet again. As he turned to take Sissi into his arms his elbow bumped against the cup which tottered for a moment then fell to the floor.

"Oh," Sissi gasped.

"Whoa!" Percy muttered, moving his feet just barely out of reach of the tea.

"I'm sorry, baby," Sissi apologized, suppressing an amused smile at his clumsiness in his haste to make love to her again.

"It's okay. It didn't break or spill on me," Percy said, bending over to pick up the mug. Reaching for the now empty mug, he paused, noticing steam rising heavily from the carpet. The tea hadn't been that hot when it was in the mug, he thought, baffled by the steam. He peeked closer and sniffed. It had an odd smell, and he wondered if it could be the carpet and his imagination at work. But then he noticed the steam had burnt a hole in the carpet. Staring at the hole, he gingerly picked up the mug and set it back on the tray. Uncertain what to think, he frowned and glanced at Sissi, his face clearly expressing his concern. Sissi's smile initially broadened beneath his gaze, but slowly it faded into bafflement.

"What's wrong?" she murmured, barely able to speak above her fear. What had suddenly occurred that would change him back into the brooding man who had arrived Friday night? Was he doubting her love again? Had he changed his mind about loving her?

Completely oblivious to her concerns, he answered, "The tea."

Sissi was confused.

"The tea?" she repeated, not comprehending his statement. He gazed down at the carpet, his eyes targeting the hole. She followed his gaze and gasped. The carpet was burnt through in a small patch where the tea had spilled from the mug. There was still a film of steam floating above it.

"What . . . what happened? What's going on?" Sissi stammered, jumping from the bed in a state of agitation. She wrapped the sheet around her and bent over to get a closer look at the hole. Percy put his hand on her shoulder to hold her back, worried that she would accidentally touch the burn that he was now sure was no freak accident.

"It's acid. Or something strong enough to be," he exclaimed, gingerly coming to his feet and moving away from the burn in the carpet.

"How in the world did acid get there?" Sissi asked with such innocence that Percy paused and stared at her.

"Are you serious? You don't know?" he demanded, his scowl increasing.

"No," Sissi answered, slightly embarrassed at the look of incredulity that crossed his face.

"I have a good idea. If this ain't crazy," he swore again, now pulling on his shirt. He hesitated and considered Sissi, who was still examining the burnt area. "It was deliberate, Sissi. There is no way that much of anything could have accidentally spilled into our drinks. Get dressed, baby," he added gently. "I'm getting you out of here before another *accident* happens."

"But . . . didn't Nicole bring us the tea?" Sissi asked, unable to believe that her best friend could want to hurt her. Still she came to her feet, suddenly exhausted. She was baffled, unable to fully understand what Percy was trying to say. Carefully she pulled on her black dress and sandals. When she was dressed, Percy gave her a reassuring glance.

"You okay?"

"Of course. Confused but okay," she answered truthfully.

"I know it doesn't make sense. But we need to get out of here and find out what's going on later. Let's go," Percy said then cautiously opened the door and glanced down the hall. It was clear and, without further hesitation, he called Sissi to his side. Holding her hand, he stepped into the hall. He didn't understand how the acid had gotten into their tea. He knew that it was also suspicious how Nicole's truck had crashed when the brakes had been fine the day before. And now he was suspicious of the fire department's theory that a smoldering cigarette had caused the fire. Could Phil had been so enraged, so jealous of Sissi that he wanted to kill her as well as her friends? Percy couldn't be sure, but that didn't explain why Nicole then had brought them the drinks. He knew only one thing, he was going to get Sissi out of the house before something else befell them.

Another glance down the hall and Percy headed for the stairs. But then Sissi hesitated, grabbing his arm and whispering in an urgent voice, "What about everyone else, Percy? We can't just leave them. They could be in danger. Phil could have lost his mind and attacked them, too," Sissi said.

"We don't know that Phil put acid in the tea. It could have been . . . it's possible that Nicole did it, Sissi. She did bring us the tea."

"Nicole couldn't be cruel like that. Phil did it," Sissi retorted, hating the very idea that Nicole could be guilty of such a horrible act.

"Look, I want to get you out of here. We can let the police figure all of that out for us later," Percy insisted.

"But we can't just walk out like this," she protested.

"Of course we can. We'll call for help from the car," he added as an afterthought to console her.

"No," Sissi hissed, snatching her hand free from Percy's hand. "It could be too late then. I don't know . . . I don't know what's going on, but we can't just leave them. I can't let what happened to Donna happen to anyone else."

Percy understood her fear and groaned in defeat. He would give in to her. She was right, and he knew he couldn't just up and leave his best friends, especially if it was going to grieve Sissi. But he didn't want any harm to come to her, and to prevent that he would sacrifice anything or anyone. He had already caused her enough suffering.

"Okay, Sissi. We'll do it your way but please be careful. I don't understand what happened here tonight, and I don't want anything to happen to you, not now. We have way too much catching up to do. You understand me, baby," Percy whispered, holding her chin up as he stared into her eyes.

Sissi nodded in agreement, her heart bursting with joy at his statement of loving her. Feeling confident that she wouldn't do anything rash, Percy started to head down the hall to Craig's and Nicole's room.

Nicole was standing just inside the doorway, her petite frame still holding her tray of tea she planned to share with Craig. At the sight of Michelle, Nicole was incensed. He couldn't even wait until they were apart before he was in that woman's arms again!

"You pathetic bastard," Nicole screamed, causing Michelle to jump away from Craig and Craig to stiffen at the sight of her. His face distorted into a snarl, and he shoved Michelle to the side.

"I'm pathetic? Who was screwing on the kitchen table with a stranger?" Craig shouted, having no qualms about humiliating Nicole even as Sissi and Percy gingerly walked up to the door. Sissi paused, shocked by the loud outburst. Nicole made love in her kitchen? With whom?

As if on cue, Nicole fired back, "At least Geoff isn't messing with everyone we know, like Michelle."

"How do you know? Huh? What? Did he tell you that? And you believed him!" Craig snapped.

"Oh, come on, everyone. Let Craig and Nicole be alone," Sissi suggested gingerly, putting a hand on Geoff's shoulder to keep him at bay as if in the heat of Craig's and Nicole's argument she'd forgotten the reason they had come in search of Nicole.

"I don't think that's a good idea, baby," Percy said coolly.

"She should, because it's true," Geoff responded, leaning against the door with a concerned frown. Nicole had decided to confront Craig after all. He should never have left her side.

"You stay out of this," Craig shouted, enraged at the very sight of Geoff.

"I can't. I love this woman," Geoff said evenly, coming to stand beside Nicole. At his words Nicole's hands trembled, and she nearly dropped the tray. She dared a glance at him, surprised at his statement. He loved her? He barely knew her. She was torn between distrust and elation that Craig was humiliated yet again.

"You love her! You don't even know her! What? You fall in love with every woman you meet over a weekend?" Craig said harshly. Nicole gasped and Sissi was embarrassed for Nicole. Craig was being deliberately cruel.

"That wasn't necessary, Craig," Sissi said softly.

"But he's right. She's trash and I've been telling you for a long time—" Michelle blurted.

"Shut up, Michelle," Craig snapped, staring furiously at Michelle.

"Nicole, Nicole," Percy whispered having gingerly moved around the crowded room until he was at Nicole's side. "We need to talk," he said gently. As he watched her, he wondered if the acid in his tea could have indeed been an accident. She looked so fragile, so damnably innocent.

But Nicole didn't seem to hear Percy, she was so infuriated by Michelle and Craig that she could barely still her trembling. "I hate you both," she hissed.

Michelle glared at Nicole then at Craig and responded heatedly. "Then leave. We don't need you. And take your new friend. But be careful, Geoff, she's also screwing her dead cousin's husband," Michelle added nastily.

Nicole blanched but managed to maintain what little composure she had. "I tell you what, Michelle. Just as a gesture of good faith, I offer you the tea I made for me and Craig. You and Craig have it instead. Toast to your future and may you rot in each other's arms." Before Michelle could respond, Nicole tossed the tray at them. Percy shoved Craig and Michelle aside, fearing that their tea had acid inside it as well. But when it fell to the floor and didn't leave a burning hole in the carpet, Percy realized that the tea he and Sissi had been given had been deliberately poisoned.

With a hurt expression, Percy stared at Nicole and asked blatantly, "Did you poison our tea, Nicole?"

Nicole was stunned by the statement and, as she stared from Percy to Sissi, she instantly realized what had happened. "Oh, Sissi, it was a mistake. I didn't mean to . . . I thought I gave you and Percy the good tea—"

"The good tea? You tried to poison me? Are you crazy?" Craig stormed, his face frowning as he watched Nicole in disbelief. Geoff was staring at her, too, surprised at the admission. Why would she poison the tea?

"No. I'm more sane than you. But I . . . I hate you!" Nicole blurted, ashamed of her wild impulse. It was a mistake, she knew that, but she was so tired, so fed up with Craig. It was the wrong thing to do, but no one had been hurt. She turned pleading eyes on Sissi, repenting as she whispered, "I never meant to hurt you or Percy. I just wanted to teach Craig a lesson. The tea was meant for me and Craig, not you two. And when I saw Michelle in here, I just, for a moment, I just lost my self-control."

"I'll say you did," Michelle snapped, staring at the tea-stain on the carpet in disgust.

Sissi wanted to hold Nicole in a warm hug, to wipe away the pain of the last few days and bring back the old Nicole, the happy Nicole, and to say she understood. But Geoff had already pulled Nicole to him and was holding her. Nicole began to sob, and Percy became extremely uncomfortable. Walking to Sissi, he whispered, "We should leave."

Sissi nodded and followed him from the room. But they were a step outside the door when Michelle shouted, "She's lying. She meant to hurt all of us. For all we know, she set that cottage on fire and killed Donna."

"No . . . !" Nicole shouted.

"Michelle, you know that was an accident," Sissi intervened. "The fire department thinks Donna accidentally caused the fire herself, from smoking."

"Yeah, right. And what about the truck?" Michelle continued. "My goodness, am I the only one around here who thinks it's one heck of a coincidence? She's crazy." Michelle's voice faded when she noticed Craig's eyes fall on her.

"Let it go, Michelle. You've made your point," Craig groaned.

"She tried to kill us!"

"No . . . I didn't mean to. I didn't start the fire. I didn't hurt Donna. Keith . . . Keith and I, yes, we planned to share his inheritance, but I would never hurt Donna for the money." Nicole's voice trembled, and suddenly she was crying as she spilled the whole story. Sissi made a motion to go to her, but Percy's firm hand on her arm kept her still.

"Come on, Nicole," Geoff murmured. Before Nicole could protest, Geoff lifted her in his arms and left the room, taking her to his room where he laid her exhausted body on the bed. She was sobbing softly, and Geoff felt pity for her. Carefully he lay beside her and held her next to him in a gentle hold. In the morning he would have to convince Sissi and her friends not to press charges. He would get help for Nicole. Of that he was determined.

Percy and Sissi were heading back to Sissi's room when they both heard someone calling Percy's name. Sissi frowned, realizing in an instant that it was Phil. She ran to the window and stared down at him. He was standing in the middle of the lawn, his hands at his side, his face turned up.

"Phil, what are you doing?" Sissi asked from the window.

"Where's Percy? You coward. Come down here now!" Phil shouted, his eyes looking over Sissi as if she wasn't there. Percy heard the call and scowled.

"I'll be back," Percy said and brushed past Sissi.

Sissi turned from the window and grabbed his arm.

"We're not children," Sissi declared urgently.

"I'm just going to reason with him, Sissi. Calm him down some," Percy said firmly. As he spoke, Eddie came up from the basement, sleep in his eyes as he looked around. "I hear nothing but racket everywhere. Now what's going on?" he asked gruffly.

"Eddie!" Sissi said urgently, running to Eddie just as Percy opened the front door. "Stop him, Eddie. He's going outside to confront Phil!"

"What? I thought that was resolved," Eddie muttered then raced out the door behind Percy. He ran up to Percy and grabbed his arm, trying to stop him. Percy yanked himself free. He had no intention of ignoring Phil. He was going to put a stop to Phil's irrational thinking before things got out of hand. He wanted Phil to know that he knew about the fake engagement.

"Back off, Eddie, I don't need your help," Percy snapped.

"Yeah? Are you sure about that?" Phil asked the moment Percy reached him.

Percy keenly assessed Phil's threatening stance and determined that it wouldn't be easy to put Phil in check. The man was angry in his menacing stance. "What?" was Percy's muttered response.

"That's right. Thought I was going to let you just take my woman in my face? Thought I was going to let that slide?" Phil's dark eyebrows were creased in a beastly scowl as he stepped into the light illuminated from the house. It was then that Percy saw the small gun. Percy hesitated and had to think quickly. He would have been lost had it not been for Sissi's scream.

"Phil don't do it. Don't shoot!" Sissi cried from the window then hastily ran downstairs in a fretful panic. She was surprised Phil was still around, and where he had gotten a gun, she had no clue. She knew only that nothing was worth losing Percy, not after all they had been through.

Percy glanced at Sissi in apprehension. She was standing a good few feet from both of them. He then gave Phil his undivided attention although worried that in Phil's state of mind, his anger could incite him to shoot at Sissi as well. And for all of his strength and love for Sissi, he couldn't fight a bullet.

Phil, never losing sight of his aim at Percy, tossed Sissi a wicked smile. "Oh, I'll shoot him, and when I'm done I'll have you again, Sissi Adams. Only this time I won't have to worry about this pest, Percy, interfering with our love," he said with such arrogant confidence that Sissi wondered how she had ever overlooked it.

"Fine, Phil. The engagement's back on. Just don't . . . don't shoot Percy. Please," she pleaded. She began to walk slowly and purposely toward Phil. Phil chuckled at her flagrant attempt to be seductive in her desire to save her lover. With a wide grin that bore only malice, Phil snorted in disgust at her pleading for Percy's safety and, ignoring Eddie, who was steadily approaching, he turned back to Percy.

"To hell with you, Sissi. And forget Percy!" Phil hissed then shot point-blank at Percy. As the shot rang out, Eddie lunged for Phil and caught the bullet in his leg. He let out a painful yell and simultaneously dropped to his knees, causing Percy to fall with him.

"No!" Sissi cried, dropping to her knees, utterly distraught.

Phil, holding the gun loosely in his hand, strolled up to Percy, a sneer on his face as he prepared to shoot Percy again. The gun clicked but no shot rang out. Enraged at Phil's open intent to assassinate him then and there, Percy shoved Eddie off him, mindful of the raging pain that must be filling Eddie's leg from the bullet. At his sudden movement, Phil hesitated and lost his footing when Percy grabbed Phil by his knees, causing the unsuspecting professor to fall on his buttocks.

Michelle watched the scene unfold from the bedroom window, realizing had Nicole been in possession of a gun she could very well had resorted to the level Phil had taken. Stung by the realization, she clung to Craig, watching in disbelief as Percy tackled Phil to the ground after the shot rang out. At the shot, Craig yanked his arm from Michelle only to have her grab it again. He was trying to release himself from her fierce grip.

"Let me go, Michelle. He shot Percy!" Craig shouted, prying Michelle's clawlike grip from his arms.

"No, don't leave me, I'm afraid," Michelle cried.

Craig scowled, tossing her a bitter look. "Afraid of what? Nicole's not going to come back, and Phil isn't thinking about you. Now let go of me so that I can help Percy," Craig commanded before with a final fierce shrug, he shoved Michelle from him. Feeling abandoned, Michelle fell to her knees, crying hysterically. Craig ignored her and ran from the room. Within moments Craig was in the yard. He came upon the scene of Percy and Phil rolling around on the ground, going blow for blow. Eddie was sprawled an uncomfortable short distance from the fight.

"You bastard," Percy was cursing as he fought Phil on the ground. Phil fought back once he caught his bearing, and the two men rolled in a grappling battle.

"Call the police, Craig," Eddie yelled at the sight of Craig walking up behind Sissi. Sissi tossed him a fretful glance before turning fearful eyes back on Phil and Percy's struggle.

"Will one of you call the police? Sissi, get up, baby. Help Percy," Eddie was instructing, incensed at both Sissi's and Craig's lack of movement as the two watched the fight in dazed fixation.

Sissi slowly came to her feet. As if in a trance and to Eddie's dismay, instead of running back to the house to call the police, Sissi walked purposely up to Phil and Percy and snatched the fallen gun before Phil could get it. She was waiting for Phil to get into the right position so that she could knock him out with the gun. He spotted her and, before she or Percy could react, he lunged for Sissi, taking the gun from her unsuspecting hands and causing her to stumble backward. Craig had run up to them by that time and instantly joined the attack on Phil to get the gun.

"Sissi, get out of the way," Eddie was yelling, seeing the three men's battle as a danger to Sissi.

Sissi turned to run to the house to call the police when she stopped dead in her tracks. The gunshot sounded, and all three men froze. Slowly Sissi turned around, fearful of what she might see, praying fervently that Percy had not been shot.

Percy lay on his back, his arms keeping Phil at bay. Phil sat half forward over Percy, the gun still in his hands as Craig, slowly, in shock, dropped to his knees.

Michelle screamed, Sissi shook her head, stunned as they watched Craig grab his arm and gape at the blood oozing from him in shock.

"You shot me," Craig choked out in agony.

"Ah, no, I didn't mean . . . I didn't mean to shoot him," Phil cried, dropping the gun as if it were diseased.

Percy instantly shoved Phil from him, scrambled for the gun, then aimed it at Phil.

"I ought to shoot you dead, you crazy bastard!" Percy yelled, angry at seeing his friends shot.

Phil shook his head repeatedly, not able to believe it as Craig moaned and groaned. Cursing and gritting his teeth in pain, Percy struggled to his feet with Sissi's help. They stared down at Phil and Craig and barely looked up when Michelle's screaming body raced past them to drop by Craig's side in a hysterical weeping mass.

"I'm all right, Michelle. Just get the ambulance here," Craig strained to say.

"Are you sure, you're bleeding so much," Michelle cried.

"I'm in pain but I'll live," Craig insisted, shoving Michelle aside.

"I'll go call . . . I'll call the police," Michelle finally stammered and went inside, truly believing that at last it was truly over between Craig and herself. Nicole and Craig were finished, Michelle knew, but Craig's eyes clearly expressed his rejection of Michelle's love. Michelle wanted to cry. Even in the face of Nicole's betrayal, in the face of his being shot, he didn't want Michelle near him. And at that moment she had to admit he never truly wanted her. She faced that fact now and with a heavy heart she dialed 911 and explained the scene that had taken place outside of the house.

Chapter
Twenty-Four

The halls were filled with hectic activity as nurses and doctors hurried down the brightly lit halls. They moved from room to room, carrying their charts and trays and displaying bright smiles and hellos to Sissi and Percy as they passed by

Sissi walked with Percy hand in hand as they made their way through the busy clutter to find Janice's room. At Sissi's and Percy's entrance, Janice sat up with a wide grin, delighted to see them. Sissi had called Janice just past ten A.M. to give her the sad news of Donna's death. Janice was at first devastated then sad, unable to believe that little Donna was dead. But what truly caused Janice to be surprised was Sissi's admission that she had lied about her engagement to Phil and had married Percy just this morning! It was incredible how things had turned out. So Phil had cheated on Sissi and was busted in broad daylight. Janice was sorry that Sissi had to be hurt by Phil, but she was glad that Percy and Sissi were able to find love once again. They belonged together and everyone knew it. At their entrance, Janice thought how beautiful a couple Sissi and Percy were.

"Janice," Sissi murmured, pleased to see her good friend wide awake and waiting for them. Janice looked great, Sissi thought in relief. Except for the bandages and the hospital setting, one wouldn't think she had been in a car accident. At Sissi's side was Percy, looking incredibly handsome even as he held on to one crutch for support.

"Sissi. Percy. I am so glad to see you two," Janice gushed. reaching her arms out to them for a hug. They complied.

"We're glad to see you up and your usual sunshiny self," Percy said, sitting on the bed beside her.

"Have you seen Eddie or Craig?" Sissi asked, sitting in the chair by the bed.

"No, not yet. But Michelle came by if you can believe that," Janice added, still amazed that Michelle had taken the time to come to see her. During their brief visit, Michelle had informed Janice of Nicole's newfound love with Geoff. It was bizarre. Nicole had finally left Craig. And good riddance, Janice said, disgusted with Craig's inconsiderate and selfish ways. Nicole deserved better. Janice wondered if Donna's death had been the final heartbreak for Nicole that opened her eyes. Who could tell with those types of things? All that mattered though was that Nicole had a chance to be happy with a man who by all appearances seemed capable of true love.

"I think Michelle's got a lot of sorting out to do," Percy suggested.

"Sure she does. Now who is she going to blame for Craig not being with her? And you know he'll never take her seriously, not after all of this time," Janice murmured, leaning back against her pillow. Sissi nodded in agreement, putting her hands in her lap to still herself from fidgeting. Janice noticed Sissi's behavior and grinned.

"So you two have something to tell me?" Janice inquired, eyeing them with a knowing glance. Percy chuckled then gently nudged Janice against her shoulder.

"I'll bet Sissi's already called you and told you," Percy said.

Sissi tried to hide a smile, but beneath Percy's probing glance she couldn't help but grin. She was ecstatic, so full of joy she couldn't contain it any longer. As if she were on trial, she blurted, "Oh, shoot, Percy. I'm sorry. I just couldn't keep it to myself."

"I knew you told her," Percy said, trying to sound stern, but he could no more control his grin than Sissi could keep from talking about their sudden marriage just a few hours earlier.

"Well I'm happy, too. You two deserve each other," Janice blurted.

"Hey? Just what are you implying?" Percy laughed.

"I think your running off and getting married like that was the smartest thing you two have done since you fell in love. I, of course, knew it was going to end up this way. . . ." Janice's words faded as Percy and Sissi stared at each other then leaned forward until their mouths caught in a sweet kiss. Janice smiled, thrilled to see that they had gotten back together.

"Why don't you two get out of here and go back to the hotel. I can see you need to be alone," Janice suggested.

"No," Sissi blurted, pulling away from Percy's kiss. "I'm not going to leave you alone. Besides, Percy and I have a lifetime," Sissi added with a sidelong glance at Percy.

"And you have a few years to make up. Go on. I'll be fine. Go make love and make lots of babies like you were meant to do," Janice said with bright expectation.

"We will, but for now we're just glad to finally be married. I was so worried Sissi wouldn't say yes. I'm so glad you did, baby," Percy added, giving Sissi a loving gaze.

"You knew full well I would marry you at the drop of a hat." Sissi laughed.

"And that's exactly what you two did, at a drop of a hat. I know Phil is steaming in prison," Janice added.

"Serves him right," Percy muttered. He hated the very idea that Phil had even come close to stealing Sissi from him forever.

"Now, Percy. You should have no hard feelings. You got the woman and were barely hurt except for your twisted ankle. So let that man simmer in peace," Janice scolded him.

Percy smirked at her comment then shrugged. "I'm just a little uptight right now. I haven't been married twenty-four hours yet, so you gotta understand," Percy said with a cocky grin at Janice.

"Well, I am happy that you two got married, I am. But you could have waited until next weekend—"

"No more weekends!" Sissi and Percy said together, putting their hands up to stop Janice from talking more.

Janice laughed. "Okay, okay. Next *week*. At least by then I would be all better and could have been your witness, maid of honor, something," Janice ended on a pout.

"Oh, Janice, baby. You know we're going to have a serious wedding later. We just didn't want to wait any longer. But you'll be there," Sissi insisted.

"Of course, I'm going to shower my sweetheart with so much love she won't have any time to prepare for a wedding. Far as I'm concerned, she's my wife now, and I can't wait to be alone with her," Percy added with a look at Sissi that was so full of love that Janice could have burst with pride for them.

Janice was glad Percy's love was able to keep Sissi's thoughts so occupied. Sissi didn't have time to dwell on the sad outcome of the weekend. Feeling lighthearted by their obvious affection and love for one another, Janice blurted, "You two go on and be alone for a while. You're choking me up. Besides, Eddie's supposed to be down here soon, and he can keep me company."

"Eddie's in with Craig right now. We just left them," Percy noted. Eddie, whose wound was not serious, was on crutches and he would be in a cast for a while. The bullet that shot Eddie had gone right through his leg and luckily hadn't caused any serious problems. Outside of the bandaging and crutch, Eddie would be fine in a few weeks. Of course, in hindsight he wondered if Phil had shot the gun just to scare him, without meaning to shoot him. It didn't matter now, though. Phil was in custody and, even if Percy didn't want to press charges, the police had every intention on seeing Phil did time for shooting Eddie and Craig.

"I'm actually right here," Eddie said loudly as he hopped into the room on his crutches. Percy glanced over his shoulder at Eddie.

"Hey, man," he greeted him.

"Ah, stay seated. I know how it is trying to move around with these things," Eddie insisted, coming fully into the room.

"Eddie, baby, I see you stopped complaining about that cast," Janice said, scooting over on the bed to give Eddie space to sit down.

"Sort of, I would be angrier but it turns out, it's endearing me to my sweet nurse," Eddie responded with a broad grin. Janice and Sissi looked at Eddie with surprise.

"What nurse?" Sissi asked.

"Some new young woman on his job," Percy answered for Eddie.

"That's right and she's interested in me," Eddie boasted. "I hadn't been able to reach her all weekend. But when I called her this morning and told her about the horrible weekend I had . . ."

"Thanks," Sissi interrupted dryly.

"Now you know I didn't mean it like that. I'm talking about what happened with everyone. Anyway, she got all worried about me and wanted to see me as soon I get back. I'm telling you, she's the one for me."

"Good. Let's hope so," Janice added.

"How's Craig, Eddie?" Sissi asked a moment later.

"He's okay. A little devastated that he lost Nicole the way he did. He's feeling real bad, I think," Eddie responded, sitting heavily on the bed.

"Well, he should," Janice retorted.

"I think he'll be fine in the end. He'll always have Michelle," Eddie added dryly.

"I still can't believe Donna's dead," Sissi said. "What in the world was she thinking?"

"She must have been pretty upset about Keith," Percy whispered.

"So upset that she tried to kill Nicole. I still can't believe she actually cut the brakes. I knew something was wrong when I saw that oil stain smudged on the hood of Nicole's truck," Janice blurted.

"She may not have meant to kill Nicole. She may have meant to only frighten her," Sissi offered, not able to see Donna as a cold-blooded calculating murderess.

"Whatever her intentions, Sissi. She was wrong and if she hadn't accidentally caused that fire at your cottage she would have probably hurt someone in another way," Eddie noted.

"She was definitely out of control," Percy commented.

"She was unhappy, like Nicole, like Michelle and . . . she wasn't thinking coherently. We have to forgive her for being human," Sissi insisted.

"I don't think so. What Nicole did was impulsive and even unintentional to a large extent. But what Donna did to the brakes was thought out and planned. She even managed to stay away when you all went to town. Besides, think about it, Sissi. When you broke up with me, you had just lost our child and you didn't attack anyone. Donna was just crazy," Percy added.

"Or Donna knew about Keith's inheritance and greed overtook her," Eddie added.

"Yeah, but I don't get why Keith would play Nicole so cruelly. She had to be crazy to trust him," Percy said.

"She was hurt by Craig. Anyone could have played Nicole, the way she needed to get away from him," Sissi responded dryly.

"Yeah, but she sure fell hard for Geoff and overnight, literally," Percy said with a wide grin.

Sissi raised her eyebrow and considered Percy. "You don't think love can happen overnight? I certainly do. Sometimes two people are natural soul mates."

"Yeah, yeah, you're right. Just look at us," Percy added, again thinking of his marriage to Sissi.

"I'll tell you what, after the trouble I went through to put you two together, we can't let what happened this weekend affect the rest of our lives," Eddie insisted.

Percy and Sissi laughed and asked in unison, "What trouble?"

Eddie paused, for the first time stumped. He had never gotten a chance to talk to Sissi and Percy after he knocked Sissi out with the drugged cloth and carried her to the cottage. He was just trying to help when he set them up together in the cottage. How could he have known it would catch on fire? That Donna in a drunken state, would burn down the cottage while they were in it? With a boyish smile, he shrugged.

"I, uh, I was the one who set you two up at the cottage."

Sissi gasped, her eyes widening in disbelief. Percy scowled, instantly angry.

"You what?" Percy repeated.

"Wait, wait. Calm down. Let me explain. I saw how you

two were acting all night and I felt you needed to come together and talk about it, so . . ."

"So you smothered me and put me in the cottage?" Sissi asked incredulously. "That was a bit drastic, don't you think?"

"Eddie. We could have been killed. What were you thinking?" Percy demanded.

"He was thinking what you two were thinking, that you belong together. He didn't plan the fire, silly. And he had no idea that Donna was even there. He was trying to help, like always," Janice interrupted, annoyed at her friends for not seeing the good side of Eddie's helping hand. "And look at you two now. Why, if weren't for Eddie you may never have gotten together. You both ought to thank him instead of complaining about what *could've* happened to you."

At Janice's words, Percy and Sissi gave Eddie a sheepish glance. Eddie grinned and gave Janice a thankful glance.

"Yeah, you're right, Janice," Percy conceded before giving Eddie a firm handshake. Sissi moved by the full impact of what Eddie had gone through just to see that she was at last happy, got up and gave Eddie a fierce hug.

"Thank you, Eddie," she said, taken with emotion.

"No problem. You two are married and beautiful together. It was well worth it. I foresee a great future for you two, that's for sure," Eddie added with a wink at Sissi.

"I love Craig, you all know that. But I'm going to be upset with him for a long time for hurting Nicole the way he did," Sissi said softly.

"I just hope she and Geoff work out," Janice added.

"If you had seen them together, you would believe they'll make it. I think they have a long future together," Sissi responded with confidence in Geoff's ability to help her friend get over Craig.

"Well, I'm glad Geoff has convinced her to seek therapy," Eddie added.

"It was the only way we could get Michelle and Craig to agree not to have her arrested for what she did to them. I'm just glad she didn't hurt anyone," Sissi retorted.

"Yeah, well I'm just glad we didn't drink that tea," Percy said dryly. Sissi glanced at Percy and sighed. He was still upset with Nicole for accidentally giving them the tea that was meant for Craig and herself. She was thankful too that they hadn't drunk the tea. It was sad how Craig had broken Nicole's spirit but Sissi was confident that with Geoff at her side, Nicole would find peace and be able to face her friends.

"I just wish I had been able to help Nicole. I should have seen it coming. I just didn't think she was hurting so much," Sissi murmured.

"It's not your fault or ours or even Craig's. That was Nicole's and Donna's thing. It's enough that we're not pressing charges," Percy insisted, reaching out to take Sissi's hand.

At his hold Sissi's frustration evaporated. She stared down at their hands, awed by the gold bands that were evidence of their marriage. Sissi Adams and Percy Duvall were finally married, just as we always should have been, she thought joyfully.

Percy noted with warmth the soft glow of happiness that glistened in her eyes. He felt proud that he could make her happy, at last.

"Okay, you two, that's enough. Get out of here. I've got Eddie, and Craig down the hall to keep me company. Go on and be alone for a while."

"I am a little tired," Sissi murmured sheepishly. Percy stood and grabbed his crutch, perfectly willing to escape with his new bride and be alone with her.

"Yeah, me, too," Percy added, putting his free arm about Sissi's waist as she came to her feet.

"All right now. Sissi, call me. Mom is going to be down in a little while, and she'd love to hear from you," Janice added. Sissi smiled and waved as she and Percy left.

Sissi lay quietly in her husband's arms. She was leaving North Carolina as soon as the police were done questioning her and her guests. Another day and they would be done, the police had informed her. Percy, her darling husband, insisted on waiting until she could leave with him before returning to New York, determined that she would come with him because he didn't want to be separated from her again. So together they lay in the queen-size bed, sure that it would be their last night in the hotel in Fayetteville. She planned to return to North Carolina after she and Percy settled down in New York. Percy knew how much the mansion meant to her. It was her grandmother's home, her pride and joy. Even with the tragic end of her celebration, she couldn't bear giving up her home. Percy knew how much the mansion meant to her and had even offered to rebuild the old cottage. Maybe they wouldn't live there for years to come, but someday when their children were grown—and she planned to have several—she and Percy would move into the mansion and retire there together. By then the mansion would be filled with new memories.

"Percy, I don't want to hold you up from taking care of business. I will be all right if you go ahead of me," Sissi whispered.

"I know you will, baby. But I'm here for you, and I'm not going to let you push me away that easily. Besides, I'm going to do everything I can to keep you safe and happy. If that means staying here through the end of the questioning, if that means coming back and forth every other day until you decide what you want to do with your grandmother's home, I'll do it. I want to give you something special this time, Sissi. I want you to never regret marrying me," he whispered with such a sense of urgency in his voice that Sissi looked up at him with loving eyes, fascinated at how beautiful he was.

"You know how easy I am, Percy. Of course I'm happy," she murmured.

He constantly spoke of their marriage, as if he still couldn't believe it had happened, that they had taken vows to be man and wife forever. For Sissi their marriage was like a wonderful dream. And each time she thought of the words "I do" she felt tingles of joy.

"I'll never trip up again, Sissi. You've got me for life," Percy said passionately, turning to hold Sissi in the crook of his arms. She cuddled against him, content and confident that this time she and Percy would last.

"I'm glad to hear that cause I wasn't planning on letting you go again."

"I love you, baby," Percy whispered then reached over her head and switched off the light.

Enshrouded by darkness, he allowed the blanket of night to warm their bodies as he slowly, passionately made love to Sissi Duvall, again and again.

BEYOND DESIRE   (0-7860-0607-2, $4.99/$6.50)
by Gwynne Forster
Amanda Ross is pregnant and single. Certainly not a role model for junior high school students, the board of education may deny her promotion to principal if they learn the truth. What she needs is a husband and music engineer Marcus Hickson agrees to it. His daughter needs surgery and Amanda will pay the huge medical bill. But love creeps in and soon theirs is an affair of the heart.

LOVE SO TRUE   (0-7860-0608-0, $4.99/$6.50)
by Loure Bussey
Janelle Sims defied her attraction to wealthy businessman Aaron Deverreau because he reminded Janelle of her womanizing father. Yet he is the perfect person to back her new fashion boutique and she seeks him out. Now they are partners, friends ... and lovers. But a cunning woman's lies separate them and Janelle must go to him to confirm their love.

ALL THAT GLITTERS   (0-7860-0609-9, $4.99/$6.50)
by Viveca Carlysle
After her sister's death, Leigh Barrington inherited a huge share of Cassiopeia Salons, a chain of exclusive beauty parlors. The business was Leigh's idea in the first place and now she wants to run it her way. To retain control, Leigh marries board member Caesar Montgomery, who is instantly smitten with her. When she may be the next target of her sister's killer, Leigh learns to trust in Caesar's love.

AT LONG LAST LOVE   (0-7860-0610-2, $4.99/$6.50)
by Bettye Griffin
Owner of restaurant chain Soul Food To Go, Kendall Lucas has finally found love with her new neighbor, Spencer Barnes. Until she discovers he owns the new restaurant that is threatening her business. They compromise, but Spencer learns Kendall has launched a secret advertising campaign. Embittered by her own lies, Kendall loses hope in their love. But she underestimates Spencer's devotion and his vow to make her his partner for life.

Available wherever paperbacks are sold, or order direct from the Publisher. Send cover price plus 50¢ per copy for mailing and handling to Kensington Publishing Corp., Consumer Orders, or call (toll free) 888-345-BOOK, to place your order using Mastercard or Visa. Residents of New York and Tennessee must include sales tax. DO NOT SEND CASH.

SPICE UP YOUR LIFE
WITH ARABESQUE ROMANCES

AFTER HOURS, by Anna Larence   (0-7860-0277-8, $4.99/$6.50)
Vice president of a Fort Worth company, Nachelle Oliver was used to things
her own way. Until she got a new boss. Steven DuCloux was ruthless—and the
most exciting man she had ever known. He knew that she was the perfect VP,
and that she would be the perfect wife. She tried to keep things strictly profes-
sional, but the passion between them was too strong.

CHOICES, by Maria Corley   (0-7860-0245-X, $4.95/$6.50)
Chaney just ended with Taurique when she met Lawrence. The rising young
singer swept her off her feet. After nine years of marriage, with Lawrence away
for months on end, Chaney feels lonely and vulnerable. Purely by chance, she
meets Taurique again, and has to decide if she wants to risk it all for love.

DECEPTION, by Donna Hill   (0-7860-0287-5, $4.99/$6.50)
An unhappy marriage taught owner of a successful New York advertising
agency, Terri Powers, never to trust in love again. Then she meets businessman
Clinton Steele. She can't fight the attraction between them—or the sensual
hunger that fires her deepest passions.

DEVOTED, by Francine Craft   (0-7860-0094-5, $4.99/$6.50)
When Valerie Thomas and Delano Carter were young lovers each knew it
wouldn't last. Val, now a photojournalist, meets Del at a high-society wedding.
Del takes her to Alaska for the assignment of her career. In the icy wilderness
he warms her with a passion too long denied. This time not even Del's desperate
secret will keep them from reclaiming their lost love.

FOR THE LOVE OF YOU, by Felicia Mason   (0-7860-0071-6, $4.99/$6.50
Seven years ago, Kendra Edwards found herself pregnant and alone. Now she
has a secure life for her twins and a chance to finish her college education. A
long unhappy marriage had taught attorney Malcolm Hightower the danger of
passion. But Kendra taught him the sensual magic of love. Now they must each
give true love a chance.

ALL THE RIGHT REASONS, by Janice Sims   (0-7860-0405-3, $4.99/$6.50)
Public defender, Georgie Shaw, returns to New Orleans and meets reporter Clay
Knight. He's determined to uncover secrets between Georgie and her celebrity
twin, and protect Georgie from someone who wants both sisters dead. Dangerous secrets are found in a secluded mansion, leaving Georgie with no one to
trust but the man who stirs her desires.

*Available wherever paperbacks are sold, or order direct from the
Publisher. Send cover price plus 50¢ per copy for mailing and
handling to Kensington Publishing Corp., Consumer Orders,
or call (toll free) 888-345-BOOK, to place your order using
Mastercard or Visa. Residents of New York and Tennessee
must include sales tax. DO NOT SEND CASH.*

WARMHEARTED AFRICAN-AMERICAN ROMANCES
BY *FRANCIS RAY*

FOREVER YOURS   (0-7860-0483-5, $4.99/$6.50)
Victoria Chandler must find a husband or her grandparents will call in loans that support her chain of lingerie boutiques. She fixes a mock marriage to ranch owner Kane Taggert. The marriage will only last one year, and her business will be secure. The only problem is that Kane has other plans for Victoria. He'll cast a spell that will make her his forever.

HEART OF THE FALCON   (0-7860-0483-5, $4.99/$6.50)
A passionate night with millionaire Daniel Falcon, leaves Madelyn Taggert enamored . . . and heartbroken. She never accepted that the long-time family friend would fulfill her dreams, only to see him walk away without regrets. After his parent's bitter marriage, the last thing Daniel expected was to be consumed by the need to have her for a lifetime.

INCOGNITO   (0-7860-0364-2, $4.99/$6.50)
Owner of an advertising firm, Erin Cortland witnessed an awful crime and lived to tell about it. Frightened, she runs into the arms of Jake Hunter, the man sent to protect her. He doesn't want the job. He left the police force after a similar assignment ended in tragedy. But when he learns not only one man is after her and that he is falling in love, he will risk anything to protect her.

ONLY HERS   (07860-0255-7, $4.99/$6.50)
St. Louis R.N. Shannon Johnson recently inherited a parcel of Texas land. She sought it as refuge until landowner Matt Taggart challenged her to prove she's got what it takes to work a sprawling ranch. She, on the other hand, soon challenges him to dare to love again.

SILKEN BETRAYAL   (0-7860-0426-6, $4.99/$6.50)
The only man executive secretary Lauren Bennett needed was her five-year-old son Joshua. Her only intent was to keep Joshua away from powerful in-laws. Then Jordan Hamilton entered her life. He sought her because of a personal vendetta against her father-in-law. When Jordan develops strong feelings for Lauren and Joshua, he must choose revenge or love.

UNDENIABLE   (07860-0125-9, $4.99/$6.50)
Wealthy Texas heiress Rachel Malone defied her powerful father and eloped with Logan Williams. But a trump-up assault charge set the whole town and Rachel against him and he fled Stanton with a heart full of pain. Eight years later, he's back and he wants revenge . . . and Rachel.

Available wherever paperbacks are sold, or order direct from the Publisher. Send cover price plus 50¢ per copy for mailing and handling to Kensington Publishing Corp., Consumer Orders, or call (toll free) 888-345-BOOK, to place your order using Mastercard or Visa. Residents of New York and Tennessee must include sales tax. DO NOT SEND CASH.